FATED SOULS

USA TODAY BESTSELLING AUTHOR
ELLIE WADE

Copyright © 2021 by Ellie Wade
All rights reserved.

Visit my website at www.elliewade.com
Cover Designer: Letitia Hasser, RBA Designs
Editor: Jenny Sims, www.editing4indies.com

No part of this book may be reproduced or transmitted in any form or by any means, electronic or mechanical, including photocopying, recording, or by any information storage and retrieval system without the written permission of the author, except for the use of brief quotations in a book review.

This book is a work of fiction. Names, characters, places, and incidents either are products of the author's imagination or are used fictitiously. Any resemblance to actual persons, living or dead, events, or locales is entirely coincidental.

ISBN-13: 978-1-944495-31-2

*This book is dedicated to all of my author friends.
This is a tough job, and I'm so grateful to you all for your kind words, support, and friendship. I feel like you are the only ones that truly understand what life is like in this career we've chosen.
And yet, we wouldn't have it any other way. We're living the dream.
You see me, as I see you. I'm here to chat. Anytime. We got this!*

PROLOGUE

TANNON LEE

A scream erupts from my throat. It's loud, shrieky, and panicked but not foreign. I've heard it before—many times.

I gasp for breath, my lungs begging for air. My chest burns as if I've been deprived of oxygen for quite some time. Extending my arms out from my sides, I feel around. Silky linens meet my clammy fingertips. A cool sweat coats my entire body. Bending my knee, I raise it from the bed. *That's where I am—in a bed.* The moistened skin of my leg clings to the sheet below me before it reluctantly releases its hold. I bring my hand to my face, tapping gently in search of something blocking my breaths. There is nothing.

I breathe deep. The night air soothes my aching chest.

My eyes blink, heavily—hours of tears and exhaustion urging them closed, but they struggle to open. Despite what I might find once my surroundings come into focus amidst this dark terror, I won't shut it out. I can't. The stakes are too high, and I can't fight what I can't see.

And I'll fight with everything I have. No one will hurt me again. No one will take what I'm not offering. *No one.*

The bed moves to my right, and that's when I feel it —soft fur against my arm. Centering me.

It was a nightmare.

Just another nightmare. Not real.

This time.

I turn toward the ball of fluff that rests against my arm, circling my other arm around the black cat that blends into the darkness. He's not visible, but he's here. He allows me to pull him against my chest and squeeze him like a child who finds comfort by clinging to a teddy bear. Only I'm not a child, and he's not a cuddler. During the day, he's honestly quite an ass. Yet when the tears surface at night, he always comes.

He allows me to hold him and pet him. Running my palm against his smooth fur brings me back from the terrors that haunt me in my dreams. It soothes me. As selfish as he seems to be, he inherently knows I need him.

I saved him once from the metal cage that held him hostage. I rescued him because he needed me. I saw the mischief in his bright green eyes, earning him the name Lucifer right from the get-go. He's lived up to his name, too. A wicked, fat thing that has me waiting on him hand and foot. At night, though, my little devil brings me back to reality, to where I'm safe. So, I suppose he saves me, too.

Six years, and I'm still not over it. *Six years.* I can't remember where I leave my cell phone at least a dozen times a day. But I remember every detail from that night, and the memories hold me hostage in my dreams. Not every night but too many to count.

A soft snore sounds from behind me, and I stiffen, clutching Lucifer to me. *Someone's in my bed.*

Think.

Pressing my face against Lucifer, I replay the events of yesterday, and it all comes back to me. It's crazy how the world is so much more terrifying in the dark, yet I'm not scared. It took me a little longer to connect the dots, but the sleep is lifting from my brain, allowing me to finally think clearly.

I'm in my room with my...boyfriend? Hookup? I don't know what exactly Jacob is to me. He's the second-grade teacher across the hall from me at school. We've been hanging out for a good month now. Last night, he stayed over for the first time. He's smart, cute, charming, and would check off all of the boxes if I were the type of girl to come up with boxes to check, but I'm not. I haven't thought about what I want in a life partner since that night in Mexico when I was a high school senior.

If I'm being honest, I have issues. Fear is something I have in abundance while my trust is scarce. I'm afraid of the what-ifs, the horrors out in the world that could break me. Trust isn't fostered when one lives in the shadow of dread. And I do. Look on a map and you'll find me, Tannon Lee, located right smack in the middle of trepidation and terror.

I'm a great teacher, a wonderful daughter, and the best of friends. I would do anything for the ones I love. I love hard and fierce. In the quiet of the night, in the moments after waking from a nightmare when my defenses are down, I can finally be honest. I need to learn to love myself.

Three realizations dawn.

#1 Jacob sleeps like the dead. Like, really, can I even take anyone serious who snores through someone screaming in terror a foot away from them? *No. I can't.*

#2 I'm not okay now, but I will be.

#3 Work is about to get a hell of a lot more awkward.

I place a small kiss on Lucifer's head. "I love you, buddy." I release my hold on him, and he immediately jumps from the bed, grateful for the freedom. Grabbing my phone on the nightstand, I see the time reads 4:00 a.m. *Good enough.* I hit the base of the lamp on the small table, turning it on.

Twisting in my bed, I face Jacob. I tilt my head to the side, admiring his face. He really is handsome. I don't question my decision, however. I know if he were the one, he'd make me feel safe. The fact that a twenty-pound fur ball that cleans himself by literally licking shit off his body comforts me more than Jacob does is a deal breaker.

I need to heal and fix myself. I know I do, and settling isn't going to do me any favors.

"Hey." I pull on Jacob's arm. "Wake up," I say louder, increasing the intensity in which I'm now shaking his bicep.

"Tannon?" he questions, half asleep. He clears his throat. "What is it? What time is it?"

"I need you to leave." My tone is assertive.

"What? Now? What—"

I halt his thoughts. "Yes, Jacob, I need you to leave now. Our relationship isn't working. I'm sorry. It's not you, it's me." The cliché rolls off my tongue as truth, and it is.

Jacob is a catch and will make some woman very happy someday. Yet that woman isn't me, and right now, his presence isn't benefiting my life. The terror I just awoke from was one of the worst yet, and it happened tonight—the first night I invited Jacob to stay. A coincidence? *Maybe.* The fact that I don't feel at all guilty in making him leave at four in the morning, a sign? *Definitely.*

"You're serious?" He pushes his hands behind him, sitting up.

"Yes. I'm sorry, but please leave."

"Oh-kay," he drawls out. "Now?"

"Now."

I pull the sheet up around my body and watch as Jacob slides out of my bed and starts to get dressed. Resisting the urge to tell him to hurry up, I bite my lip. He's moving at a snail's pace, but in all fairness, he's still waking up. He's peering around like he doesn't know what he's doing.

When he's clothed, he turns to me with what appears to be a sad expression. It's only been a month, so I know I'm not breaking his heart or anything, but regardless, a blanket of guilt engulfs me. This is a pretty unorthodox way to end a relationship. Yet my Marie Kondo game is stronger than my guilt. I study him, and he doesn't spark joy, only bone-deep restlessness.

He needs to go.

He pulls at the short hair at the nape of his neck. "Do you want to talk?"

I shake my head. "No."

It's cruel of me, I know. He deserves an explanation, but I promised myself that I would do what's right for me. Right now, the best thing for me is that he leaves. I don't owe anyone anything out of perceived obligation. I've played that game before and lost.

"Okay." He huffs out a sigh. "I guess I'll see ya."

"Bye," I respond.

When the apartment door closes with an air of finality, I turn off the small light on my nightstand and lay back against my pillow.

I know I can't keep living like this. Something has to give. Bad things happen to good people all the time—

every day—and it doesn't destroy them. People move on. Heal. I can heal, too. I won't allow his or his friends' actions to break me. I'm stronger than that. I must figure out what I need to let it go and feel whole.

Tragedy is a burden of many, but it won't weigh me down anymore. I will no longer allow the sadness and regret to take residence in my heart and mind. Without my tears, without my fear...the memories will have nothing to hold on to. They'll be left a faint whisper, one I won't hear.

Sleep won't find me again tonight. I sit up against my headboard and reach down to where my laptop rests against the side of my bed. Pulling it onto my lap, I open it and click on Microsoft Word.

My fingers race against the keys, and I watch as words materialize on the screen. So much in my head demands to be heard, and I type as fast as I can to give it a voice.

CHAPTER 1

TANNON

3 YEARS later

Spring break changed my life forever. It was a passage I could have lived without, a rite I would have forgone if I had known then what I know now. I would have made different choices. The words materialize on the screen of my laptop, and my skin pebbles at the memory. Visions of that time in my life are never welcome. Most days, I don't grant a moment from that week any space in my mind, not even for a second, because that's all it takes. One simple inhale of regret produces an exhale saturated with sorrow, and I tumble into the abyss of darkness. The obscure weight so heavy with the what-ifs that will never find an answer.

Yet here I am writing about it in painstaking detail. Why? Clearly to torture myself. I let out a sigh. No, that's not true. I write about it because I can't not write about it. The idea for this book came to me some time ago, and I ignored it. Well, in reality, a few years ago, I sent my boyfriend packing at four in the morning and typed out my story the entire day. My fingers had pressed against the keys of my laptop, creating the words that my heart wanted to release—and my mind wanted to forget—for the next eighteen hours. Save for a couple of bathroom and food breaks, I couldn't stop writing. I cried and wrote and cried some more until the story—my story, materialized. Then I deleted it all, every last word, and went to bed.

The thing about a writer's brain is that a book demanding to be written can't be ignored forever. The voices within won't be silenced. They're strong and dedicated. They come as a whisper at first, a gentle nudge providing me with the illusion that I have a choice in the matter. When I choose not to listen, the voices scream louder until they consume my every waking thought.

They're not real voices or alternate personalities. I'm not crazy, at least not most days. They're like thoughts that never leave. I think about this book in the shower, when I'm making breakfast, grocery shopping...all the damn time. And, truth be told, I don't want to think about this book anymore because it hurts.

I'm not sure of the process of other authors, but mine is personal. All of my novels are somehow rooted in my reality. When plotting a new book, I think of an instance in my life and take a visual screenshot, a photograph, of that time. Then I build a story around it.

So, no, the romance novels I write aren't autobiographies by any means, but a piece of them is real. The part of my current work in progress that's real hurts all the way down to my soul. I'm hoping that writing it will somehow free me of the pain and maybe help one of my readers, too.

My roommate, Cassie, explodes from her bedroom and practically skips into our living room. "Look at this premade I found on Emily's page!" She references one of our favorite cover designers as she tilts her laptop in my direction.

"It's awesome," I agree, the conversation a welcome distraction. I close my laptop. "Good timing. I need to take a break."

"I think it's perfect. I'm going to message her and snatch it up for your next book." She grins wide.

"No," I protest. "It's a great cover, yes, but not for me. Seriously, for the last time, I am not putting a man chest on my cover." I shoot a mock glare of annoyance at my best friend.

She squints in my direction, and her bright hazel gaze screams of exasperation and judgment. "Let's look at the facts. Shall we?" she quips, her fingers typing rapidly against the keyboard of her MacBook like it personally offended her and deserves to be punished. "Your author buddy Susie released her book three days ago as well. Her book is also a second-chance romance, same as yours." She presses the index finger from her right hand against the one from her left, counting out the similarities.

"Her cover is mainly blue, like yours." She ticks off the second point by touching her right index finger against her left middle. "Both contemporary romance," she says, pointing out the third similarity. "Both advertised as angsty, sweet, and spicy. You both used the same expensive-ass PR firm for the release tour. You did takeovers in the same reading groups. So many similarities, right? You want to know what's not the same?" Her voice rises an octave.

"Is no an acceptable answer?" I ask with a bite of my lip, trying to suppress a giggle as my bff's face becomes redder.

I feel like a guilty child getting schooled by her parents. Though I'm actually six months older than my closest friend and publicist, Cassiopeia "Cassie" Davenport. Cassie and I have been inseparable since we were paired as roommates in the University of Michigan dorms during our freshman year. Being older was cool when we were twenty because I could score us alcohol a whole six months earlier. Though, now at twenty-six, I'd take the later birthday. I mean, at this point, who wants to be older sooner. *Am I right?*

"Did you hear me?" she asks.

"Um..."

She lets out a sigh. "I said that the differences are the fact that you are a way better writer than she is. Her books are crap. You have a larger following on all social media accounts. Yet...she sits pretty with an Amazon ranking of twenty. Where are you, again?"

"Ten thousand?"

Cassie shakes her head. "Nope, that was yesterday. Today, you're at twenty thousand...three days after release. Twenty thousand isn't going to cut it, Tannon. You can't make a living off that."

"My brain hurts. Stop yelling." I sigh, grabbing a pillow from the sofa and covering my face.

"I'm not yelling, and you need to see this," Cassie insists.

"What?" I say, my voice tired.

"Do you know what the only difference between your marketing plan and Susie's marketing plan is?"

I drop the pillow to my lap. "No, but I'm guessing you're about to tell me?"

Cassie turns her laptop around so I can see it. It shows Susie's book cover on the screen.

"Man. Fucking. Chest." She slices her hands through the air like she's a "mic drop" gif.

I roll my eyes with a grin.

"I've done it before, and I can do it again." I shrug, and it's true.

Two years ago, in the third year of my teaching

career, I wrote a book that made it to number twenty on the list of top-selling books and didn't hit a hundred for six months. I've always loved writing, and I've been an avid reader my whole life. An idea came to me, and I wrote a novel. Then I published said novel, and for some crazy reason, it did really well. So well, in fact, that I decided to leave teaching and focus on my writing career. Two years later, I'm still living off the money I made from my first book. I've written ten books since my debut, but each new release does a little worse even though I think my writing has actually improved. I'm down to the last bit of money in my savings account. If my sales don't start to increase, I'll have to go back to teaching.

And I really don't want to go back to teaching.

Don't get me wrong. I liked it enough. I love kids, and I always wanted to be a teacher—second to my main dream of being a writer. I just never thought being a writer, and actually making money, was attainable. So, I went with my number two dream.

Then I wrote a book, and I made money. So now that I've lived my number one dream, I can't go back. I can't settle for anything less than my dream. *I can't.*

The marketing firm I work with has been trying to get me to make my covers sexier, which is where Cassie's obsession with me putting a half-naked man on my books comes into play. Currently, my covers are what I would call beautiful. They're colorful, pleasing to the eye, and basically works of art. Some of them have couples, and some don't. And for the ones that do have a couple on the cover, they're not the focal point.

My book covers definitely set up my brand, and I love everything about them. The covers are as beautiful as the words within. Admittedly, the words are a little spicier than the exterior of the book suggests, but my readers know what to expect.

When I started this journey, I swore to myself that I would never put a hot, sexy, naked dude on my covers. I know...what kind of romance author am I? But I want my covers to be like art and my stories to speak for themselves.

"I've never needed a man chest cover. If you recall, I made a lot of money off my first book—which has the most G-rated cover of them all," I tell Cassie.

"So much has changed in the book world in the last two years. You have to evolve with it."

"No, I'm not going to be a sellout, Cass. I'm not. I've built a beautiful brand. I'm not changing it to fit someone else's mold."

She nods dramatically and pouts out her lips. "Right. You mean the reader? You're not going to market your books toward those who will one-click? That's not a very sound plan, Tan. I get it, your books are beautiful, but they're not as marketable as they could be."

"How about we remove the spotlight from me and talk about your book for a minute?" I raise an eyebrow.

Cassie graduated from the University of Michigan with a double major in business and English. She's had a book written for years that she refuses to publish. In fact, one of the main contributing factors to me writing my initial book was the fact that my bestie had written one. She inspired me to write my own. Currently, Cassie isn't using either of her degrees—well, besides the help she gives me, her only client. She's a barista at the Starbucks below us.

"How about no?" She pins me with a stare. "You don't pay me as your publicist to talk about myself."

I can't help but laugh. "I barely pay you as it is. Believe me, it's okay. We can talk about you for a while."

She closes the screen of her laptop. "Sorry. That's a no. We're going to come up with a new marketing plan for you. It's going to be epic." She waves her hands through the air as she says the last word. "But, first, I have to go serve coffee. Are you coming down to write?"

She jumps off the couch and grabs her green apron from the back of the chair.

"Did PSL's come back yesterday?" I ask, knowing full well that the question is rhetorical. Everyone knows that pumpkin spiced lattes are back—anyone with social media, a TV, or a radio, that is...So basically everyone.

"You know they did." She grins, throwing her long brunette hair back into a ponytail.

"Then you know I'll be there."

"You're such a basic bitch," she says as she grabs her keys and cell phone from the table and tosses them into the front pocket of her apron.

I hold my hand to my heart. "Aw, thank you so much for the compliment."

"Anytime." She blows me a kiss before stepping out of our apartment. "See you soon."

After Cassie leaves, I reluctantly stand from our comfy couch. I should make my way down to Starbucks because I really need to get some more words in today. That's the thing about living the dream—I always need to be writing. It's been three days since my last book release, which means that my die-hard readers are already waiting for my next book—you know, the one that hasn't been written yet.

I scan myself in the full-length mirror.

Yoga pants—check.

Form-fitting *Star Wars* tee—check.

My long blond hair up in a messy bun—check.

No makeup for the "just rolled out of bed" author look—check.

This writer is ready for her day. The only thing missing is coffee and a lot of it.

I'd have to say it's pretty convenient for both Cassie and me to live above a Starbucks. We have the best work commute ever. Being right downtown in the heart of Ann Arbor, Michigan, means we're walking distance from anything of importance.

I grab my laptop, charger, phone, and keys, kick my feet into some flip-flops, and head out. It's still summer—late August—despite what the PSL campaign would have us all believe. In another month or so, I'll be able to sport my UGGs—which will round out my basic bitch status. But since it's eighty degrees out today, flip-flops are the next best option.

"Hey, Tannon." I'm greeted by a deep male voice when I step into the hallway. Everett, who lives in the only other apartment up here with his best friend, Asher, greets me.

"Hey, Ev. Going down to get some work done?" His laptop rests under his arm.

"Yep," he answers as the two of us walk side by side down the hall.

Everett created my website, so I know he does something with technology. I couldn't tell you what else he does, though. He's told me before, but once someone starts to speak "technology," I lose focus. They might as well be speaking a foreign language, and I guess for all intents and purposes, for me—they are.

Everett and Asher are the "Chandler and Joey" to Cassie's and my "Monica and Rachel." They are our best friends, who conveniently live across the hall. Though we all graduated from college the same year, we never actually met until the four of us moved into these apartments four years ago.

"You working on one of your dirty love stories?" he asks as we enter the stairwell.

"You know it. You working on some technology crap?"

"Absolutely." He grins and opens the door to Starbucks for me. "Remember, no work on Saturday night. Ash and I are having that party."

"Right." I nod. "You are penciled in. We'll be there. Well, have a great day, babe," I tell him.

"You too. Make sure to pound out some brilliance on that keyboard."

I shoot him a smile. "I'm going to try."

CHAPTER 2

JUDE MARTINEZ

"Fuck you, Jude!" Stacy screams from my driveway, kicking the front tire of her Honda Civic in anger. Why she's taking her fury out on her car, I don't know. She's already grabbed a basket of clean clothes from the sofa and scattered my clothes around the yard.

My front yard is a scene from a drama-filled love gone wrong 90s flick where the crazy girl throws her ex's shit out from a two-story apartment window. Only I live in a family-friendly suburb where Stacy's kind of crazy is a rarity. Who am I kidding? The Stacys of the fancy suburbs exist. They just hide their crazy more.

This Stacy, on the other hand, wears her insanity proudly.

Mrs. Anderson, my nosy next-door neighbor, steps out onto her front porch, wide-eyed and judgmental. *Just a typical day for her then.*

"Good morning, Mrs. Anderson." I wave cordially, a content smile across my face as Stacy drops some more f-bombs while continuing to kick her car.

Mrs. Anderson glares disapprovingly with a shake of her head and retreats back into her home.

Holding my wrist up, I check the time on my watch. *Is she almost done? Maybe I should go make some coffee?* I would be worried that one of my neighbors was about to call the cops. Stacy is a poster child for disorderly conduct and disturbing the peace but seeing that my police cruiser is parked in front of her now beat-up Honda, there'd really be no point in calling 911—and they all know that.

I should arrest her myself for being an obnoxious bitch, but I won't. I just need her gone. Why do the insane ones always find me? I'm pretty levelheaded. Isn't like attracted to like? Granted, they all hide their true colors initially, but the stripes always come out sooner or later. Maybe the irrational get off on the idea of being with a cop.

I let out a dry chuckle, ignoring the one-woman circus in front of me. If that's the case and the committable chicks seek me out, I'm screwed. It's utterly ridiculous because I know how to treat a woman. I was raised by my grandmother, mom, and five sisters. I speak girl drama and aced honors PMS. I excel at it, in fact. I'm the most understanding motherfucker you'll ever meet. I'm not scared away by a little attitude or emotions. I respect women and all they bring to the table. But this? Shooting a glance toward my driveway, I never realized how much Stacy resembled Godzilla. I can't get on board with this.

All right. Enough.

I make my way toward the screeching banshee. "That's enough, Stacy. Go home."

"Oh, now you want to talk?" she yells in my face, her spittle wetting my skin.

"I've always been willing to talk. I've never been interested in a screaming match with you, and you're not dragging me into one now. You've made your point. You're pissed I broke things off. But if you think this behavior is going to change my mind, you're wrong." *And insane*, though I leave that thought unspoken.

"Fight for me! Fight for us!" she hollers, tears drenching her cheeks.

Yeah, I think I'll pass.

"There is no us." I know that statement will fuel her unstable fire, but I'm over it and need her to leave.

"You bastard!"

"There are people in this neighborhood who just want to enjoy their day. Enough with all of this." I motion toward her and my yard full of laundry. "We're over, and that's not going to change. You need to go home and not come back. If I need to arrest you to get you to leave, I will. Now go."

"You can't arrest me," she spats.

"Try me."

She narrows her eyes at me with so much raw hatred

present. "You will regret this. You will never find someone who loves you as much as I do."

I highly doubt that, I think. Though I'm smart enough not to poke the bear when she's about to retreat. So I don't say anything. I simply wait.

And she leaves. Her tires screech against the pavement as she pulls away.

"I'm a nice guy. I don't get it," I say to myself, dragging the back of my hand against my face to wipe the remnants of Stacy's spittle off. Grabbing the laundry basket lying on the grass, I start to pick up my belongings.

"What in the hell?" Jane leans out of her driver's side window, laughing, as she pulls in.

"Don't ask," I answer, holding a pair of boxers in my hand.

"I'm guessing she didn't take it well?" Her lips tilt up in a smirk.

"No, she didn't."

The thing is, I won't miss Stacy at all. We'd hardly dated, and her true colors began to show right off the bat. She was one of those girls who constantly picked fights. She tried to make me jealous and irate, but I'm not down for that. I'm not taking the bait. The more I wouldn't bite, the more she tried to stir shit. I'm twenty-eight and ready to find "the one," as cheesy as that sounds. I'm done playing games. I want the true love, and family—kids—all of it. I know it's out there because I've seen it with my grandparents, parents, and my sisters and their husbands.

Being single has its advantages, sure. Yet I think if I found a person I was compatible with, the settling down part would be so much more fulfilling.

"Well, I know what will make you feel better," Jane says.

Jane is my partner at work and one of my best friends. We graduated from the academy at the same time. She's a tiny little thing and took a lot of shit from the other guys at the academy, but she never let it get her down. She trained harder and worked her ass off to graduate as the top female in our class—in everything. She holds a lot of power in her small frame, and I wouldn't trust anyone else to back me up on the job as much as I trust her.

"What's that?" I shoot her a grin.

"Leg day." She returns the smile. "Our legs will feel like Jell-O when we leave."

"I do love a good leg workout."

"I know. Right?" she quips.

Jane quickly helps me finish picking up my clothes. I dump the clothes into the washer. They're technically clean, save for a few errant blades of grass, yet Stacy touched them all as she threw them about in her rage. Once I wash her off the items of clothing, I'll never think of her again.

It's a relief.

Maybe I don't need to go looking for my future wife

just yet. It will be nice and so much less stressful to be single for a while—perhaps a long while. Besides, I have time.

After mixing up a couple of protein shakes, I hand one to Jane and grab my gym bag.

"Let's do this."

CHAPTER 3

TANNON

N*OTHING*. *Nothing. Nothing. Nothing.* I type the word out four times for emphasis. Given that the meaning of that word is "not anything," once should be sufficient. Though it's not. Writing the word one time couldn't adequately convey how much nothing I felt, how I literally couldn't feel anything down to my soul. An empty vessel. *Absolutely nothing.*

I drag the back of my hand across my cheek, wiping the tears that are falling. My chest heaves in sobs. A sense of relief comes over me as I sit back in my desk chair and hit save. I'm not deleting it this time. It was painful and horrible in the worst of ways, but at least that part is written. The next chapter is going to hurt like hell, too, but there's a semblance of relief that at least that chapter is finished. I wrote it exactly like it happened, word for word. This section of the book is vile in the worst of ways, but it's freeing too. I feel lighter.

I don't know how readers will take it. Maybe they'll hate it. I've accepted that this is a real possibility, but I honestly think I'm okay, even if that's the case. I had to write it. Maybe there's a girl out there, like me, who needs to know she's not alone. Yeah, this chapter was hard, but with each word, my character will become more free. *I'll become more free.* Perhaps one of my readers will become more free. And that's worth it. Happily ever afters exist even for the most broken.

"I'm ready," Cassie sing-songs as she swings my bedroom door open. Her red-lipped smile drops when she sees my face. "Oh, my God, Tannon. What's wrong?" She rushes toward me as I close my laptop and stand.

"Nothing." I shake my head. "You know…just wrote an emotional part."

Cassie wraps her arms around me, supplying a quick hug. "Authors are so high maintenance." She laughs. "Are you okay?"

I nod with a sheepish grin.

She sighs in relief. "Couldn't you wait until later to write that chapter? Your makeup was done already."

"Hey." I pucker my lips, catching her in my stare. "It's your fault that you took forever getting ready. You know I have to write when inspiration hits. It's fine," I quip, walking across the room to my vanity. "I'm wearing waterproof stuff anyway."

I dab my face with a tissue before reapplying some powder.

"So, it's an angsty one?"

"Aren't they all?" I chuckle. "It's all I know how to write."

"Give me details," she pleads.

"You'll be the first to read it when I'm done."

I never tell Cassie any of the details of my books as I write them. It's another part of my process. I feel like I can't share my characters until they're ready, until their story has been told. I think I'm just the type of writer who needs the words to flow from deep within, from my heart. I don't want to risk the story being altered by outside opinions. I feel it helps my characters remain authentic to my readers. At least, I hope so.

I look over my reflection in the mirror. My lashes are still on point, thanks to fabulous waterproof mascara. My blue eyes seem brighter after a good cry, an added bonus. My long blond hair falls in beachy waves that say, I woke up with these luscious curls, which is the desired effect. Yet any girl would know that it took loads of expensive product and a good amount of time with my curling iron to acquire such a carefree result. When I'm satisfied I don't look like I've been crying, I follow Cassie out of my room.

"Who's all going to be there?" I ask Cassie as we exit our apartment.

She shrugs as she steps across the hall and turns the

handle to Asher and Everett's place. "I have no idea. It's different every time."

"So true," I agree.

Our neighbor boys love to throw parties. Asher is a physical trainer at the gym down at the end of the block and has a ton of clients. So the last party was nothing but us and gym bunnies. Sometimes, the parties are full of friends or old fraternity guys from college.

We all have full-time jobs, but in a way, we're still living like we were during college: roommates, parties, and zero commitment. It's nice that I'm not alone in my endeavor to stay single. Right now, I'm focused on hitting the New York Times, not starting a family...much to my mother's disapproval.

If my mother had her way, I'd go back to teaching and marry a nice principal, and the pair of us would have 2.5 children and live in the burbs. Maybe someday, that life will be for me—well, at least the husband and kid part...probably not the rest. Right now, I'm happy living up the single life with my girl Cassie.

Scanning the apartment for familiar faces, I see none. "Randoms," I tell Cassie, and she nods in agreement.

Sometimes, Asher and Everett's guest list has no rhyme or reason at all. I have no idea where they find these people.

"Let's check on the porch," Cassie says, her voice loud so I can hear it over the music.

We find our friends on the small porch that overlooks the back alley. It's the one perk that their place has over ours. Otherwise, the floor plans are the same. Our apartment faces the street, and unfortunately, Starbucks isn't going to want a random porch hanging over their sign, so we don't have one.

They each hold a beer while they chat next to the grill as burgers sizzle over the flames.

"Ladies! It's about time you got here," Asher says and takes a swig from the amber bottle.

"You told us ten." I look down at the screen of my cell phone. "It's ten."

Everett grabs two bottles of alcohol from a cooler of ice and hands them to Cassie and me—a beer for her and a fruity drink for me. I've never been much of a beer drinker.

"Yeah, well, I told people all different times. I forgot," Asher answers.

"Who are these people? I don't recognize anyone," Cassie says.

Asher puckers his lips. "You know, friends from here or there."

I raise my eyebrows in question. "So you actually know everyone in your apartment right now?"

"Well, no. You know how it is. You invite someone, and they invite a few friends, and so on." He circles his free hand in the air.

"So, Tannon, how was your book release this week? I saw your book everywhere on social media, so I'm guessing it did well?" Everett asks.

"It did—"

Cassie cuts me off. "Horrible."

I shoot her a glare. "That's not true. There are millions of books on Amazon, and not even a fraction make it to a ten thousand ranking."

"And that's fine for the rest of them, but not for you. You should be selling more," Cassie chastises me, and I know it's out of love and concern for my career, but I just need one night where I can drink happily and not think about sales.

"Can we not?" I beg. "Not tonight."

"Maybe they aren't spicy enough," Asher offers. "Are your sex scenes juicy...like really juicy?"

I roll my eyes. "They're fine."

"Because I'm kind of wondering how you write these scenes since you never have sex. You need to spice up your life, so you can spice up your writing." Asher quirks a brow.

"Would you stop?" I smack him playfully on the chest. "My spicy scenes are fine. They're good. There are other ways to get inspiration, you know? Some call it...imagination," I say slowly, tapping my finger on my temple. "Plus, everyone on this porch is single. So, I don't want to hear it."

"We may be single in the commitment sort of way, but we all have fuck buddies. Just because we don't want to be in a serious relationship doesn't mean we don't get our needs met in other ways." Asher shoots me a creepy smile that I'm assuming was meant to be sexy.

"You're so gross." I laugh.

"Okay, prude. Aren't you the one who writes about sex for a living?" Asher throws his head back with a deep chuckle.

"No, I write about love and life, and beautiful journeys that happen to involve sex, but that's not the main focus. I write love stories. Not that you, Mr. Fuck Buddy, would know about any of that," I retort.

"Thank fuck for that," he scoffs.

"Who are you sleeping with now?" My question is directed at both guys.

"Erin, a girl I met at the gym," Asher says.

"Of course you are. What about you, Ev?"

"Julie," he answers.

"Julie from my work, Julie?" Cassie asks.

"The very one." Everett nods.

Cassie puckers her lips. "She didn't tell me that."

Everett drops his empty beer bottle in the recycle bin and grabs another cold one from the cooler. "That's because we're screwing, not getting engaged. It's not a big deal."

"With girls, it's always a big deal," I say.

Everett shakes his head. "Not true. Plus, Grandpa Henry is banging Cassie, and she's not serious about him. Prime example." He motions toward Cassie. "Not a big deal."

"Stop calling him that. He's thirty-five," she says of her Starbucks manager. "He's only nine years older than us." She shakes her head in a laugh.

"He seems older. Plus, he's all serious and frowny and 'would you like a grande or venti?'" Everett says in a whiny voice, apparently imitating Henry.

Cassie smacks his arm. "He doesn't sound like that, and he's just doing his job."

"Let's not digress," Asher says. "The point is that our girl here is best-selling author, Tannon Lee, writer of word porn, yet she's seeing no action in bed. There's a serious problem."

"I do not write porn!" I yell and turn to the side to see three wide-eyed girls staring at me. "It's romance," I tell them with a smile. They nod awkwardly and return to their conversation.

"I'm just saying that maybe you need some real-life inspiration to spice up your writing a bit." Asher shrugs.

"I had Brad," I blurt out.

"The Brad bootie call was like a year ago, babe," Cassie says.

"So, I have other things and stuff," I say with a pout.

"Like BOB." Everett chuckles.

I regret the day Cassie and I explained to the boys who or what BOB was. They love to bring up our "battery-operated boyfriends" any chance they get.

"Whatever. BOB is better than your MOG any day. You're just jealous because I don't have to work so hard," I say.

"Huh?" Everett asks for clarification.

"Manually-operated girlfriend...aka your hand. In

the shower. Everyday. Suck it, loser," I say with a gloaty confidence that probably isn't warranted.

All three of my friends burst out in laughter.

"You really need to work on your comebacks, Tannon. I love you, but you do." Cassie giggles.

"Whatever." I roll my eyes in mock annoyance. "How about we change the subject?"

"Yes!" Cassie wiggles, doing a giddy happy dance. "Did you talk to him?" she asks Asher.

"I did. He's in." He shoots her a wink.

"Who? What?" I ask.

Cassie turns to me, grinning. "I've been setting something up with Asher. It's a surprise for you. You'll find out next week."

"Uh...I want to find out now. I don't trust you two."

Cassie gasps and holds a hand to her chest. "That hurts. How can you not trust me?"

I narrow my gaze in her direction. "Tell me. What are you two cooking up?"

She presses her lips together in a wide grin. "It's a surprise, but I promise...it's a good one."

"You can't bring it up in front of me and then not tell me. Come on, please?" I bat my eyelashes, causing Cassie to laugh again.

"You'll find out when the time is right. I'm not giving you the chance to shut it down," she says.

I drop my head back and stare up at the roof's gutter with a sigh. "That means it's going to be bad. Is it work-related?"

"Maybe," Cassie sing-songs.

"Then you have to tell me. I need input on these things."

"As your publicist, I say no."

"You can't say no," I scoff. "I don't pay you to say no."

She shrugs. "Well, as you said before...you barely pay me. So you'll find out this week, and you'll like it whether you want to or not."

"Um, I think you're going overboard with your duties and getting a little pushy if you know what I mean." I lift an eyebrow and shake my head slowly.

"I don't think I do...know what you mean." She winks and takes a sip of her beer.

CHAPTER 4

JUDE

Holding the iPad in my hand, I pull up the Google doc of the class participants. I always hate calling out names like a kindergarten teacher. Logically, I understand that there's nothing wrong with it, and it's important to know if someone doesn't show so that we can offer the spot to a woman on the waiting list. Yet I hate it nonetheless.

"Is that the list of names?" Jane questions.

"Yeah," I answer, looking at the class roster on the iPad. "You're calling them out this time. I always butcher a pronunciation and look like a fool."

She chuckles, taking the iPad from my hand. "Remember last month when you completely screwed up Siobhan's name? *See-oh-bon?*" Jane says the mispronounced version of the name in a low, goofy voice, apparently imitating me.

I shoot her a glare. "Come on. You have to admit that name is spelled weird and sounds nothing like it looks."

She shrugs. "It's Irish."

"And that matters why?"

"I'm just saying everyone knows how to pronounce Siobhan." Jane puckers her lips in amusement.

"I guarantee they don't, and you know what? You're the designated name-caller for every class from now on."

"Okay, grumpy butt," Jane kids.

I press my lips together in a tight smile, remembering my *See-oh-bon* moment. *I'm an idiot.*

Scanning the gym, I count the ladies in attendance as they start stretching. I'm pretty sure they're all here. This self-defense class is quite popular and always fills up. There's a waiting list, but there haven't been too many times when we've actually pulled someone from the list due to a no-show.

Jane and I have been running this class for two years and don't charge anything to those in attendance. All women should know how to defend themselves. Growing up with five sisters and listening to the cries of one who was hurt by a man fostered a fierce desire to make sure I help as many women as possible so they can protect themselves if the need arises. Studies say that one in five women have experienced some form of rape in their lifetime. That's fucking infuriating.

"Welcome!" I yell out to the gym of women before me. The ladies stop chatting and turn to face the front of the large space where Jane and I stand. "I'm Officer

Martinez, and this is my partner Officer Grenada." Jane waves. "Welcome to self-defense for all ability levels. Whether you're here to brush up on previous skills or learn new ones, this class is beneficial for both past participants and newcomers. Over the course of the month, Officer Grenada and I will be splitting you up into ability levels to help you get the most out of your time here. Today, though, we're going to be going over the basics. Even if you've learned them before, practicing the fundamentals is crucial. You want to know these moves inside and out. If the time ever comes when you need to employ any of these tactics, it's important to do them instantly without thought. Seconds matter." I pause for emphasis.

"Officer Grenada is going to start by taking roll call." I nod toward Jane, who smirks subtly.

"Michelle Cable."

"Here."

"Amy Everetts."

"Here."

"Kristy Parks."

"Here."

I find the women's faces in the crowd as they confirm their presence. It brings me a satisfaction that is hard to beat, hoping that these women won't be victims, and if they already have been, they won't again.

"Tannon Lee."

"Here."

My gaze lingers on Tannon's face as Jane continues

to call names. There is something about her that is entirely intriguing. My heart picks up pace as I stare in her direction. She has a natural flawless beauty. Her blond hair is swept up into a bun atop her head. Her skin is pale and perfect. I imagine it being as soft as silk to the touch. She smiles and whispers something to her friend at her side, her blue eyes shining with mischief. If we were anywhere else, like a club, I'd approach her a hundred percent. She's drop-dead gorgeous without even trying.

Her eyes find mine, perhaps sensing the presence of my stare, and I force my attention to someone else.

Fuck. What a creeper.

I'm sure the last thing this Tannon chick needs is a dude ogling her during a class where I'm supposed to teach her how to take a man my size down. It's just been a long time since I've had such a visceral reaction to someone based solely on appearance.

Jane finishes reading off the list, and I step forward to start the lesson.

"Today, we're going to focus on escaping from an arm grab, a grab from behind, a chokehold, and a hair grab. In all of the maneuvers, the main component is your ability to be quick. Do not hesitate. We are going to practice these escape techniques so much that they will become rote memory. Your life may depend on quick thinking and fast movements. The truth is that you won't always be able to out-muscle the perpetrator. Jane and I are going to show you how to act fast, use leverage and your core strength, and strike where it will have the most impact." I tick off the four strike areas on my fingers. "Eyes, nose, throat, and groin."

Jane takes a step forward. "I'm going to grab Jane's arm, and she's going to show you how to escape. We're going to demonstrate two techniques. The first one is to be used in a more aggressive situation."

Leaning forward, I grab Jane's wrist. She swiftly steps in and brings the palm of her hand toward my nose in one smooth motion, kicks at my groin, and when I release her hand, she runs away.

"Did you see when she stepped in quickly, it forced my wrist to bend. That's crucial because it gives you leverage over your attacker by weakening their hold. Before I could register what she was doing, she had struck my face and kicked my groin. It doesn't matter how much stronger your attacker is, those two consecutive moves will startle him and cause enough pain that he'll release his grasp, giving you the window to get away. And that's crucial—get away. As soon as your attacker is off balance and has released you—run to somewhere safe or public. So pair up. We're going to go through the steps together, slowly."

Jane and I demonstrate the move again.

"Step, pull, hit, kick, run," I say as Jane completes the steps. We go through the process in slow motion as the women work with their partners. "Step. Pull. Hit. Kick. Run," I repeat, walking the women through it and observing their moves.

"Good," I say to Tannon as she pulls her arm free from her partner. I ignore the way I feel around her and focus on the task at hand because I'm a professional. "It helps to grab your fist with your free hand to assist in pulling it down or up, depending on how you're being held. You always pull against the space between the attacker's thumb and forefinger."

I've already explained this, and I know that Tannon gets it, but man, I just have to talk to her.

"Thanks." Her gaze holds mine, and I swallow. The hue of her irises is so rich. They're blue like the ocean, yet not the shallow part but near the shore where it is more of a teal. No, Tannon's blue is the color of the water that resides over the deepest part of the ocean. I want to stay and stare into her waters. The woman behind the intense gaze fascinates me.

I know that the woman before me has a story to tell. In my profession, I've become good at reading people. Because of this, I know that Tannon isn't simply a pretty face. She's good and kind. She's sensitive and warm. She has layers waiting to be peeled back and discovered. I see a guard up around her, weighing her down. She's been hurt. I'm not sure how I know this exactly, but she has. I just hope she has someone to confide in and help her lighten the load.

I give her and her partner, a brunette woman, a nod and continue to the next couple to check in on their progress. I have to watch myself around Tannon over the next few weeks. I think next class, I'll have Jane take the side of the room where Tannon is. I've already committed the exact color of her eyes to memory, which is more than I've done with my last fling. Nothing can ever be with Tannon because I won't approach a woman I've met in one of my classes. It just seems...wrong. If a woman can't be free from a man's advances here, where can she?

No, Tannon's off-limits. Hopefully, when I see her in the next class, that fact won't sting as bad.

CHAPTER 5

TANNON

COFFEE IN HAND, *I switch my iPod back on as I exit the coffee shop. Looking up, I freeze, stunned, and the most gorgeous man I have ever seen walks down the sidewalk toward me.*

Lame.

I suck.

This chapter is boring. I'm a failure. My teaching certificate hasn't expired, so it's not too late to switch my career back to something that will make money. I mean, I won't become rich as a teacher, but it's enough to get by.

Annoying girl meets gorgeous guy. Cue butterflies. Nope. It's predictable. Perhaps, I should mix it up a bit. Switch genres. I could write a zombie novel. *Geez, Tannon. Focus.*

I'm tired.

Lying across our leather couch with my MacBook in

my lap, I yawn obnoxiously. I find that sometimes it helps me to wake up if I make my yawns as loud and irritating as possible like a lion or, more accurately, an ostrich in heat. Do birds go into heat? I don't know. But if they do...I think they'd sound like I do right now. If I annoy myself enough—surely, I won't be so tired. It makes sense.

I should get up. Maybe go for a walk. Do some jumping jacks. Find a way to lift this brain fog. I'm too tired, though. This happens when I'm writing a book, usually around the midpoint. I get stuck in this no makeup, yoga pant, sloth-like existence where all I want to do is nap or eat. But I can't nap because if I do, then I won't write, and then I won't publish, which means I won't make money, and I'll have to go back to teaching. It's a vicious cycle.

"Uhhhhh." I yawn loudly again, stretching my arms over my head.

I'm met by an evil stare from Lucifer, my cat. He sits under the coffee table, judging me. When I rescued this pure black puffball of a kitten from the Humane Society three and a half years ago, I had no idea he'd turn out to be the worst cat in history. That's the thing with cats. They come into the world with their personality in place. They don't have the need to please like dogs do. Frankly, they don't care.

That's not entirely true—he's not the worst cat. He has his moments. He loves me in his own cat-like way. At least he loves me when I need him the most. When I first got him, that was a lot. Many nights. But, after some therapy, a change in careers, self-defense classes, and I suppose maturity, I began to heal. I'm not without issues. I'll probably always have insecurities where my past is concerned, but at least Lucifer doesn't need to rescue me at night as much anymore. In fact, I can't remember the last time he curled up next to me after a nightmare. It's been many months.

Truthfully, I think I'm a dog person, but dogs and apartments are a lot of work. Plus, I live in Michigan, and taking a dog for a walk every few hours to go to the bathroom in the arctic tundra that is our winter doesn't sound fun. At least cats are pretty low maintenance.

I close my laptop with a sigh and set it beside me. Maybe I need more coffee? I place a foot down hesitantly and eye Lucifer. His eyes narrow as he takes in my socked foot.

"Don't even think about it," I hiss. "I'm serious."

I set my other foot down on the ground. Lucifer hasn't attacked. So far, so good. He has a thing with biting my feet when I'm getting onto or down from chairs, sofas...my bed. He's not picky with the location of his assaults. He's not consistent either. Sometimes, he goes weeks without mauling my toes when I get out of bed. Then out of the blue, he charges and scratches me to hell. He's such an asshole.

He extends his paw from below the coffee table to taunt me, and it works. My heart picks up a beat, and I lift my legs back onto the couch.

"I will give you away to a stinky man with lots of dogs who only feeds you generic dry food. No Fancy Feast for you—ever again. I'm serious." I glare at him.

He stretches out his other paw with a lazy yawn. He knows I'm not serious. I love him too much.

"You're right. I won't, but please don't attack me. Your momma is having a bad day. Be nice," I plead with my cat.

I hesitantly place my feet onto the floor again and watch Lucifer. He eyes my feet and then raises his gaze to my face.

He's going to let me pass freely. *Phew.*

I quickly step around the coffee table and into the kitchen to make more coffee. I really feel like some Starbucks right about now, but I have mascara running down my cheeks from two days ago, and I'm not in the mood to wash my face. So, a K-Cup will have to do.

Lucifer purrs against my ankle and then meows like a crazy animal.

"No. You've had your wet food today. You have a whole bowl of dry. Go eat that."

He meows again, and this time, it's louder and more assertive—a warning. He will not ask twice.

I owe him because he let me get off the couch in one piece, and he's come to collect. My life is ruled by this cat.

"Fine. One more can of food, but that's all for today. You're going to get too fat, and that's unhealthy. And you have to promise to be nice to me for the rest of the day. I have to get some words in, or I won't be able to afford all of this fancy wet food that you love so much. Okay?"

He paces beside me as I open the can of food, swishing his tail back and forth. He meows again, this time in truce.

"Thank you," I tell him as I place the bowl of food on the floor.

Cassie comes sauntering in through the door. "Look what I have for you!" she holds up the large white cup with green writing.

I hold my hands to my chest. "Oh my God, thank you! I needed a pick-me-up."

I leave Lucifer in the kitchen and meet Cassie by the couch. I take the cup of goodness from her and plop down on the soft cushions.

"You don't know how much I needed this," I say into the cup as I take a sip.

"How'd writing go today?" she asks, sitting in the lounge chair across from me.

"Eh." I let out a grunt. "Two hundred words."

"Two hundred words in the six hours since I've left?"

I frown. "You know how it is. Sometimes, they flow. Sometimes, they don't."

"Maybe you need to put this book aside and start another one...a more exciting one." Her eyes go wide with mischief.

"I like the one I'm working on. I think it may end up

being the best book I've written." I don't know if that's true, but it's definitely very meaningful to me.

"That's nice, but will it sell? What's the exact genre?"

"Angsty Contemporary Romance, heavy on the feels," I answer.

"So, exactly like your others."

"Oh," I add with some excitement. "There are hot firefighters."

"Mmm. Well, that is a bonus. Firefighters have a decent reader fan base. But maybe you should write to market more. I've been doing research on what's in right now."

"Okay." I urge her to continue.

"Well, stepbrother went out a while ago, but it's still a good seller."

"Pass."

"Then we have bully romance, which is huge right now."

"What's bully romance?"

"You know, like the one we read by your author friend in Indiana? It's a guy in high school. He loves a girl but is an asshole to her like ninety percent of the story, and then they get together and have hot sex and live happily ever after."

I shake my head. "Absolutely not. That's not me. I know those types of stories are huge right now. I can't write them, though." I scrunch up my face, thinking of my younger brother, Branson. "I mean, my brother and his friends are all seniors in high school. They're all pimply and awkward and..." I shiver, making a face. "That is not romantic."

Cassie laughs. "Well, in general, the romance genre is based in fiction, Tannon. You can't think of real-life high school guys."

I furrow my brows. "I can't help it with that genre. It's too close to home. Next."

"All right, well the other huge one right now is reverse harem."

"What in the hell is reverse harem?" I chuckle.

"You know, one girl, three or more guys. No jealousy." She looks at me hopefully. "Do you know how many reverse harem books are in the top 100 of romance?"

I let my head fall back against the couch with a sigh.

"What?" Cassie giggles. "You have to think outside of the box a little. Writing to market is a smart strategy. Trust me."

I groan. "I'm sure it is, and I appreciate you looking out for me, but I can't." I shake my head. "Nope. I can't write a book that doesn't resonate with me. Those genres aren't me."

"I knew you'd say that," she says on a sigh. "It was worth a shot, though."

"You're going to love the one I'm working on. The readers will too. I promise."

Cassie kicks her legs up on the coffee table. "It's not a matter of the readers liking your stuff. They always do.

It's marketing it. Grabbing the attention of new readers. You need something...a little umph. You know what I mean?"

I pat her leg. "I'm sure whatever marketing strategy you do for my next release will be brilliant. I have no worries." I shoot her a wink.

She presses her lips together in a smirk. "Well, I am working on something."

"You always are. I have complete faith in you." I grin with a shake of my head.

She removes her feet from the coffee table and stands suddenly. "Oh, I almost forgot. You need to go shower and get ready." She claps her hands together excitedly.

I eye her skeptically. The way she's rocking up on the pads of her feet excitedly can only mean she's done something I'm not going to like. "What did you do?"

She holds up her hands in surrender. "Hear me out, okay? Know that I only have your best interest at heart and just keep an open mind."

"I hate you already," I say with a roll of my eyes.

"So, there's this guy..."

"Nope." I stand from the couch. "Not interested."

She grabs my wrist as I start to turn away. "You promised to hear me out," she whines.

"I did not." I chuckle.

"It was implied." She shrugs. "Anyway, there is this guy who comes into work all of the time. He's so dreamy, and he's an architect. So, he's all super creative, too. I know you'll hit it off."

"What kind of coffee does he order?"

Cassie and I have a coffee scale for men. The men worth dating order their coffee black. Plain black coffee means the man is strong, secure, steady...dating material. Then we have a sliding scale for the other types. Espresso is also very good, but it's not as good as plain black. A guy who orders an espresso has all the qualities of a black coffee kind of guy, but he tries a little too hard. He can be overbearing and bossy.

I'd think about dating a cappuccino guy, though they can be a little airheaded and noncommittal. A cappuccino dude is kind and romantic, but he often chases unattainable goals and can be a tad clueless. If there was an attractive man who checked all the right boxes off on my dating checklist but thought he could make a living by following his childhood dream of becoming an ant farmer—he probably drinks cappuccino. It's hit or miss with them.

Now, if I see a white chocolate mocha with extra whip dude? I run—far, far, away from him. No one needs that hot mess in their life.

Cassie's lips curve up into a wide smile. "Black!"

"And he's dreamy too?"

"So dreamy. I think you'll hit it off, and if not—he's totally worthy of a one-nighter. He's yummy. You need to get out, break up the routine, and maybe get laid. It will help with your writer's block. Malcolm can help. Just go out with him. I promised him you would."

"Well, you shouldn't have." I lower my stare. "But he sounds decent. Even though you know I hate when you try to go all matchmaker on me, I'll give him a chance."

"Yay! Okay, good!" She jumps up. "So go shower. He'll be here to pick you up in an hour." She presses her lips in a tight line to stop a laugh from erupting.

"Cassie." I groan.

"Just go. It's too late to cancel, and you already agreed." She waves me off toward the bathroom.

I snatch the coffee up from the table and cradle it to my chest. Even though I now know this coffee was an attempt to butter me up before she dropped her blind date bomb on me, I'm still going to enjoy every last drop. It's not the coffee's fault my bff is a manipulative little shrew.

"Fine, but you're getting a little too much power in this relationship." I motion back and forth between us. "Oh, is this what you and Asher were planning at their party?"

She waves me off. "Oh, no. You still have that to look forward to."

"Great," I grumble as I head toward the bathroom. I feign annoyance, but the smile on my face is completely genuine.

CHAPTER 6

TANNON

M&#65533;&#65533;&#65533;&#65533;&#65533;&#65533; &#65533;&#65533;&#65533;&#65533;&#65533;&#65533; all of my first impression requirements with flying colors. He looks eerily similar to the way I wrote my main male character earlier.

His grin, sexy and beautiful, is disarming, and his sea-blue eyes shine as they hold my gaze. I think back to the way in which I introduced my main male character today. He's dreamy, real book boyfriend material.

Malcolm is very easy on the eyes. *Real-life boyfriend material? Maybe.* He has a beautiful smile, perfectly disheveled hair, and blue eyes that twinkle—like literally twinkle. Though it could be the bright spotlight over our table that is practically blinding me with each second that passes.

He's kind and polite. He loves his family and his job. He has a rescue pit bull puppy and everything. Wasn't I just thinking this afternoon that I was meant to be a dog person?

However, if this was a romance novel, I should totally be feeling this pull toward my lady parts, but I'm not. My loins are not throbbing. *Hmmm.* Maybe if I asked him to lift his shirt so I could drool over that inverted 'V' that I always write about, the one that makes real-life women fall for fictional men, then I'd feel the clench in my groin.

Hey, Malcolm. Can I see your abs? I practice the sentence in my head to see if it sounds crazy. Verdict—it does. Dammit.

Can you pass me the breadsticks and your shirt, please? Not any better.

Let's play a game? Every time you take a bite of your food, you remove an item of clothing. Start with your shirt. Ugh, still crazy.

"So, Cassie tells me that you write romance novels for a living?" His question pulls me from my abdomen-obsessed fantasies.

"Yeah, I do."

"That's cool." His response is the most common reaction I get to that question.

I think it's a safe reply. People tend to want to gauge my reaction before they commit to judging or praising me too much for writing books with sex.

"It is. I've always loved writing and telling stories. I get to make my own schedule and work from home. My books are spicier than, say, Nicolas Sparks, but nowhere near *Fifty Shades* level." I want to smack myself the second the words leave my mouth. I don't know why, but I always want to compare my novels to other authors to give them validity of some sort. It's dumb. My work can stand on its own.

I also have a habit of downplaying the spice so others don't judge me too harshly. What I need is a T-shirt that reads, *I write books with lots of sex. So what?* Then I need to wear that baby loud and proud. But I never would. I'm not one for confrontation. A part of the reason being an author suits me so well is because most of my time is spent in the comfort and safety of my own home. I think a lot of authors are closeted introverts to be honest.

"Sounds like a great gig. I think Rachel reads those kinds of books. I'll have to tell her so she can check you out."

I'm not entirely sure who Rachel is, but I don't ask, probably a sister. I have a feeling he mentioned her while I was fantasizing about ways to get his shirt off. I'll look like a jackass if he realizes I wasn't listening to what he was saying.

"So what kinds of buildings do you design?" I ask.

He regals me with descriptions of his past and upcoming projects. I listen attentively, trying to feel a spark, but still come up empty. I think I'm broken. Writing about love has ruined me for it.

Why am I even thinking about love? I don't need love. I have my dream job, a roommate I love, friends I adore, and a devil cat. A perfect life. I'm not missing out by not being in a relationship. Sure, some sex now and then with anyone other than BOB would be ideal, but not necessary.

I take in Malcolm's features as he talks. Everything about him is romance book beautiful. I don't need to have a love connection to sleep with him. Right? I'm just not feeling it, and I'm not a one-night stand kind of girl, as exciting as that sounds.

What is more attractive than a hot guy with a puppy? I've seen the memes. Let's move the conversation back to that. Maybe I can convince my brain that I'm into him enough. "How is having a puppy and living in the city? Is he crate trained while you're gone at work? We had a pittie mix when I was young, and every time we left him at home, he'd chew up something. He was so anxious." I smile, thinking back to my childhood love, our dog Elvis.

"Yeah, he loves to chew, but luckily, he's never really home alone. Rachel works from home, so she can take him out anytime," Malcolm shoots me a dashing smile, but for some reason, it gives me the creeps.

Does he live with his sister? How did I miss this whole conversation?

"I'm sorry if I missed this earlier, but who's Rachel again?" I ask casually before taking a bite of my lobster.

"My wife," he says without missing a beat.

Holy hell.

I inhale the chunk of food in my mouth and start

coughing to dislodge it. I smack my chest, water filling my eyes.

"Are you okay?" he asks, leaning forward.

"Yeah. Food. Wrong pipe," I choke out, continuing to cough with full-on tears falling now.

I cough the seafood out of my lungs for what seems like an hour. I don't even care how ridiculous or stupid I look. *The asshole has a wife.*

I take a drink of water, finally able to breathe again. "I hate when that happens," I say as I wipe under my eyes with my napkin. "I gotta say, Malcolm. I'm kind of surprised that you wanted to go out with me given that you're married."

"Why? Cassie gave me the impression that you didn't want anything serious. Just some fun. I'm down for some fun." He winks at me, and the food in the pit of my stomach threatens to come back up.

I'm going to kick Cassie's ass.

"Right, but what will Rachel think of this fun?" I ask.

Malcolm shrugs with an air of nonchalance. "Nothing. She won't know about it." His voice is completely unaffected by the subject of infidelity. People get more riled up about the weather than he's getting about the prospect of an affair.

"Huh. Yeah." I nod, at a loss for words.

What do I do? What do I do? Yell at him? Excuse myself to go to the bathroom and leave?

His phone buzzes, and he picks it up.

"Hey, babe. Just having dinner with a client." He shoots me another wink. *Cringy AF.* He addresses me now. "Will you please excuse me? I need to take this. I'll be back." Getting up from the table, he walks toward the back of the restaurant and disappears around the corner.

I flag down the waiter. "Hi. Can we please order your most expensive bottle of...well, what's more expensive here, wine or champagne. We're celebrating our anniversary and want the best." I smile wide.

The waiter grins. "We have a vintage 1993 Dom Perignon for $500."

I gasp with faux excitement. "Oh my gosh. That's the year I was born. That'll be perfect. We'd also like to order every dessert on your menu, please. Here." I reach for Malcolm's wallet that he left on the table and pull out the American Express in the first sleeve. Go ahead and ring us up. But can you bring the champagne right away? I want it to be at the table before my hubby gets back. The desserts and credit card slip can be brought anytime." I wave him off. "Hurry! He'll be back any minute."

I stare toward the back of the restaurant. Whatever Rachel needed to talk about is taking a while because Malcolm hasn't come back yet. The waiter returns a minute later with a bottle of champagne and an entire chocolate cake.

"I brought the cake because it was ready. The other items need to be plated. I hope that's okay, Mrs...." He drops his stare to Malcolm's credit card, reading the last name. "Stone."

"Perfect. You know what? Can you add another one of these cakes to the bill and write the word *Fidelity* on the top with melted white chocolate. It's the most important pillar of our marriage. We'll probably need that one in a to-go box, though." I smile.

"Absolutely, Mrs. Stone. I'll just need to take the card back to charge the additional cake."

"No problem. Take your time."

He leans in to pour the champagne. "Can you just leave the bottle? My husband likes to pour it. Something about bubbles." I chuckle, waving my hand through the air.

"Absolutely." The waiter nods and retreats to the kitchen.

I ball up an unused napkin from the table and stick it in the top of the bottle, where the cork once was. Then I slide the bottle into the side of my MK bag, and put it over my shoulder. I grab the plate with the cake, stand from the table, and I walk the fuck out.

Peace out, Malcolm.

A short Uber ride later and I'm back home.

"Home so soon?" Cassie asks. "And with a cake?" She sounds confused.

"Did you know he was married?" I snap at her as I kick the door closed behind me.

"What? He's married?" Cassie gasps. Of course she

didn't know. I never thought she did. It just seemed like the appropriate way to begin this conversation.

"Sure is and was very open about how he was all for having some fun with me behind her back."

Cassie covers her mouth. "Oh my God. I'm so sorry, Tannon."

"I mean, whatever, I wasn't into him anyway. He's cute and all, but I couldn't make myself dig him. But when I found out about his wife, I was so mad—for her. What a fucking douche!" I set my purse down on the kitchen counter and take out the bottle.

"Wow. Such a disappointment for a black coffee drinker." She frowns.

"Totally."

"He's really going to skew our coffee rating system." She sighs.

I nod. "I know. We may have to re-evaluate the scale. Though, let's not get too hasty. He could just be a random outlier."

"True."

I grab two wineglasses and two forks and meet Cassie at our dining table. I set the cake between us on the table and hand her a fork. I pour us each a full glass of champagne. "Have you ever had $500 champagne?"

"Um, no."

I hand her a glass of the bubbly. "Cheers to firsts." I smirk while clinking our glasses together.

"Where did you get a $500 bottle of champagne?" she wonders, her mouth hanging open.

"Malcolm bought it for me and this cake." I grin wide. "So, all in all, I'd say it was a pretty good date."

Cassie takes a long sip from her glass. "It tastes like..." She stops to think of the right word.

"A twenty-dollar bottle of champagne?" I finish her thought, and we both laugh.

"Yes!" she agrees. "What the hell?"

"I know. I thought it'd taste magical somehow." I giggle. "Oh, well...I feel pretty amazing." I dig my fork into the cake and take a big bite. "This," I say through a mouth stuffed with chocolate, "tastes like a million bucks."

Cassie rolls her eyes back and groans as she takes a bite of the cake. "Ah-maze-sing. So, I need to hear the details."

"Definitely, but first, you have to promise me something."

"What?" she asks.

"Don't ever set me up on a blind date again."

"Ugh. Fine. Now, tell me everything."

CHAPTER 7

TANNON

If a man's looks are too good to be true, it means his appearance is merely compensating for the evil hiding inside, and I have to stay the fuck away—far, far away. I think of the last line of the chapter I finished last night. I can thank Malcolm for that inspiration. My female character is in a very *I hate men* place right now. I'm digging it.

I throw BOB into my bedside table drawer. "See you later, friend," I tell the pink device as I stand and stretch.

It's a shame that my blind date didn't turn into at least a quickie. Who am I kidding? I would've never been able to go through with a casual hookup, even if he wasn't a cheater. What's wrong with me? None of my friends have issues with casual sex, but I've never been into it for various reasons. Yet...I'm the one who writes romance.

Maybe that's my problem. I'm holding out for the swoon-worthy book boyfriend when, in reality, the world is full of Malcolms. Are romance books ruining my life? Am I setting my expectations too high? Plus, if legit heartthrobs actually do exist, I'm not going to find him in this apartment, which is where I spend ninety-nine percent of my time.

Cassie is being abnormally loud this morning. She's been moving about the apartment and chatting on the phone with whom—I don't know. There's music playing and dishes clanking. About twice a year, she goes into this cleaning frenzy and deep cleans our apartment from top to bottom. In autumn, it usually happens in November before we put our Christmas decorations up. So, if she's out there with a Q-tip, dusting between the rungs of our chairs, it's a little early.

"Can't anyone sleep in anymore?" I address Lucifer, who's sprawled out across my dresser.

He glares at me and swipes a pair of my earrings off my dresser.

"Rude. Yeah, I know it's eleven, but I was up until after three in the morning writing."

Lucifer growls and lifts a leg before he starts cleaning himself where his balls once were. It's a message. He's very good at communicating, though he doesn't actually speak English.

"Fine. I was on Instagram and TikTok. I wasn't writing. Are you happy?" I huff. "Whatever. I finished a chapter at least."

Making my way toward the bedroom door, I adjust my tank top before opening it. Half of my left boob was hanging out, which always happens when I sleep. I look down. My tight booty shorts are covering all the essentials and both nipples are covered by my top. I'm good to go.

I open the door and stroll out. Pulling the hair tie from my wrist, I lift my arms and wrap my hair into a messy bun. It takes a second for my eyes to adjust to the brightness of the space.

Squinting, I turn the corner toward the living room and walk right into a shirtless guy. My hands splay across his chest to stop myself from falling into him. I quickly remove my hands from his skin, knowing immediately that this isn't Grandpa Henry.

"I'm so...I'm sorry," I stutter, stepping away from him.

Now that my eyes can fully focus. I take him in—tall, tan, stunning green eyes, short dark hair. Oh, and there's a pull. There's a definite pull—all the way down to my needy lady parts. And then there's the flips in my belly—a hundred horny butterflies, going insane at a disco party—right in the center of my stomach because A.) He's hot AF. And, B.) I've seen him before.

Two thoughts enter my head simultaneously. One—he's here with Cassie. I need to pull my dirty mind out of the gutter. These thoughts are so not appropriate. Though, how could she? Then again, we both mentioned that he was hot. I can't blame her. And, two—I've suddenly become very aware that I'm barely dressed, and my nipples are hard as rocks against my thin, white tank top.

"It's fine. No worries," the guy says, and dammit, I'd be lying if I said I haven't dreamed about that sexy as hell voice since I first heard it last week.

I cross my arms over my chest and take a step back just as Cassie's cheerful voice addresses me. "Tannon! Hi."

Tannon? Hi? Why does her voice sound all squeaky?

I finally pull myself together enough to take in the scene unfolding in our living room. There are hanging white backdrops, lights, boxes, and a very expensive-looking camera on a stand being looked at by some dude —who if I had to take a guess—I would say is a professional-ass photographer.

There's a fucking photo shoot happening in my living room, and I'm practically naked.

"Tannon, I want to introduce you to your model. This is Jude Martinez," a tight smile crosses her face. "Jude, this is Tannon Lee, the author."

I'm seriously kicking her ass this time.

"Yeah, I remember you from last week in class." He smiles warmly as if he's not looking down at a train wreck and extends his hand.

I remove one of my arms from my breast area and shake it quickly. "Right. The instructor. Small world." I dart a sheepish smile in his general direction before addressing Cassie. "Cassie, can I talk to you a minute?" I turn and retreat to my bedroom.

"Uh, sure," she says nervously and excuses herself.

She steps into my room and shuts the door behind her, pressing her back against it with a horrified expression on her face. "I can explain."

"I cannot even believe you right now," I whisper-shout, aware our apartment walls are extremely thin. I've been embarrassed enough for one day. "You set up a photo shoot. In our apartment! Without telling me? With our instructor?" I raise my hands in disbelief. "And you introduced me as 'the author,' which can only lead me to believe that this shit is all for me?"

Cassie raises her hands in surrender. "I get why you're mad. But just listen. Okay?"

"Whatever." I roll my eyes.

"Asher is Jude's personal trainer, which is how I found him. Obviously, he's a police officer but also a part-time model. I was telling Asher how I wanted to make your covers a little more spicy and was looking for models. He mentioned that he knew one. Asher asked Jude if he'd be interested in shooting for a cover of a novel, and he agreed. I didn't know it was Officer Martinez from class. Asher just said Jude."

I open my mouth to protest, but Cassie cuts me off.

"Wait. Let me finish. So, I wasn't going to tell you until right before they got here because I knew you'd want to cancel the shoot. But I really think this is going to help you with marketing, Tan. My job is to help you."

"No, your job is to be my friend. Friends don't embarrass one another. I look like an idiot. I go traipsing out there in next to nothing. My hair's a mess. I probably have mascara running down my face. I look like shit, and I'm pretty sure he saw more of my nipples than any man has in over a year. I can't work with him now—even if I wanted to—which I don't."

"Your face looks great, no smeared makeup. You're all fresh, and..." I shoot Cassie a death glare which halts her thought. "The funny thing is that I thought we were shooting at one, but apparently, when I texted the photographer, I added an extra one, so they showed up at ten thirty, thinking we were shooting at eleven. It was an innocent mistake. I was just about to get you up and tell you about the day when they knocked. I'm sorry."

I shrug. "Innocent mistake or not, I can't go back out there now."

"Yes, you can. We're paying them. They're doing a job for us. We can show up in a clown outfit and a red nose if we want. Who cares?"

"I care," I deadpan. "Plus, he's like our teacher."

Cassie nods. "Not really. I mean, technically, yes, but it's a free self-defense course, not a college class. He's our age. It's not weird. We've seen him before, once, for an hour. He said a handful of words to us about a grab, and that was all. All that matters is that they get paid for the job they were hired to do. If they judge you for your initial meeting, it's on them. Plus, after today, you'll never have to see these two people again. We can quit the defense class. It's not like you don't know that material inside and out anyway. You've taken a hundred of those types of classes. Please just get dressed and come back out. It will be worth it once we have these pictures. I promise."

"You know what?" I glare toward Cassie. "You have a meddling problem. None of this would be happening had you not decided to do a photo shoot for a cover that I specifically told you I didn't want."

"That is neither here nor there," she sing-songs with a wave of her hand, no longer pretending to be apologetic. "Get dressed and come out. See you in a minute." She raises her eyebrows teasingly before slipping out of my room.

"Unbelievable," I whisper to myself.

I walk over to my dresser where Lucifer lays right where I left him a minute ago. "Can you believe her?" I pet him and he starts to purr loudly. "She's something else. Good thing we love her so much." I stare off as I pet Lucifer, listening to Cassie and Jude talking through the wall. I must get too close to Lucifer's belly because he lunges forward and bites me.

"Ouch!" I jump back and hold my assaulted hand to my chest. "Jerk," I hiss. My cat does his sound that's a mix between a forceful meow and a shriek. "I know. I'm getting ready now. Stop being so mean."

I'm over halfway through my twenties, yet my life is ruled by an overbearing best friend and an asshole cat. I really need to evaluate my life choices. But, first...I need to get through today.

CHAPTER 8

TANNON

I take a deep breath, and press my palms down my outfit in a nervous attempt to flatten any nonexistent wrinkles. My outfit's fine, I'm just stalling.

Get yourself together. God knows what you're paying for this. Go out there and make sure you get your money's worth.

My inner voice is so smart and brave. I really should listen to her more often.

"Okay," I say to myself in the full-length mirror.

I'm wearing a gray tapered pair of slacks, and a simple black, form-fitting V-neck. I ran a brush through my hair, and pulled it back into a tame bun. Cassie was right, my face is fine, completely void of streaked makeup and I decide that I'll leave it that way. I don't need to impress the guys in my living room. At this point, makeup would be a waste of time. Let's just get the show on the road.

I swing my bedroom door open and step out, a small smile plastered to my face.

"Yeah, that looks good." Cassie is talking with the photographer. "We need enough to have options, especially if she turns the book into a series. Plus, we need images for teasers."

"Should we re-do introductions? Pretend the previous one didn't happen?" the shirtless model, aka Jude my instructor, asks in an attempt to cut the tension.

I shoot him a genuine smile, and wave my hand through the air. "Eh. It is what it is at this point. But, in my defense, had I known that anyone was here or that we were doing this today, I would've been more prepared. I'm usually more professional—or—at least I think I am. This is my first cover photo shoot, and I just found out about it." I look down to my wrist at a nonexistent watch. "like fifteen minutes ago."

"That's different," Jude says with a raise of his eyebrow. "But you're the author."

"Yes, that's true." I nod. "But, she's the evil best friend publicist that likes to run the show and set up projects when I told her no."

"That sounds like an interesting dynamic." He chuckles.

I grin at Cassie. She's intently studying the small window on the photographer's camera.

"Too much shadow here. Not enough light on the

abs. You can't even tell he has a six-pack. It's just like, straight. More lighting, maybe?" She's barking out suggestions as if she's a professional photographer herself, and I love her a little more.

"She means well and, despite my resistance, is usually right," I tell Jude and then side-eye him. "Did you slather up with oil since the last time I saw you?"

"Yeah, helps everything stand out more."

By everything, he's referring to his muscles, and holy hell, are they yummy.

"Right," I answer.

"So, police officer by day, instructor by night, with some modeling thrown in for good measure? You seem to keep busy." I raise an eyebrow. "This isn't weird, is it? You being our teacher? In Cassie's defense, she didn't know that when she hired you. I hope this isn't uncomfortable for you."

Jude chuckles. "Nah, I'm good. Though Asher oversold my modeling 'career.'" He holds up his fingers in air quotes. "This isn't a regular occurrence for me. I only agreed because Asher's a good guy, and I wanted to help him out. And as for the class." He shrugs. "I'm cool with it if you are."

"Okay, yeah." I nod in agreement.

Jude is beckoned over by Cassie and instructed to stand in front of the white backdrop. He's barefoot and only wearing a pair of faded jeans that rest just under his pelvic bones, right where that hot as hell inverted v resides. Stealing glances at him the other day at the gym during the class, I knew he'd have one of those.

I swallow.

He places his thumbs in his front pockets and looks into the camera like he's going to mount it and start humping it—hard and rough.

He is yummy, I admit. Hell, I'd buy a book with him on the cover for that simple fact alone. I wouldn't even read the synopsis. I'd just one-click that sucker immediately. Maybe Cassie is on to something here after all.

I capture the sight of his body in my mind and close my eyes, willing my brain to commit every single glorious detail to memory. In my mind, I can see his hands on me, his warm, taut skin against mine. I breathe in deeply. This vision, me, and BOB—tonight—it's happening. Truthfully, it already has, but now I have a clearer picture to work with.

"Tannon!" Cassie's voice invades my mind, and I snap my eyes open. All three of them are staring at me as if Cassie's called me more than once.

Jude's grin tells me he knows exactly what I was just doing. Or at least he thinks he does. I could have been envisioning my grocery list for all he knows, or maybe I sleep standing up. He doesn't have proof of anything.

"Do you think we should shoot some shots in his boxer briefs? Just in case?" she asks me.

Just in case what? You want me to combust from need right on the living room floor? I swallow the lump in my throat. "Um, sure." My voice comes out breathier than I would've liked.

It dawns on me that I don't have to remember every detail of Jude's body because I will have the pictures. I'll literally own the rights to them. Even if I never use them on a cover, I can drool over them for all eternity. *What am I? A pubescent teenage boy? Professionalism, Tannon! Geez.*

Jude locks his greens with my blues as he slowly unbuttons his jeans. I pull my bottom lip through my teeth before I realize that I'm doing it. *So cliché, Tannon.* Shaking my head, I break my stare with Jude and head into the kitchen for a glass of water where the tall lights block my view of the photo shoot. It's probably for the best.

One thing's for sure. If I do use Jude's photos on my cover, I'm going to have to write my main male character a hell of a lot sexier. I empty my glass and then fill it again. Leaning against the counter, I drink slowly as the sound of a camera clicking sounds behind me.

When Cassie is satisfied that we got the shots we need, the photographer starts to pack up.

Jude finds me in the kitchen staring into my water glass.

"Hi," he says, pulling me from my water trance.

"Hi. All done?" I ask for the sake of saying something. We both know he is.

"Yeah, I was wondering if I could use your restroom to change? This went a little longer than I anticipated, and I have to dress for work." He chews on the corner of his lip, drawing my attention to his mouth.

"Of course, it's back there." I wave in the general direction of the hallway.

"Do you have any paper towels I can use to wipe off some of this oil?" He motions toward his chest, and my gaze gets stuck on his pecs.

I speak directly to them—the pecs, that is. "Yeah, um. There are towels in the closet in the bathroom. Use whatever you need. Just drop it in the hamper when you're done, and I'll wash it."

"Are you sure? A paper towel is fine." His husky voice pulls my attention from his chest back up to his mouth.

I nod. "Yeah. I'm sure. Mi casa es su casa." Ridiculous words fall from my mouth, per usual.

"Hables español?" he asks, the foreign language rolling off his tongue with ease.

"Um, no. Only phrases that can be found on a standard Bed, Bath & Beyond welcome mat." I chuckle. "But obviously, you do."

"Yeah, my dad and his parents came here in the eighties from Mexico."

"Oh, cool. Is your mom from Mexico, too?"

He shakes his head. "No, Indianapolis."

"Gotcha." I grin. "From the great foreign land of Indiana."

"Exactly," he says, his smile disarmingly beautiful. "Well, thanks."

He turns and grabs his duffel bag from the living room. I watch as he strolls down the hall, admiring the way his ass looks in his jeans.

"Oh my gosh." Cassie comes barreling into the kitchen, clapping her hands together. "Your cover is going to be so fucking hot."

"Not that I've agreed to a man chest cover. Remember?"

She waves me off. "You will, once you see the final result. I have faith in your good judgment." She gives me a wink.

"Well, that's good because my faith in yours is lacking."

She laughs. "It is not. You know I'm right. You just need to jump off your high horse and admit it."

"I'm not on a high horse, but you do know that if I do a man chest cover, it won't go with my brand—like, at all."

She shrugs. "So what? It will sell, and that's what matters. Sex sells, babe. It's fact."

I shake my head with a grin.

Cassie leaves me to pay the photographer. Jude exits the bathroom, and I'm sure my eyes bug out of my head like a Bugs Bunny cartoon. Half-naked Jude barely holds a candle to uniformed police officer Jude. His dark navy shirt stretches over his muscled biceps, and I want to wrap my hands around his arm, just to—well, for no reason at all, actually. Just because.

"Thank you," I manage to get out as he approaches.

"Anytime. I hope your cover turns out great."

"I'm sure it will."

"Take care, Tannon Lee." Hearing my entire name come from his lips makes the pull within my belly so much stronger.

"Bye."

He exits my apartment followed by the photographer, who I now realize didn't even speak to me in my Jude-induced haze.

I drop onto the sofa with a sigh. "I love him," I say to Cassie.

"I know. He's so cute, right? Asher wasn't overselling him at all. What a small world, too. We were seriously just drooling over him last week, and now he's going to be on your cover."

I turn toward her. "No...like...I love him, Cassie. He's...just...so..." I'm lost for words.

Her eyes go wide in realization. "Oh, you're smitten. Did you give him your number?"

I lean back away from her. "No! Of course not. I hired him—well, you hired him—for a job. It wouldn't have been professional to hit on him, and there's the whole instructor thing. It would've been weird."

"Eh." She dismisses the thought. "Who cares? You totally should've. We can have Asher talk you up to him at the gym."

"No, don't." I shake my head. "I'm sure he thinks I'm a hot mess. Plus, I guarantee you that he's seeing someone, probably a gorgeous little gym bunny."

"Well, you won't know unless you ask," she urges.

"No, it's fine. He'll just be forever in my highlight reel of hotness, stored safely within my mind. Plus, I'll have the pictures as backup." I quirk an eyebrow.

"Hell, yeah. They're going to be so yummy, too. I can't wait to see them."

"Me either." I sigh.

Cassie taps her fingers against the screen of her phone. "Guess what his name stands for?"

My bestie has a thing for the meaning of names. She knows the definition of all names belonging to anyone important in our life. She gets this trait from her mother, who named her Cassiopeia after the very beautiful and vain Greek goddess who now exists as a constellation in the sky.

She lives up to her name, as beautiful as they come with a personality as bright as the stars. She's tall with long brunette locks, a slim model-esque body, and flawless tan skin. Yet she's not vain in the least. My parents didn't share the same affinity toward name meanings. Cassie has looked deep in an effort to turn mine into something more profound than a boy name derived from Tanner or the German term for fir tree. Nothing is interesting about it, though.

"What does it mean? Hottie with perfect abs? Green-eyed God?" I question.

She pouts her lips in a smirk. "The praised one."

"Yeah, I'd say that's about right."

CHAPTER 9

TANNON

The boys are over for Taco Tuesday. It's our weekly tradition because tacos are the best food ever invented. I could live off Mexican food—authentic Mexican, Taco Bell, Tex-Mex—if it contains beans, cheese, and salsa in a shell, I'm in heaven.

Cassie got the edited digital files back from the photographer and took the liberty of printing off every single picture. The enormous pile of half-naked Jude lies sprawled across the counter as the four of us look through them.

Everett holds up a picture with a sly grin. "If I were gay, I wouldn't kick him out of bed."

I let out a laugh and take the photo from Everett. It's one of Jude in his boxer briefs. His expression exudes sex, yet it's not overdone or cringy like some model expressions that I've seen.

"Same," Asher agrees. "These are great, girls. I think they'll take your whole marketing strategy to a new level. Good call, Cass."

"Thanks! Yeah, I'm so excited about it. Thanks for finding him for me. He's perfect," she says.

Asher drops the photo on a pile of others. "All right. We ogled over your model. Can we eat now?"

"Yes, we can." I walk to the other side of the kitchen and grab a bowl of cheese and sour cream and carry them to the table. The others follow suit and bring the rest of the taco ingredients over.

Cassie runs back into the kitchen to grab the pitcher of margaritas because what's taco night without a little tequila sweetness.

"Everett, do you think you can help me remodel Tannon's website? I want to give it a new look." Cassie asks.

"Of course. Are you scheduled tomorrow? I can work on it down there for a while," he says before taking a big bite.

"I am. I'm working open to two. That would be great! I want to start teasing the readers with pics of Jude. You know how Taylor Swift leaves little Easter eggs around before an album drops. I want to do that, but with him."

"Right, but posting a picture of him is like giving it all away. It's not an Easter egg, but the whole Easter basket." I chuckle.

"You're right. Maybe I'll just post segments of him...

like his abs." She raises her eyebrows.

"Well, that would be a good place to start." I address Asher. "Has he been in to the gym since last week? Did he say anything about the shoot?"

Asher nods, and a big pile of shredded cheese falls from his taco shell. "Yeah, he comes in almost every day. He said he had fun. He's excited to see the finished cover when it comes out."

"Is that all?" Cassie asks.

"What else should he be saying? Is there something particular you're wanting to hear?" Asher looks between Cassie and me, narrowing his eyes.

"Did he say anything about Tannon?" Cassie says, and I smack her on the arm. "Ouch." She shoots me a glare. "You know you were thinking the same thing."

I shrug. "True. Did he?"

"No," Asher says slowly. "But if I'm being honest, we don't talk about stuff like that. We're guys. I'm his trainer, not his dating coach. So, you're into him, Tan?"

"Uh, no." I roll my eyes dramatically. "I just think he's cute, is all. Anyone with eyes would think the same. It's not a big deal."

"She's totally lying." Cassie cuts in. "She's obsessed."

"I am not!" I say with a laugh. "You're so ridiculous."

"Didn't you tell me that you're both taking a class with him? You could talk to him yourself, you know," Asher offers.

Cassie scrunches up her lips. "We had to skip class this week so we haven't seen him since the shoot."

"Why'd you skip?" Everett questions.

"That new girl who Henry hired didn't show up for her shift, and Henry needed me to cover. He needed to leave for a doctor's appointment."

"Colonoscopy?" Everett asks grimly.

"What?" Cassie squints.

"Grandpa Henry's doctor's appointment? You know everyone should get one when they turn fifty."

Cassie rolls her eyes. "Very funny. No, he had to get...something removed."

"A wart?" Everett guesses.

"A third nipple?" Asher asks.

"No," Cassie groans with a wave of her hand. "A bunion."

"A bunion?" the boys question simultaneously.

Cassie throws up her hands, and I stifle a laugh. "Let me guess? Bunions are more common in older people?" she asks exasperated.

Everett shrugs. "I mean, I've never known anyone our age to have bunions."

"Young people get them, too," Cassie argues.

"If you say so." Asher provides us with a devilish smirk. "So, why didn't you go to class, Tan?"

Before I can answer, Cassie responds, "Because she's crushing on him and didn't want to go alone."

"That's not true. I was writing. I was busy," I say in defense.

Cassie shakes her head. "Sure. We're all buying that."

I groan. "You know that when I'm really involved in a chapter, I just can't get up and leave, or I'll lose my rhythm." Though, Cassie is a hundred percent right. I couldn't face Jude alone after I'd last seen him standing half-naked in my living room.

Asher taps my hand with his. "Well, we'll give little Miss Tannon the benefit of the doubt. If she says she was busy writing, then she was busy writing. Though, back to Jude, I will say that he's with this one chick a lot."

Cassie whips her head around to face him. "Are they dating?"

"Once again, I'm just his trainer. We don't talk about girls."

"Well, you should. We need the details. So he's with this girl a lot at the gym?" Cassie asks.

"Yeah." Asher pours himself another margarita.

I take a sip of mine, emptying the glass. "Do they kiss?"

Asher throws his head back and laughs. "Have either of you ever been to a gym? It's not the middle school playground. We don't make out or talk about our latest girl crush. We work out. You know? That's kind of the point."

"And grunt," Everett adds. "There's always one douche who grunts when lifting."

Asher lifts an eyebrow and nods toward Everett in agreement.

"Please tell me Jude doesn't grunt," I plead. I've seen some compilation videos on social media of guys at the gym making insane noises. It shouldn't matter to me, but I hope Jude isn't one of those guys.

Asher shakes his head. "No, he doesn't."

"So, no kissing either? Just wanted to clarify," I say before pressing my lips together.

"No. No kissing that I've seen. They lift together almost every day, but that's all I know." He raises his hand as if swearing before a judge.

Cassie grabs the now empty pitcher of margaritas and carries it over to the kitchen. "Do they flirt?" she calls out while tossing ice in the blender.

Asher tosses a tortilla chip in his mouth. "No, but once he bent her over the weight bench and fucked her from behind. It was quite the show."

I gasp, and both Asher and Everett start laughing.

"Ha-ha. Funny boys," Cassie says. The sound of the blender fills the space, and a moment later, Cassie is refreshing our drinks. "I just think that even though you may not talk about girls or dating, you should be able to tell. Those who are romantically involved act different with each other than those who aren't."

Everett speaks up. "Why don't you just text him and ask him if you're that interested?"

"Because I'm not—that interested. Just curious."

"Sure." Everett doesn't sound remotely convinced.

"I don't even know what I'd be interested in. I mean, he's hot but probably not relationship material. I'm not into one-night stands. So what's the point? Plus, it sounds like he has someone. Not to mention, I'm sure I'm not his type," I say.

"So gorgeous isn't his type?" Everett lifts a brow.

"I have curves. I'm not a super thin gym bunny. I can't even jog a mile. Like, legit...I'd die. I'm sure the girls he dates have six-packs and toned legs for days," I grumble.

Asher drops his fork. "News flash. Guys fucking love curves. You have meat in all the right places."

"Ew. That's gross. I do not have meat." I scrunch my face in disgust.

"Seriously, she's not beef brisket. Who says that...? 'You have meat.'" Cassie lowers her voice to sound like a deranged creep as she mimics Asher.

"Baby, you're a fine slab of baby back ribs," I tease in a low voice with a Southern accent. For some reason, my man imitation is from the South.

Cassie lowers her gaze. "I want you like I want a double quarter pounder with cheese."

"You're a sexy ass pork roast," I groan out in dramatic fashion.

"I want to grab your hindquarters and barbecue you up right." Cassie's man voice now sounds like he's from Texas.

"You smell like a lamb chop on a sunny day," I grumble.

Cassie hits her hand on the table. "What in the hell does a lamb chop on a sunny day smell like? Rotten?" A tear from laughter rolls down her cheek.

"I don't know." I hold my stomach as I laugh. "I was running out of cuts of meat that sound sexy."

The two of us work out our giggles while the boys pretend to ignore us and shove some more tacos into their mouths.

When we're settled, Asher speaks. "It was meant as a compliment."

"I know it was." I pat his arm. "And as weird as it sounded, I appreciate it. I just don't think that Jude and I would jive. Even if I were interested."

"But you can obsessively fantasize about him. We do have like a thousand pictures of him to hang around your room if you want," Cassie says.

"Yes! I can have Jude Man-Chest Martinez as my wallpaper." I grin.

Everett shakes his head. "If you ever want to get laid again, I wouldn't."

I stand from the table and start to clear out the dishes. "All right, let's halt this conversation right now. My sex life is off-limits for the rest of the night. I'm not like you three. I don't need to be constantly hooking up with someone to be fulfilled."

"Bullshit," Asher calls out. "It's called biology, Tan. We're born with the desire to procreate."

"It's called, we're done with this subject." I place the dishes into the sink. "By the way, it's the boys' turn for dishes tonight. Don't think we forgot."

A grumble comes from the table.

"We'll give you five bucks to do them," Asher offers.

"No."
"Ten."
"No."
"Twenty."
"No."

"I don't know, Tannon. It will take us five minutes. Twenty is a pretty good deal," Cassie admits.

"It's not about the money. It's about the guys being lazy. We can't baby them." Walking back toward the table, I take the empty pitcher from the center. "Girls will make more drinks and set up the show. Boys...the dishwasher is in there." I motion toward the kitchen.

"Fine. Come on, Ash. We got this," Everett says.

"There's the winning attitude." I shoot Asher the smile of victory, and he glares in mock disgust.

Cassie and I plop down on the couch with our newly refreshed drinks. I turn on the TV and scroll through our streaming service to find *Survivor*. We have "family TV time," as we call it, a few times a week after dinner with the guys. We've watched the entire series of *Friends*, *How I Met Your Mother*, and *The Office* from start to finish. I was all for rewatching *Friends* again, but the guys wouldn't have it, so we settled on *Survivor*.

I've seen every episode of all the seasons already, but the other three haven't. My parents, brother, and I watched this show each week without fail. It's fun going through it all again, though. Truthfully, my memory is so bad that I can't remember most of the seasons. I remember my favorite characters—like it's Rupert in the season we're on—but I don't recall the outcome.

The episode we're on is cued up. We wait for the guys to finish in the kitchen.

"It's always been my dream to be on this show," I tell Cassie. "I even made an audition video when I turned eighteen, right before I came to college. I never sent it in, though."

"Why not?" Cassie asks.

"I don't know. Honestly, I think I'd suck. I'm not very sporty. Plus, I hate being uncomfortable. These people don't get to shower with soap or brush their teeth for thirty-nine days. I don't know that I could do it—even for a million bucks."

"I bet they smell so bad." She grimaces.

"Oh my gosh, you know they do."

"But, man…it makes for some good TV," she says.

"It sure does." I nod.

The guys make their way toward us from the kitchen, chanting the opening song of *Survivor*. Everett drops beside me, and Asher sits in the chaise lounge chair next to Cassie. I hit play on the remote, and all thoughts of the hot model are gone.

Okay, that's a lie.

Most thoughts are gone.

It's silly for me to spend any more time than I already have thinking about him. I'm pretty content with my life as it is. I love this family of mine, and I don't want anything to change.

CHAPTER 10

TANNON

I NEED to walk away from this one and forget that I ever met a beautiful girl named Cam. But then, I notice the dimple above the corner of her smile on the right side. Damn. Yeah, there's no forgetting this girl.

I step outside the building, my mind alive with images from the chapter I just finished in the male character's point of view. I love writing from the male POV. There's just something about creating the ideal man that gets my writing juices flowing. I may not be able to find him in real life, but I can write the hell out of him. My current main male character, Deacon, is perfection. I love him.

Exiting the alley behind the apartment, I turn the corner onto the sidewalk in front of Starbucks. My foot lands atop a bright red leaf. Bending down, I pick it up and hold it in my hand. The vivid scarlet foliage is out of place amongst a street lined with nothing but greenery. Lifting my gaze, I scan the area to find a maple tree with one branch of red leaves.

"Slow your roll, buddy," I say to the lone branch attempting to rush autumn.

I love fall. It's my favorite time of year, but it's also the most fleeting. It seems like the second the leaves start turning, I blink, and they've all fallen to the ground, leaving a barren winter in their wake. Truthfully, I still have a little PTSD from last year's seven-month winter. It was brutally cold and seemed to last forever. The summer sun has barely thawed me out, and now this little jackass is rushing fall. I glare down at the leaf in my grasp. Almost immediately, my lips tilt into a smile because it's such a beautiful red. I can't even be mad. That's how autumn gets you—with its beauty. It makes one forget about the coming nightmare of the never-ending frigid, sunless days.

I drop the leaf and cross my arms over my chest. A cold front has moved in since yesterday's eighty-degree day. The breeze picks up, and it makes me think I should have grabbed a sweatshirt. I hesitate a moment, wondering if I should go back up and grab one, but I don't. I'm only going two blocks to the corner convenience store to pick my devil cat up some more gourmet wet food. I've been feeding him more cans than normal so he'll leave me in peace while I try to finish this next book. I'm an enabler to his horrible behavior. I've accepted that fact.

College students with heavy backpacks and earbuds in place pass me on either side, most likely heading home after a study session. Living in a college town is oddly calming. The hustle and bustle of it has a therapeutic quality. Someday, I'll move out of downtown Ann Arbor—live on my own somewhere I actually need a car, but not anytime soon. I love it here.

The bell chimes above the door of the store as I enter.

"Hola, niña," the store owner calls out, a smile across his face.

"Hola, Fedé." I grin back.

"Can I help you find anything?" he asks.

I shake my head. "Oh, I know exactly where to find what I need."

"I see. Then you're heading to the pet aisle, I'm guessing."

"You're guessing right. You know me so well."

"Well, Lupita made some tamales. Would you like me to bag you up some?"

I halt and turn to face him. "Yes, please. Oh my gosh. You know how much I love her tamales! Do you have any Lift?" I ask about my favorite pop.

I don't drink pop all that often, but when I was on spring break in Cancun back in college, I tried this soda down in Mexico called Manzana Lift. It's basically an apple-flavored pop, and it's so good. A couple of years ago, I was talking to Fedé about his time growing up in Mexico, and I asked him if he ever had the "Lift." He got such a kick out of that conversation that he special ordered the beverage for me as a surprise.

Now, he always carries it in a little refrigerator behind the counter just for me. He's become my apple pop dealer, and I can't get enough.

"For you, siempre," he tells me. When I raise an eyebrow in confusion, he clarifies with, "Always."

"Okay." I smile wide. "Thank you. I'll return in a minute to collect."

The bell above the door chimes as I make my way back toward the cat food. Fedé starts talking to someone in Spanish, and I can't help but grin. I just love him. My grandparents died when I was young, and I don't remember much about them, but I like to imagine that my grandpas were kind and loving like my favorite store owner. Fedé is everyone's adopted grandpa. He loves this community and makes an effort to show the people in it that he cares.

I reach for the smallest yet most expensive containers of cat food for my little Satan. Only the best for him. He'd make me suffer if I chose to save a little money and get him anything else. It's not worth the fight.

Tossing a few more containers in, I fill up my basket with enough food to last him a couple of weeks. My step quickens as I make my way back up front, thinking about the tamales and Lift that await.

A uniformed police officer talks with Fedé, and it stops me in my tracks because I'd know that ass anywhere. I've seen that round derrière in jeans, boxer briefs, and that very uniform, and it is unforgettable.

"Mi niña!" Fedé calls to me, and I have to double-check that my mouth isn't hanging open as Jude turns around to face me.

His lips morph into a mix between a pucker and a smile. "You're the girl my abuelito always talks about?"

"I guess." My voice comes out more shaky than I would like.

"The one he's choosing to give the rest of my abuela's tamales to even though she told me to swing by after work to grab them?" He lifts an eyebrow.

Fedé smacks him on the arm. "Don't make her feel bad. It's not her fault she got here first."

"I see how it is. A pretty girl comes in here, and you forget about family," Jude teases his grandpa.

"Oh, she's smart, too. She's a writer," Fedé says, his chest puffs with pride.

"I know." Jude grins in my direction. His green gaze captures mine, and I find it hard to breathe.

"You've met mi niña?" Fedé asks Jude.

"I've run into her a couple of times," he says with a sidelong glance in my direction.

Fedé shrugs. "Well, if you've met her, then you know she's special. And next time, you need to get here sooner."

"Yeah, I do know," Jude responds. It's a soft declaration, but the words reverberate loudly within my mind, causing a chill to run down my spine.

"Come. Come." Fedé waves me forward, and I place the basket of cat food on the counter.

Jude steps to the side, just a fraction. Suddenly, I'm painfully aware that I'm in my work uniform, which consists of a makeup-free face, yoga pants, an old T-shirt, and a messy bun atop my head. *Why must I be such a slob?*

Fedé packs up my cat food and hands me another bag that holds my six-pack of Lift and tamales. It doesn't escape my attention that he only charges me for the cat food, so I give him an extra twenty-dollar bill.

"This is too much, mi niña." He attempts to hand me back the money.

"No, it's not. You failed to charge me what I owe. Please keep it." I reach forward and squeeze his hand. He shakes his head with a grin and puts the money in the cash register.

"I'll see you soon. Please tell Lupita thank you for me," I say to Fedé before supplying Jude with a weak smile. I quickly turn and walk out of the store before I can do or say anything embarrassing, which, for some reason, comes easily when I'm around Jude.

The bags full of canned soda and cat food are heavy, and I'm grateful for their weight because at this moment, I need the force that holds me down to earth. My head feels light and airy—almost dizzy. I can't believe one of my favorite people in this town is related to Jude. Ironic? Yes. Weird? Absolutely. Intriguing? Definitely.

"Let me help you with those." The deep voice pulls

me from my thoughts, and I let out a startled yelp. "I'm sorry." Jude chuckles as he takes the bags from me. "I didn't mean to scare you."

I shake my head, clearing my thoughts. "I was just thinking." I drop my eyes to my bags, now in his hands. "And you don't have to carry those. I only live two blocks away. I'm fine."

"Yeah, well...it's getting dark. I should make sure you get home safely."

"It's Ann Arbor." I laugh. "I hardly need a police escort."

He grins down toward me. "It's best to be safe. So, small world, huh?"

"Yeah," I agree. "I've known your grandpa for eight years, since my first week of freshman year. I can't believe I've never run into you in there before. Besides my couch, bed, and Starbucks...his store is my top-visited location.

"Your couch and bed?"

"Mostly. They are my work locations. Writer life. You know?"

"I couldn't stand a job that required so much sitting." He walks beside me.

"Well, I got one of those treadmill desks once. I spent over a grand on that thing and almost died the first day. I cannot think, type, and walk at the same time—even on the treadmill's slowest setting."

"That bad?"

"Uh, definitely." I nod. "I fell and skinned up both

shins. Then after the treadmill spit me out at the end, I got stuck between the wall and the treadmill belt, and when I went to get up, I put my finger too close to the moving belt. It got sucked under, cutting and spraining it pretty badly. I was a hot mess for a couple of weeks after that. My whole body was bruised and cut up. I sold that stupid thing for a hundred bucks on Facebook marketplace. I literally used it once."

Jude lets out a laugh. "I'm sorry for laughing, but the visual..."

"I know." I grin. "I'm something else."

"That you are." The laughter's now absent from his voice.

We pass the entrance to the Starbucks and walk around the side of the building where the door to the steps up to the second level is.

I hitch back my thumb. "Well, this is me." I totally run my eyes up and down Jude's body. What is wrong with me? I have no shame. "Thanks for getting me here safely." I give him a wink.

"Anytime." He presses his lips in a line, gifting me with a small smile.

I take my bags from him. There's an awkward silence between us, and I dwell on it longer, not wanting to walk away but knowing I should.

I should, right?

Yes.

I chew on the inside of my lip. "Okay. Well, bye," I

blurt out with a nod of my head before opening the door and stepping inside.

I start the ascent up the stairs. Why do I feel equipped to write romance when I'm so ridiculous in real life? At this very second, I realize I'm a fraud. *Eh, whatever.* My writing and my words consume me almost every second of every day. Yet right now...I don't want to think about any of that. All I want is to be in the same space as Jude again.

My eyes drop to the bag in my hand. Descending the steps, I swing open the door to find Jude right where I left him.

"Um, I...I have plenty of tamales to share. Do you want...to...come inside?" I motion toward the stairwell.

Smooth, Tannon. Real smooth.

Jude's mouth breaks into a devastatingly beautiful smile, and I think I sigh. Hopefully, it was a silent one. "Yeah, sure." His answer sounds so much more confident than my question.

He takes the bags from me again and follows me up the stairs. I'm anxious to get inside the apartment. Depending on the outcome of tonight, I may or may not be sharing it with Asher and Everett. So I need to get out of this hall before one of them sees us.

Cassie is staying the night with Grandpa Henry...I mean Henry. I told her I'd stop calling him the nickname that the boys gave him, but habits die hard and all that.

So, it's going to be Jude and me alone in the apartment. I'm not sure how I feel about this decision. My mind is trying to weigh out the pros and cons of this idea, but my heart is beating too loudly to allow me to focus on rationale.

I don't overthink. I simply open the apartment door and let Jude in.

CHAPTER 11

TANNON

"Make yourself comfortable," I tell Jude as we enter the apartment, and I take the two bags from him. *Do people still say make yourself comfortable?* I'm so awkward it's embarrassing. Everything I know about conversation and life I've learned from nineties sitcom reruns. I should seriously invest some time in current shows—or get out of the house more. Spending my days writing about others' lives has made me inadequate in my own.

Setting the bags on the counter, I pull out Lucifer's food first. Priorities. The second the container's seal is broken, the black fur ball is at my feet, screeching like a baby raptor set to attack.

"He may sound like he's starving, but he's not. This is his third can of soft food today, and he always has a full bowl of dry available. He just likes to pretend his life is hard." I make excuses for my cat's behavior. "Do you have any pets?"

"No. I'd like a dog, but I'm not home that often. I don't think it'd be fair to him." Jude stands across the counter.

"Yeah, I get that. I'd like a dog too, but I want to wait until I'm out of the city and have a house with a yard. I'm too lazy to walk him multiple times a day." The words leave my mouth before I can stop them. I have to remember I'm talking to a guy who practically lives at a gym.

I raise my gaze to Jude's face, I'm expecting to find judgment or something other than the warm expression that greets me. It's disarming. I quickly dart my eyes to the cabinet door, open it and grab two plates.

I split up the tamales, setting them on the plates before handing him one. "Would you like a Lift?"

"Water's fine." Jude takes the plate from me.

"But...it's Manzana Lift." My voice is a tad more whiny than I'm comfortable with, but come on—best pop ever—special ordered for me.

Jude chuckles. "I know, it's great. I try to limit my sugar, though."

I hand him a glass of water, noticing the way his biceps threaten to break out of his shirtsleeve. I suppose a body like that takes a strict diet.

I normally eat my tamales and drink my apple pop in front of a classic episode of *Friends*. I find it strange to be sitting across from a uniformed police officer instead. It doesn't make it any less weird that I have a picture of him in his underwear in my bedside table drawer.

Speaking of the pictures. "Have you seen the pictures from the shoot?"

"No. They turn out okay?"

"Oh, yeah. They're awesome. Cassie may talk me into using you on my cover after all. So, how often do you model?"

Jude swallows the bite of food in his mouth before answering. "Well, that was my first time."

My mouth drops open. "No, it wasn't!"

"Yeah, it was." He chuckles. "I was serious when I spoke to you the day of the shoot. Modeling is definitely not a regular occurrence for me."

"Why'd you do it?"

He shrugs. "I'm not sure. Asher's a cool guy and has helped me a lot over the years. He said that one of his best friends needed help. So, I agreed."

"Will it be weird if I put you on my cover in nothing but your boxers?"

"Maybe a little, but I doubt most of the people I see on a daily basis spend their time reading. There's no doubt the guys at the station will catch wind of it and tease me, but that won't bother me. It was fun."

I shake my head with a chuckle. "Well, you should model more often. You're good at it. I'll have to show you the pictures later. I mean, they're amazing."

Chill, Tannon.

If Jude notices my puppy-eyed fangirling, he doesn't

let it show. His voice is cool and collected when he shrugs. "I don't know if it's my thing. It was fun, but I'm not sure I'll do it again."

My eyes go wide. "But you should. You're seriously made to model." *OMG. Enough.*

I shove a bite of tamale into my mouth and clamp my lips closed tightly as I chew. New plan—keep my mouth full in an attempt to limit the idiocies that spew from my lips.

The conversation over dinner is easy. I learn that Jude is the youngest of six kids and his five siblings are girls. His parents, paternal grandparents, and three of his sisters live in Ann Arbor. He's wanted to be a cop since he could walk. He's twenty-eight, lives alone, and is dreamy as fuck. Well, that last part is implied.

I tell him about my parents and brother. I explain how I met Asher, Everett, and Cassie. I briefly go over my short stint as a teacher and how and why I started writing, or at least the non-personal reasons. The conversation is casual and easy. He smiles a lot. I do, too.

Is this a first date or a friend thing? I don't know.

Do I even want it to be more? Not sure on that one, either.

Am I a hot mess? The answer is yes.

Both of our plates are empty, as is my can of pop. Pleasantries have been had. I don't want to make this weird for either of us, so I should wrap it up. A wise woman once said that the key to being normal is knowing when to end a maybe first date. It's me—I'm the wise woman.

I push away from the table and stand. Reaching across the space, I grab Jude's plate and then my own before heading into the kitchen. He follows me. He should go. Doesn't he understand the key to being normal? He's going to make this weird, or more aptly—he's giving me an opportunity to do so, and I will make it so weird. I can't help it. It's who I am.

Clearing my throat, I say. "Make sure to thank your grandma for me. She's seriously the best cook I know. Let's share a tamale another time—or not. Either is fine. Whatever." *And there it is.*

He needs to leave before I say anything else that I'll regret. Releasing a sigh, I turn to face him. Peeking up, I expect to see something—perhaps an expression filled with amusement or even pity would be fitting, but what I don't expect to see is desire. I know I'm rusty with this, but I'm pretty certain Jude's exuding a hundred percent pure lust—for me. His green eyes are darker, a shade of emerald, and they linger on my mouth.

On instinct, I lick my lips, imagining Jude's mouth on mine. His chest rises in response, and he grabs my waist. I stare into his eyes expectantly. He doesn't make me wait long. Bending toward me, he captures my lips, and I literally groan—loud and needy—into his mouth. It's been so long since I've been kissed, and I've never been kissed like this.

Jude pulls me against his body as his lips continue

their beautiful assault. I thread my fingers through his short hair, pulling his face closer to mine. Our tongues dance as if they've been waiting for an eternity to do so. The kiss is frantic and hot but powerful at the same time. It's making my heart race and my body numb to everything but the pull in my gut—the need. I write about this feeling all of the time, but words could never do it justice. It's so physically intense that it hurts, but I don't want him to stop. God, I want him to touch me and take me—again and again. I want him to pound me so hard that this intense craving will be sated.

Without thought, I start to unbuckle the belt of his pants, which elicits a moan from somewhere deep within his chest. The sound vibrates down to my throat, which hastens the movement of my hands. I unzip his pants before grabbing the waistband of his pants and boxers and pulling them down over his hips, never stopping the kiss. I can't believe I'm doing this, but I can't stop my actions either. I feel his length against my stomach first, and then my hand finds it, circling the girth.

Jude lets out a guttural groan and pulls his mouth from mine. Panting, he rests his forehead against mine. "Are you sure you want to do this?" His voice is a husky whisper. "You don't have to, Tannon."

"I'm sure." I stroke his length, marveling at his size. My heart races, feeling his smooth skin under my touch. God, I'm sure. I've never wanted anyone more than I want Jude right now.

Reality hits me when I realize Jude is standing still, his forehead still against mine as if he's contemplating his next move. Doubt creeps in. "Oh." I gasp, releasing my grasp. "Do you not want to do this with me?"

Jude stands tall. He takes hold of the bottom of my T-shirt and pulls it over my head, dropping it to the ground. His stare holds mine as he reaches around my back and unclasps my bra. He drops his eyes to my shoulders as he slides the bra straps down my arms until that garment, too, is falling to the floor.

His fingers trace my skin lightly, moving over my arms, up and down my neck, across my collarbones, and down to my breasts, where his thumbs rub my taut nipples. "I want to. I definitely want to," he whispers, "but promise me you'll say something if you want me to stop, at any time."

"I don't want you to stop," I moan as his fingers pull against my nipples.

"But if you change your mind, tell me. Okay?" Leaning down, he circles his mouth around my nipple and starts to suck.

Oh my God.

I pull his head into my chest. "Promise me," he says against my breast. His warm breath across my wet skin causes goose bumps to erupt down my arms.

"I promise."

Jude pebbles kisses down my abdomen and teases the skin beneath my waistband. A warning goes off in my head.

Crap!

I grab his shoulders and stop his movements. "I didn't shave." I sigh. What has it been, a week? Why am I not prepared for random post-tamale sex with the local hot model/cop? I should always be ready. I hate myself right now.

Jude surprises me by letting out a laugh. "I don't care, Tannon."

"But it'll be all pokey, and it could irritate your skin."

Stop talking, Tannon. He said he didn't care.

"I can handle it." He shoots me a wink. I start to protest again when he quickly slides his hand into my panties. When his finger enters me, all of my fight leaves.

I warned him. It's all I can do, I think as my head falls back with a moan while he works his magic inside me. I whimper when he pulls his hand from my underwear. The disappointment doesn't last long, though, because he removes my last pieces of clothing. I lift my feet, one at a time, to help and kick my yoga pants to the side.

I yelp when his hands grab my sides, and he lifts me onto the counter. He pushes my knees out to the side, and then he drops to his knees, his face stopping between my legs. The first lick of his tongue causes me to cry out. He inserts one finger and then another into my opening and starts to fuck me with his hand while his tongue does all of the right things to the exact spot that needs it the most.

Oh my God.

I lean back, resting on my hands. My entire body hums with pleasure as my core starts to shake. There's a half-dressed cop in my kitchen licking me into submission.

This is not how I saw this day going.

"Fuck! Yes!" I scream as the wave of ecstasy rushes through me. My entire body convulses on the granite, and my cries fill the air. I come so hard. I have no control of my vocal cords as I continue to moan in the sweetest pleasure I've known.

My fingers thread through Jude's hair, and I attempt to push him away as the sensation grows. It's almost too much. He doesn't budge. His tongue worships me until the last wave of my orgasm passes, and I fall back in a sated lump on the counter, every muscle in my body spent.

Jude kisses up my body until he's sucking on my neck. "Do you have a condom?"

"Bedroom," I manage to get out as I'm lifted into his arms.

He sets me down when we cross the threshold into my room. I watch him undress like he's my own personal Pornhub fantasy. Every inch of his toned, tan skin is perfection.

"Oh," I say, splaying my hands across his abs because I freaking can. "We have to run and jump into the bed."

He raises an eyebrow, the corner of his lip tilting up. "Why?"

"My cat's hiding under there, and he'll run out and attack our feet. It will be a real damper on the mood."

"Seriously?"

"Yeah, he's quite the asshole."

"Um. Okay, ladies first." Jude motions toward my bed.

I do something that would normally be completely out of my comfort zone, and I lean in and place my tongue against that hot as fuck inverted V and lick up his abdomen until I reach his pecs. I pull his hard nipple into my mouth and flick it with my tongue.

Then I turn and jog toward my bed until I'm close enough to leap onto it. I bounce up off the mattress as Jude lands beside me.

I let out a giggle, which falters the second Jude's lips are back on mine. He proceeds to explore my body with his mouth, and I return the favor—kissing and licking every inch of his skin.

"Where's the...?" He starts to ask when both of us are panting with need.

I reach my hand into my side table and snatch up the box of condoms before closing the drawer quickly, not wanting Jude to see the picture of him I keep in there.

Jude has the box open and the condom on before my head has hit the pillow. He presses his palm against my chest and drags it across my skin, burning me with his touch. "You are amazing, Tannon. So fucking beautiful."

When he enters me, I cry out. His length is impressive and fills me up the way I've always needed but didn't know to want. I've had sex plenty of times in my life, but I've never had this. The way Jude moves is indescribable. He's deep, and slow, and fast, and needy...and so very perfect all at the same time. I'm lost in a drunken euphoria of lust.

We're all skin, sweat, and sobs of pleasure. When the orgasm hits this time—it's even better than the first somehow. Jude chases his release, and holding him as he comes almost sends me over the edge again. He turns me on in a way that no one else ever has.

The night is spent kissing, and fucking, and making love with Jude until my body is limp, and I can't stay awake any longer. He wraps my naked body in his, and I fall into slumber with a smile on my face because I finally know what it's like to live out an epic chapter in a romance novel. It's so much better than any words could ever be.

Because it's real.

CHAPTER 12

TANNON

I STRETCH my arms out above my head with a long sigh. My entire body aches in all the right places. I smile as memories of last night flash through my mind. Who knew? Who freaking knew that a trip to get cat food would end with the best sex of my life and Jude by my side?

Wait.

I extend my arms to the side. My heart starts to hammer within my chest when it dawns on me no one is in bed with me.

I sit up. The rays of sun shining through the blinds light up the room. I look around, and a lump in my throat forms when I realize he's gone. The piles of his clothes on the floor—gone. I just had a one-night stand, and now I want to cry.

This is why I can't have one-night stands. I get invested. It hurts my heart that he's gone even though it shouldn't. He didn't promise me anything. Last night was solely based on an immense amount of lust, which was clear, even then. I knew it was just sex, but I let myself believe it was more anyway.

The darkness that I've worked for years to bury, or more aptly—release, returns. Heavier than ever. Tears of remorse stream down my cheeks. So much regret. I feel dirty and wrong. Insecurities and doubts pound within my chest, and my heart hurts. Last night with Jude can't even compare to my demons, but somehow, it brings it all up. Jude is good and kind and sexy...and I wanted him. Even if I had known it was for one night, I would've wanted him still. And that's okay, or at least it should be.

I should be able to sleep with who I want when I want and not have this all-encompassing shame shove me down.

Fucking A. I swipe the back of my hands against my cheeks to brush away the errant tears. I'm a mess. I knew better.

I have no idea what time it is because my cell phone isn't in my room, but it doesn't matter. I have nowhere to go. So, I let the tears fall and feel real damn sorry for myself. I think the most depressing part of all is that I can never go back to BOB after last night. BOB's orgasms are a joke next to Jude's.

Dammit! I've ruined everything.

I cry into my pillow until sleep takes me once more.

There's ice cream and tacos, and coffee, so much coffee because my head is pounding. I'm about to bite into the delicious taco when Cassie's voice cuts through the air, calling my name. I look around the circus. There's a basketball game taking place on one side of the floor. Brad Pitt shoots from half-court and scores. What appears to be a dance-a-thon is happening on the other side. Rory from *Gilmore Girls* dances with Dean. *Aw, Dean's so sweet.* A lion lies sprawled out on the ground a few feet in front of me. He yawns and then gives me a nod of his head as if to say, "It's cool." So, I open my mouth to bite the taco again. And there it is—Cassie's voice. I turn to Harry Potter sitting beside me, and he shrugs. *Can't a girl eat a taco at a circus anymore?*

"Oh, my God!" Cassie shrieks louder this time, pulling me from sleep. I open my eyes. "Why are you naked?"

I blink until the scene before me comes into focus. Cassie is standing at the entrance of my room, holding out a hand toward me and shielding her eyes with the other. "For the love...close your legs, Tan, and maybe pull up the sheet."

My eyes dart down, and I'm suddenly aware of my very naked and exposed body. *Whoa.* I grab my comforter and cover myself.

"Okay," I call out.

"It's safe?" Cassie asks. "I can look?"

"You can look." I chuckle, imagining the scene that must be burned into my best friend's mind now.

She drops her hand from her face. "That's if you didn't scar my vision for life," she complains with a shake of her head. "Much better." She nods in approval at my now covered skin. "So, it's noon. Your thong is on the counter, dangling from a box of Fruity Pebbles, and the rest of your clothes are strung about the kitchen. I'm greeted with a clearer crotch shot than I get in most porn videos, which, by the way, I'll probably never be able to erase from my mind. I think you need to throw on some clothes, remove your undergarment from my breakfast, and tell me what the hell happened here last night."

"Yeah, okay."

"Does this story require mimosas?" she asks with a raise of an eyebrow.

"Probably," I admit. "But can we start with coffee? My head is pounding."

"Sure." Cassie leaves me to get dressed, closing the door behind her.

I swing my feet over the side of my bed and stand with a groan as I stretch my arms up over my head and then twist from side to side, satisfying back cracks sounding with each movement. My entire body literally aches. *I'm seriously out of shape.*

I throw on some clothes and look around my room. There's no sign he was even here. If it weren't for my sore muscles and the four condoms in the trash, I could convince myself that it was all just a dream.

I glare toward the garbage can. "Damn you, Man Chest."

Stepping out of my room, I'm greeted with a large mug of coffee and Cassie's obnoxious grin.

"What are you so happy about?" I inhale the goodness coming from my mug.

"You do know that the only exciting stories I get are from the boys. I've been waiting for this day!" she claps her hands together, and I follow her to the couch.

"Hey! I'm interesting." I feign annoyance, but she's right. I'm pretty boring.

"So who was it?" Her eyes go wide.

I sit at the end of the couch and face her. I take a long sip of my coffee.

"Do I know him? How did it happen? Was it good? Tell me everything!"

"How do you know it was a guy?" I ask.

Her mouth falls open. "It was with a girl?"

"No." I throw a couch pillow at her. "I just mean... how do you know I was with someone last night?"

She shakes her head and sighs. "Tannon, don't make me beg for details."

"Fine," I relent. "It was the model guy, Jude."

"What?" she shrieks. "How did it happen? How was he? Oh. Em. Gee."

"I know," I say with a grin.

I tell her about going to get cat food and Jude being Fedé's grandson. I supply all of the details about dinner and our pretty basic conversation.

"Then I thought he was going, and the next thing I know, we were kissing, and then he was eating me out on the kitchen counter." I press my lips into a line and raise my eyebrows in anticipation of her response.

Cassie jumps up from the couch and threads her hands through her long dark hair. "What the actual...Oh, my lord...I can't believe this."

"I know." I shrug with a grin because I can't believe it either.

"And then?" she asks, pacing the room.

I supply her with all of the details because she's right —she deserves it. She's given me tons of gossip over the years, and I've never had much to offer in that department. That wasn't fictional anyway.

"He made you come five times?"

I nod. "Once in the kitchen and then four times in my bed during sex."

"And he was the best?"

"The best I've ever had, better than I knew existed... better than I could ever explain." My face falls, and the knot in my throat returns.

Cassie squints toward me, confused. "This makes you sad...why?"

I place my now empty coffee cup on the end table. "Because it was so good that it didn't feel like a hookup.

It felt real and meaningful. It was like a come to Jesus moment for me—I thought this is the guy I've been waiting for. He's the one. But then he snuck out before the sun was even up. It wasn't meaningful for him. It was just a hookup, a one-night stand."

Cassie places her palms over her face and drags them down her cheeks. "Tannon." My name comes out as a sigh. "This isn't one of your insta-love stories. It wasn't love at first fuck. It was lust. You do know the difference, right?"

"Yes. Of course I know the difference. It didn't feel like just lust, though, is what I'm saying."

"Tannon, Tannon, Tannon." Cassie shakes her head. "You've seen the guy a few times in your life. You shared a couple of words over tamales, and then you had sex. Where in that whole scenario did you think he fell in love with you? Can't you just appreciate it for what it was? A great night of sex. What you felt is sexual chemistry. You find him hot. He finds you hot. Your bodies worked well together in bed. End of story. Doesn't mean you're going to run off and get married tomorrow."

I drop my head back into the sofa cushion. "You're right. I didn't think we were in love, but I thought it was leading somewhere, like maybe we'd start dating? I didn't think it could be like that with just anyone."

"Well, it normally can't. Most hookups are nowhere near as satisfying. You found the holy grail of one-night stands. You should be celebrating, not throwing yourself a pity party."

"That's true. I mean, it was pretty epic."

"Yeah!" Cassie cheers. "Exactly. You can play last night in your mind's highlight reel for a while. Plus, you know he's good in bed, but other than that, he could be a douche. Right? Honestly, you probably dodged a bullet. Plus, didn't Ash say that he's always with a girl at the gym?"

My mouth falls open. "You're right. Oh my gosh, I just helped him cheat."

She puckers her lips. "See? Douche."

"Well, that makes it worse."

Cassie stops pacing and plops down next to me. "Don't let it. It's not like you remembered that last night. You didn't seek him out to make him cheat. That's on him. You just had an enjoyable night. Don't worry about it for another second. Instead, provide your bff with more details. So, obviously I saw most of him at the shoot —and yum."

I nod with a sigh because despite his questionable character—Jude Martinez is definitely delicious.

"How was he under his boxers?" Cassie tilts up an eyebrow, and I can't help but laugh.

"Even yummier," I admit.

"I'm assuming we're not going back to that self-defense class?"

I shake my head. "Oh, definitely not."

I'm trying to come to terms with being the type of girl who's cool with having a one-night stand. Yet I know myself well enough to know that I'm also the kind of girl who would dive behind a garbage can, if one were available, to hide from said one-night stand. Taking a class where he's my instructor won't work for me. With any luck, I'll never see Jude Martinez again, in real life anyway.

But I'll hold on to his pictures. Just in case.

CHAPTER 13

JUDE

I look around the gym, hoping to see her but know I won't. She hasn't called since that night, and in truth—it sucks.

A highlight reel of that night spent at Tannon's has been running on repeat in my mind since I left her apartment. It was fucking amazing. Hands down the best night of sex I've had. Based on her reaction, I thought it was pretty awesome for her, too.

I'm not sure if my heart or my ego is more upset with her lack of response. It can't be my fucking heart because I barely know the girl. There are no true emotions there. It's not possible for them to be there already. Logic says it's my ego, but that feels like a lie. I felt something different with Tannon. Sure, there was a shit ton of lust involved, but it wasn't just that. It didn't feel like *just* sex. It felt like more.

What is it about her that has my insides twisted up? She's sexy as hell, yeah, but this town contains countless beautiful women. Why does she alone elicit this response in me? I don't like it, this feeling of unease and desperation. I crave her to the point of obsession. *Why?*

Something's off.

Perhaps this is classic Jude going for the unstable ones again. It seems to be my pattern as of late. Though she doesn't seem crazy like the others. She's unfiltered; every word that falls from her mouth is the truth regardless of how awkward it is. I find her blatant honesty endearing. In my experience, the lunatics are usually liars. I've misread people in the past, but I really don't think Tannon's a liar.

I should just let it go. I mean, what other options do I have? I left my number, so the ball is in her court. It'd probably be wise to take the hint and move on. She's not contacting me for a reason. She doesn't owe me an explanation. She doesn't have to call if she doesn't want, and that's how it is. I need to accept it.

I told myself that I needed to start looking for someone to spend my life with. I want a wife and a family. Casual sex—though enjoyable—isn't my endgame. I want it all. I want what my sisters, parents, and grandparents have. I'm ready. Pining after a woman who doesn't want me, regardless of how mind-blowing our connection was, isn't a part of the plan. I just thought she felt what I did, but I guess I was wrong.

"Everything okay, Jude?" Alma, the owner of this

place, stands across from me. Her boyfriend Amos and friend Ollie, along with a little redhead stand beside her.

I found The Lion's Lair, an organization Alma owns and runs, a little over a year ago. It's a center for kids and teens that helps with just about anything. In addition, she rents out spaces to local nonprofit organizations free of charge. The gym here is perfect for our classes.

"Yeah, I was looking to see who was here." I smile.

"I wanted to introduce you to a friend of mine," Ollie says, nodding toward the redhead. "This is Clementine. This will be her first class."

"Awesome. Welcome." I extend my hand and shake hers. "We'll have women of all abilities here tonight ranging from first-timers to some who have been coming for years. You'll fit right in. We break out into ability groups, so no need to worry."

"Cool," she says. "I thought this was a month-long class. Why have some women been coming for years?"

"Well, you'll be pretty comfortable with the basics after a month, but the more you work on the moves, the more rote they become. I think some women just like working on the steps so much that if they ever needed to use them, they wouldn't even have to think about it. It would be automatic. It makes them feel safer, you know? Then others just come because it's fun and a bit of a workout."

Clementine nods. "Okay. So what should I do first?"

"We have a few minutes before we start. You can

just find a spot and stretch. We'll explain everything once we get started."

She shoots me a smile. "Cool," she says again. She gives Ollie a look and then turns to find an open space.

"You going to stay for the class today?" I ask Alma.

"No. I have to get home to Love." She mentions her three-year-old daughter. "My mom just called and said something about making banana peel bacon for dinner, so I need to get home and make sure Love has something appropriate to eat." She chuckles.

"What is banana peel bacon?" I raise a brow.

She shakes her head. "I have no idea. Apparently, you can soak banana peels in spices and cook them, and they taste like bacon?"

"There's no way banana peels could ever taste like bacon," Ollie says as the rest of us nod our heads in agreement.

"I know." She shrugs. "That's my mom, but she's trying, and honestly, the carrot hot dogs she made last week were edible."

"If you say so." I laugh.

She grins. "Right? Anyway, Amos is going to stay and lock up when you're finished."

"Sounds great. Thanks."

Ollie and Amos follow Alma out of the gym, passing a frenzied-looking Jane as she jogs over to me.

"Cutting it a little close, don't you think?" I ask with a tilt of my lip.

She rolls her eyes. "You'll never believe the afternoon I had. Peterson called me in to give a statement."

"A statement for what?"

"Remember last month, that guy we picked up on 4th who was running the streets naked?"

"The one high on meth who gave you a black eye and a concussion?"

She releases a sharp exhale, her lips pursed. "The very one. He decided he wants to sue the city and the department. Said I was mean to him."

"Mean how?"

She raises her hands, palms up. "I have no idea. I doubt he remembers much of that day in general. Anyway, I gave my statement, and Chief pulled up the video from the dashcam. The guy's lawyer read him my statement and showed him the video along with the pictures of my face and the medical report. Needless to say, he decided to drop the lawsuit."

"You think? Wow."

"I know," she groans. "I'm just pissed that I spent the whole afternoon on my day off dealing with this mess. He was so high that day he's probably confusing me with a girlfriend. I bet he got in a fight with his girlfriend prior to him streaking through the streets of Ann Arbor. Remembered being arrested by a woman and confused the two incidents."

"Very likely." She sighs and walks toward me. I pull her into a hug. "I'm sorry."

"I may be a little rough with you during the demonstration tonight. You know to relieve stress," she teases.

I step back from our embrace. "Hey, how is this my fault?"

"Fine," she mumbles, grabbing my hand. "Can you at least take me out for some drinks afterward? Play some darts? I'm stressed."

"That I can do." I squeeze her hand. "Grab the iPad. You still gotta do roll call."

"Ugh. I hate you."

"Lies." I laugh.

Jane grabs the iPad and pulls up the class list while I give my introductory spiel to the participants. She starts calling out names. My eyes dart toward the gym of women when she says, *Tannon Lee.* But there's no response.

CHAPTER 14

TANNON

I admit it. I want him. He is so annoyingly sexy—from his genuine kindness, charming humor, and love for his family to his smoking hot body, dreamy eyes, and stunning smile. I crave him, and I hate it.

It's interesting how I wrote Deacon, the main male character in my current WIP—work in progress—so similar to Jude even before I'd met Jude. They're so similar in both their demeanor and appearance and job, too. I wrote Deacon as a firefighter, which, in terms of hunky book heroes, is similar to a cop. Little coincidences like this make me wish Jude was real-life boyfriend material. Everything about him carried a "meant to be" vibe, but he and I are clearly not destined to be. Like my main female character, I hate that I'm so inherently attracted to Jude. Insta-love isn't real, but I suppose my consolation prize is that book-worthy sex does exist, and I've experienced it at least once in my life.

Sitting by myself at Starbucks, I flip back and forth between the two covers that Cassie has sent to me. She wasted no time getting Jude's photos made into covers. Now, it's my job to tell the cover designer which one I like best. Even though I'm not even done writing the book, Cassie wants to do a cover reveal right away. She feels that getting Jude's cover out in front of the readers will drive pre-orders, and she's probably right.

I can't decide. The black and white cover is sexy as hell. It's clean and current with cover trends. It's an incredible cover, but it's just not me. The second one is simple with Jude's body on an orange background and blue writing. Cassie has informed me that the blue and orange combination is in. Once again, it's a good-looking cover, but I'm not feeling it.

Honestly, either would work and do well, I'm sure. My issue is probably more to do with the guy on the cover than the cover itself. It's been a week since my hookup with the hottie, and OMG...I want to do it again. I had Jude in my bed one night, and I have a hangover so bad that I can barely take it. It's all I think about. Though I shouldn't.

I casually asked about Jude at dinner with the guys the other night, and Asher informed me that he's seen Jude every day with the little blonde at the gym. So clearly my Adonis in the sack is a giant dickwad in real life, and well—not mine.

I've played our night together in my head so many times that I think it may be time to seek professional help. I can't stop thinking about him or the sex. It's seriously a problem. I'm starting to question my mental stability when it comes to Jude. I'm definitely the mental case heroine in my own personal teen novel. If I were the lead character in a young adult novel, the readers would be ripping the book apart in the reviews.

Tannon, the main character is so weak. Why did the author write such a stupid character? Why is this a YA novel anyway? She's twenty-six.

The writing was okay, but the main character made me DNF. She's annoying.

Ugh, I hate insta-love stories. This one is the worse because the girl was delusional.

Weak character. Cliché. Stupid. DNF. Why is anyone buying these books? The author needs to jump off a cliff and take that whiny Tannon character with her.

. . .

The last one is harsh, but it would happen. It's actually been written already about another one of my novels... but let's not go there. I've had therapy to let that review go. I've moved on.

Sort of. A little. Okay, not at all. Fine...I still cry about it in my sleep.

Whatever.

I drop my head onto the keyboard of my laptop and let out a moan.

"Dramatic much?" Cassie says.

I lift my head to find her standing beside my table with a fresh cup of coffee. "PSL?"

"Of course." She hands it to me and sits down next to me.

"Didn't you just take a break?" With a grin, I hold the paper cup to my nose and breathe in the perfect pumpkin smell—created just for basic bitches, like myself, in some lab.

Cassie waves her hand in the air. "Eh. What's Henry going to do? Fire me? No." She shakes her head and then tilts her face to address Henry, who is standing behind the counter. "I'm taking a break!" she calls out and then turns her attention back to me before her boss has the chance to answer.

"Plus, I had to come over here. You looked like you were on the verge of a breakdown. You really need to work on controlling your facial expressions when you're in public." She chuckles.

I smile at her words. I've been told many times that

everything I'm thinking is evident on my face at all times. In fact, I can't lie. Like—seriously, not even a small little white lie. My face gives me away. My dad says he used to love to watch me read books because he could follow the mood of the story through my expressions. He says it's endearing. I think it's annoying. What I wouldn't give to have a RBF. Because if I did have the classic *Resting Bitch Face*, everyone would leave me alone. But no...instead, my roommate is taking her second break in an hour to make sure I'm okay.

Cassie looks down toward my laptop. "Is it the covers? What don't you like about them?"

"They're really great covers," I say, honestly. "The designer did a fantastic job. I just don't feel like they're *me*. You know?"

"Right. Isn't that the point? We're trying to rebrand?"

"Yes," I tell Cassie. "I still want them to feel like my books but just with a more sexy edge to them."

Cassie presses her lips together and squints her eyes. "This is about Jude, isn't it? Do we need to find another model? Are you still having issues getting over the hookup?"

No.

Yes.

No.

I shake my head. "No. He's perfect for the cover. Really. This isn't about him." I drop my gaze to the covers on my screen again. "What if...?" I formulate the thoughts in my head before addressing Cassie. "What if we use Jude's sexy picture, but the background of the cover is still colorful and pretty? So we'll have the man chest, which will make you happy, and then we'll have the pretty colors to make me happy. A combination of styles, if you will."

"That could work." She taps her lip, staring off behind me. "Yep, that's doable. I'll shoot the designer a message and see what she can whip up for us."

"Thank you."

"Oh, dear. What's that?" My mother's voice makes me jump.

I shut my laptop. I knew she was meeting me here, so I shouldn't be startled. My parents and brother live an hour away from Ann Arbor, but my mom makes it over to see me at least once a week to catch up in person. We usually start with coffee and then chat over Thai food at the restaurant next door.

"Hi, Mrs. Lee. I was just finishing my break." Cassie stands from her chair and offers it to my mom. "Can I get you a coffee?"

"What are you drinking?" my mom asks me.

"A pumpkin spiced latte."

"Is it sweet?" she asks.

"Yes."

"Does it taste like pumpkin?" she asks with a slight grimace.

"Yes."

"Oh, no. Then I don't want that." She turns toward

Cassie. "How about a regular coffee with skim milk and the pink sugar packet?"

"Mom, you should try stevia. It's all natural. The pink packets cause cancer," I tell her.

"Everything causes cancer, Tannon. I'm going to drink what I like."

"Okay," I say. Cassie excuses herself to get my mom's coffee.

"So were those pictures of a naked guy on your computer screen? You're not putting those on your book, are you?"

My mom knows that I write romance, and I've told her that my books are spicy. She's never read one even though she proudly displays all of my paperbacks on the bookshelf in the study back home. I feel like she takes in the pretty covers and just pretends I write something other than what I do. She tells all of her friends that I'm the new Nicolas Sparks, which is so not true. His writing and mine are not remotely similar. Plus, I don't kill off all of my characters. Well, I have killed off one, but she wasn't a very nice person.

"We're looking into rebranding my books," I tell her.

"Why would you do that? Your books are beautiful. You said you'd never put a naked guy on your covers." She hits the pink packet of fake sugar against her fingers.

Cassie quietly sets the coffee down and then backs away, shooting me an amused expression.

"First of all, Mom, he's not naked. It's a torso. You

can see one at any beach you go to. It's not pornographic."

Her big blue eyes that mirror my own almost pop out of her skull before they dart around the room to make sure no one heard me. I have to hold in a laugh.

My mom is my biggest supporter. She loves me and has always wanted me to do what makes me happy. When I told her I was leaving my teaching job three years ago, she was all for it. But she's a little reserved. She actually just published a book of her own. It's her tale of how she found Jesus and spreads His light each day. I'm not even kidding.

She speaks in a hushed tone now. "You've built a beautiful brand, Tan. I don't think you should lower your standards now."

"Mom, it's not about lowering my standards. It's about producing a book that the readers want and making money. If I don't want to go back to teaching, I have to make more money."

She shakes her head. "Well, I just think that your books are beautiful, and you should stay classy."

"I promise I will stay classy," I reassure her.

My thoughts go to last week and my bare ass up on the kitchen counter with Jude's face between my legs. I'm pretty sure I just lied to my mother. Her expression is one of approval which can only mean that she believes me. *OMG...I guess I can lie!* Well, that's an exciting development.

"Mrs. Lee. So good to see you." Everett now stands next to the table.

"Hello, Everett. How are you?" Mom stands to hug my friend.

The two of them talk, and I try to ignore them. My mother thinks that Everett is the best man to walk the face of the earth and doesn't know why I'm not marrying him. Everett finds it all very amusing and sucks up to my mother every time he sees her.

"Yes, I'll talk to her. It's so important to stick to one's moral code," he says, and I let out a loud sigh. "By the way. I read your book, and it was touching. It really moved me, and I feel closer to God because of you. I can't thank you enough for your gift to the world."

I am going to puke.

My mom's book is great. She's a wonderful writer, and it's full of great tips for those wanting to delve deeper into their faith. But Everett didn't read a word of it. He's so annoying.

I shove my laptop into my purse and stand from the table. "You know, Mom. I'm starving. Do you want to head over to the restaurant now?"

"Sure. Everett, do you want to join us?"

"Oh, he can't," I say before Everett can answer. "He's fasting in preparation for his colonoscopy. He got something stuck up there last week, and his doctor wants to make sure nothing was damaged."

Everett's mouth drops open, and I grab my mom's

hand and pull her toward the door before he can say anything.

"I just don't know why you're still single when you have such a nice boy living across the hall from you. He's so handsome and smart. You know computers are the way of the future. That's a great field to be in. He'll always have a job."

"I know, Mom, but he's just my friend," I repeat what I've told her many times before.

We step outside. It's a perfect seventy-five-degree autumn day. The warm wind is rustling through the trees, and the sun is shining.

"How did he get something stuck up there?" she asks quietly now that we're outside.

I press my lips into a line to stop myself from laughing. "Not sure. Says he fell in the shower."

"That's very unfortunate," she says.

"Yeah, it really is."

CHAPTER 15

TANNON

"Can I use your straightener?" Cassie calls from her room. "Mine died."

"Of course," I yell back from the couch. I'm sprawled out against the comfortable leather, throwing pieces of popcorn into my mouth.

I'm on season two of my *Gilmore Girls* marathon. After my weird dream about Dean and Rory dancing at the circus a couple of weeks ago, I felt compelled to watch it again. I wonder how productive I'd be if life didn't consist of rewatching my favorite shows multiple times. The thought makes me tired. Netflix is my dealer, and I'm their number one customer.

"What in the hell are you doing?" Cassie snaps.

"Watching Dean get all jealous of Tristan."

"Why aren't you showered and getting ready?"

"I'm not going," I state.

Cassie's eyes open wide. "Yes, you are."

"It's the 'Romeo and Juliet' episode. Remember Dean goes to all of the rehearsals? I love this one." I toss a handful of popcorn into my mouth.

"I'm not going to the party without you. You're going."

I tap the spot next to me on the sofa. "Stay here with me."

Cassie stomps over to the TV and manually shuts it off. "No. We told the boys we were going, so we're going. Plus, you need a change of scenery. It will help with your writer's block."

"Everett and Asher's apartment is hardly a change of scenery. We're over there all the time." I chuckle. "I'm not in the mood to go hang out with a ton of people I don't know."

"You won't be. You'll be hanging out with me. Now, get up and get ready, or I'm calling your mom to tell her that you're in a funk and won't leave the apartment."

"You wouldn't." I narrow my eyes.

"Oh, I would."

I sit up with a groan. "Fine."

I have to admit that once I'm showered and getting ready while listening to Taylor Swift blasting through my Bluetooth speakers, I actually do feel better. One needs a night of makeup and straightened hair every now and again to break up the slob days, and I have a lot of those.

"Look at that hot ass," Cassie cheers from the entrance to my bathroom.

I palm my jeans-clad butt cheek. "I know. Right? I bought these last spring, and it's my first time wearing them." My new jeans and black tank top hug my curves perfectly. I smack my cherry-red lips together in the mirror, admiring my reflection. "I look good," I say in a serious tone before breaking into a chuckle.

"That you do. There's nothing like a little mascara and lip color to take one's beauty to the next level."

"You're gorgeous, too," I tell my bestie.

"Thanks. Are you ready to head over?"

"Yep!" I snatch up my phone from the countertop and turn off Taylor before sliding it into my back pocket.

"So, want to take any guesses as to who's going to be at this party?" Cassie questions as we walk toward our apartment door.

"No clue. Seriously, who do they hang out with besides us? I don't get their need to throw parties for randoms all of the time," I comment as we close our door behind us and step into the hall. Post Malone can be heard coming from the guys' apartment.

"At least they're playing good music today," Cassie says.

"True. Though, I liked listening to Meatloaf last time. It reminded me of my dad. He loves that guy."

Cassie laughs. "That may be true, but no one plays Meatloaf at parties. Not in this century, at least."

We're greeted by faces of people who we don't know as we enter the apartment.

"Total randoms," Cassie calls back to me, loud enough so that I can hear her over the music.

I shriek as Everett pulls me into a bear hug, lifting me off the ground. "Tannon, baby! You're looking fine. Did you go through all of this trouble for me? Your mom will be so happy."

"You know it." I supply him with a smirk as he sets me down. "I want you. Right here. Right now."

He lifts his arm, his hand rubbing the nape of his neck as he feigns remorse. "You see...I would. It's just that there are some hot-ass girls here who haven't seen me cry at the *Survivor* elimination this week. So I'm going to have to pass."

"Probably a good call." I take a drink from Asher's extended hand. "Thank you. What is it?"

"A mojito. Just for you," he says.

"Oh, yum. You know they're my fave." Ever since having one in the Bahamas on a cruise I took with Cassie a few years ago, I've been obsessed with mojitos.

"That we do," Asher says to me before shooting a warm smile to Cassie, who also has a red Solo cup filled with what I'm sure is a mojito in her hand.

"Who are these people?" Cassie asks the guys.

"Mainly people from the gym," Asher says, his eyes scanning the crowd.

"Your friends?" I ask.

Asher shrugs. "Friends. Clients. Some randoms."

"Always randoms." I laugh. "What would one of your parties be like if half the people here weren't strangers?"

"I don't know. Strange, I think." Asher grins.

"Definitely weird," Everett agrees.

Lifting the cup to my mouth, I take another sip of my drink and suddenly can no longer taste the sweet mint beverage. I freeze, my senses singularly focused. He's a room away. Dancing bodies, loud music, and dim lights separate us, yet I see him and only him, so clearly it aches. A barrage of memories engulfs me—the way he felt, sounded, and smelled—the way he made me feel. The unbelievable highs and the desperate lows of that night collide, and I'm left gasping into my cup.

"Tan, you okay?" Asher asks, placing his fingers against my wrist. He pushes my raised arm down, removing the cup from my mouth.

"You invited him?" I finally get out once the shock subsides.

"Who?" He squints toward me, confused.

I shouldn't be surprised. He's Asher's client, after all. Plus, the guys don't know about my one-night stand or the insane and sudden feelings I developed for the hot cop during said one-night stand. As far as Asher knows, Jude is just the guy who posed for my cover who Cassie and I found attractive.

Cassie follows my stare. "Jude." The whispered name coming from her lips is more of a declaration than an answer to Asher's question.

"Jude? The guy you hired as a cover model? Yeah. So? He's a client." Asher looks back and forth between Cassie and me. "Am I missing something?"

I shake my head. "It's fine. Just odd seeing him again, is all." I definitely don't want to go into details about my night with Jude or cause the guys to suspect something and dig deeper. It's unusual because I share most aspects of my life with them. Besides Cassie, they are my closest friends. There's just something about my night with Jude that I want to keep to myself. Even though I know it was meaningless and just a hookup, I can't let it go. And the part that won't leave me, I want to keep for myself.

"Are you sure? You don't look well," Everett states.

I don't feel well because Jude is leaning over talking to a tiny blonde who I now realize is his co-instructor, Officer Grenada. "I'm fine. Is that the girl you were telling us about a couple of weeks ago? The blonde he's always talking to at the gym?"

Asher leans his head back to get a peek at Jude and the girl. He nods. "Yeah, that's her."

"Lovely." I sigh.

Asher pulls his bottom lip through his teeth, a cocky grin now present on his face. "Something happened. Tell us."

"Nothing happened." I chug the remainder of my mojito in an attempt to break eye contact with Asher. He's trying to catch me in a lie, and if I look at him, he will.

"Look at me." Asher chuckles.

I peer down at my feet. "No. I need another drink."

Everett lets out a loud laugh. "You are hiding something, Tan. You know we'll find out. In fact, I think I'm going to go have a chat with model boy over there."

I throw my arm up and grab Everett's wrist. "Don't," I snap under my breath. "Please, Ev. Just leave it."

"Yeah, let's go get some drink refills," Cassie suggests.

Asher and Everett exchange looks.

"Okay. Two more mojitos coming up." Asher takes our cups from our hands, and we follow him into the kitchen.

"You need to chill," Cassie says to me as we hang back a few steps from the guys.

"I'm fine," I reassure her.

"Don't make it weird," she chastises.

"I'm not."

"You kind of are."

I roll my eyes. "No, now you are."

"Okay, I'll drop it if you do."

"Seriously?" I sigh. "I dropped it back there."

"Good. Just think of him as another random person in this party of strangers. Don't give him a second thought." She squeezes my arm reassuringly.

He's not and too late.

"I know," I say instead.

"Great. Let's get our drinks and head out to the

balcony. You won't have to deal with him out there." Cassie takes off to stand next to Asher.

I stand at the kitchen entryway and keep my eyes focused straight ahead on Asher as he smashes mint leaves into my cup. I don't dare look around. Truth be told, I should just go home and plop myself down in front of another episode of *Gilmore Girls*, but I refuse to be weak and let a one-night stand drive me away. I'm closer to thirty than I am to twenty at this point. It's about time I grow some balls.

Jude had some nice balls, and I don't even like balls.
No! Stop it.

I shake my head in an attempt to clear my thoughts and return my attention to Asher as he finishes up our drinks.

Mint leaves.
Soda water.
Lime juice.
Sugar.
Lots of rum.

My friends return to me and place the drink in my hand. I immediately take a sip.

"Balcony?" Cassie questions. She doesn't wait for my nod before she begins to make her way through the crowd of people in the living room. I follow eagerly, ready to get out of this space before I have to confront Jude.

"Tannon."
Too late.

I'd recognize that voice anywhere. It's deep and beautiful with the perfect amount of husky and sexy. I could get lost in that low timbre regardless of the words, and I want to. It's dangerous and wonderful at the same time. I want to surrender to the sound, but I can't.

So I ignore it.

CHAPTER 16

TANNON

"Tannon," he says my name again.

Nope.

Just keep walking.

"Tannon." My name is a plea, and it pulls me in. He's said it three times, but this time, I stop.

I release a sigh and steady myself before I turn to face him. When I do, his emerald eyes seem confused—sad even—and it throws me off. I plan on being cold or indifferent, but in actuality, I simply want. I want him. My body aches so close to his. My breaths come more slowly as my chest rises to pull in air that seems suddenly thinner.

There's no hiding the fact that I still crave Jude. My mind knows he's off-limits—for me anyway—yet my body is still waiting to receive that memo.

"Hey," I answer, the greeting steadier than I feel.

He leans in so I can hear him over the music. "How are you?"

"Fine. You?" My response is rote.

"Do you think maybe we can go talk over at your place?"

Is he freaking serious? "Uh, no."

He raises his hand and grasps the back of his neck. I allow my eyes to drop, just for a second, to his waist, which is peeking through the crack between his shirt and jeans.

"Okay." His eyes dart around the room. "Can we go over there?" He motions toward the far side of the apartment near Everett's bookshelves, where one guy stands moving his thumb against the screen of his cell phone. "Where it's quieter? I want to talk to you."

I point toward the sliding glass door that leads to the porch. "Cassie and the guys are waiting. I should head out there."

"Please. It will only take a minute," he pleads, and of course, I can't say no.

"Fine," I relent and follow Jude over toward the other side of the room. In reality, it's not that much quieter, but without all of the people standing around us, it seems like it is.

The guy on his phone looks up from his screen and then leaves us alone.

Jude wipes his palms against the front of his jeans. "I wanted to make sure you're okay and apologize for leaving so early."

His words aren't what I expected. "Yeah, I'm fine, and whatever. It is what it is. That's how it works, right?"

"I had to report to work at six, so I needed to head home to shower and get ready a little before five. I wanted to say goodbye, but I didn't want to wake you."

"Okay," I say for lack of anything better. I suppose my anger for him sneaking out so early starts to dissipate. The guy had to work. I can't hate him for that.

Jude shakes his head before dropping it back with a tilt of his lips. "This whole conversation feels so stupid. I should just let it go. I mean, I'm making it awkward. I wanted you to know that I don't normally do that. I mean, I do *that*, but it usually happens a little differently." He presses his fingers into his temples. "I'm making a mess of this. I just wanted to tell you that when I walked you home, it wasn't because I wanted all of that to happen. I guess that's not true. Of course, I wanted it, but I didn't expect it, nor do I usually sleep with girls the first time we hang out. I'm normally a pretty good guy."

"Okay," I say again slowly. I'm clearly coming off as real brilliant in this conversation.

Jude raises his hands in surrender. "I get it. One night was all you wanted. I'll let it go. I just wanted to talk to you...just in case."

"I'm confused." I mean to say it to myself, but the words slip out.

"With?" Jude asks.

"Everything. What do you mean one night was all I

wanted?" I can't wrap my mind around why he's saying this to me.

"Well, you didn't call or text, so I assumed..." he answers.

"You didn't call or text either."

Jude peers down toward me. "I don't have your number."

"And I don't have yours."

"But I left it."

I cross my arms over my chest. "What are you talking about? No, you didn't."

"Yeah, I did. I wrote you a note with my number on the back of the picture of me that I found in your nightstand drawer."

My eyes go wide. What in the hell is he talking about? He saw the picture? The sexy as fuck picture of him wearing only his boxers that I keep in my nightstand with BOB in the drawer that I haven't had the heart to open since my night with Jude.

"I haven't opened that drawer," I respond. There's no point in hiding the fact that I kept a printed photo of him nearly naked next to my vibrator. He obviously saw it.

"I left it on your bedside table." He bites his bottom lip.

I shrug. "I didn't see a note."

"You didn't see a note?" he repeats.

I shake my head.

"So you thought I hooked up with you and then left?"

"Well, you did," I state.

"Because I had to go to work, not because I wanted to."

I drop my arms and place my hands on my hips. "Listen. It's fine. It happens. No hard feelings. We don't have to make it weird. We had sex. I thought it was great. I'm not sure how you felt about it. Now, we can go about our own way."

Jude's voice lowers. "I thought it was better than great."

I swallow.

"I think about it every day." He steps in closer toward me. "If you want to know the truth, I can't stop thinking about you and us together that night."

His gaze drops to my mouth and then lifts to my eyes. He moves in closer, and I press my hands against his chest to push him back, but once my skin is on his, I'm frozen there.

"Have you thought about us? The way our bodies fit together? The way you screamed my name as you came? Have you...?" His voice trails off, and he licks his lips.

I shake my head.

He quirks up an eyebrow. "You haven't thought about that night at all?"

"No," I say breathlessly, pulling my stare from his face.

"Has anyone ever told you that you're a terrible liar, Tannon?"

I close my eyes. My chest rises and falls more quickly now.

"No."

"Somehow, I doubt that." Humor lines Jude's voice.

I should open my eyes. I should remove my hands from his chest. I should go home. But I don't because Jude's so close to my mouth now that I can feel his warm breath against my lips. I release an involuntary whimper before Jude crashes his lips to mine. I slide my hands up his chest and around the back of his neck until I'm pulling him further into me.

He grasps at my waist, his fingers dig into my skin as his tongue greedily moves into my mouth. He tastes of beer and mint, and I melt into him. Our mouths are desperate, and our kiss is needy. I kiss him with all of the pent-up lust and desire from the past two weeks. Moans vibrate from my mouth into his. I need this kiss like I need air.

Maybe this is an apology. Maybe it's a goodbye. I don't care because it's everything. He's right; I have thought about him. I've thought about him every second of every day since I woke up without him that morning. I've never had anyone who fits as perfectly as Jude Martinez inside me before, and I know I'll never feel anything like him again. So I can't stop to think about what this kiss means because it might be the end. And right now, I just need it.

Jude.

This kiss.

This moment.

It will probably all be over the second his lips leave mine, but right now, he's kissing me like he's afraid of the end too.

All at once, I pull away when she pops into my head, the blonde. I hate her and Jude, and his magical lips. I hate them all.

"You know, you're an asshole." I work to make my voice steady when I feel anything but.

Jude assesses me, confused. "I...what?"

"You're an asshole," I say louder. "Did you hear me that time? You were right before. I did think about that night. We do have chemistry, but I will never be with someone like you. Or at least now that I know the kind of person you are, I'll never be with you again."

"What kind of person is that?" Jude narrows his eyes.

"A cheater," I spit out.

"I'm not a cheater, Tannon."

"Would your girlfriend agree if we called her over here?"

"I'm thinking, no, since I don't have one." He glares at me, and I can't deny that I don't like it. I miss the way his eyes captured me with only desire moments ago.

"The blond girl you're with, Officer Grenada. I saw her. I know you're together. Asher sees her with you every day at the gym."

Jude scans the room. "You mean her?" He points toward the other corner of the living room, where Officer Grenada is lip-locked with some other guy. "Yeah, that's my partner and best friend, Jane. I am with her a lot, but we're not a couple."

"Oh," I say. Damn, I feel like an idiot. Why do I turn into a complete dumbass every time I open my mouth around this dude?

"Well, I actually need to get going," Jude says, his voice emotionless. "It was good seeing you, Tannon. Take care."

I open my mouth to respond and then close it again as he walks away. I'm so disappointed in myself. I've reached a whole new low. It boggles my mind how I can make a living writing about fictional characters' love and relationships because I haven't a clue about any of it in real life.

CHAPTER 17

JUDE

I don't have it in me to call her crazy because I know she's not that. She'd never stand in my driveway kicking a car and screaming. That's not her, but it doesn't mean she's relationship material because she's not. At least, not for me. She's jealous, untrusting, and kind of rude. The three combined still earn her more points than crazy Stacy—but not enough.

And it sucks.

My body had all sorts of visceral reactions going on at the mere sight of her tonight, and that kiss...fuck me. I sure as shit didn't see it ending the way it did, with a cheater label thrown in my face.

Move on and let it go.

"Hey!" Jane runs up from behind. "Where are you going? Why'd you leave so fast?"

"I'm going home."

"And you're just going to leave me there alone?"

I narrow my gaze. "First of all, you could kick anyone's ass there. Secondly, you were preoccupied. Looked like you were having fun." I raise a brow.

"I have no idea what you're talking about, but you shouldn't just bail. It's kind of rude."

"Sorry. You were kissing some guy. I thought you were having fun." I keep walking.

"It was just something to do, and no, I wasn't having fun. Just let me know if you're leaving a party that you invited me to, okay?" Her tone is snappy, and I don't like it, especially with everything I'm feeling about Tannon right now.

I halt my steps and face her. "Asher invited us both to the party at the same time when we were at the gym today. You weren't there as my guest. You were there on your own accord, and usually, if I have my tongue down someone's throat, it's because I want it there. So please don't come at me. I'm not in the mood."

She smacks my abs playfully. "Fine. Sorry. Didn't realize you were having a night."

"Well, I am."

"Let's go to the bar. Just the two of us."

I shake my head. "I'm just going to go home."

"All right. I'll come with you. We can hang out, play a game, watch a movie. Whatever."

I continue the path to my car that's parked along one

of the side streets. I don't feel like hanging out with anyone tonight, but I don't protest. I just want to get away from Tannon and all the memories that come along with her.

"Fine," I answer.

Once we're back at my place, Jane goes through my cupboards. "There's vodka, rum, and tequila. What'll you have?"

I flip through the streaming channels on the TV, looking for something to watch.

"I'll just have a beer from the fridge," I call back.

"Okay, suit yourself. I'm going with vodka."

Jane returns to the couch with drinks in hand. *The Terminator* plays on the big-screen TV. One can't go wrong with *The Terminator*.

"So what's going on?" she asks. "I need details. Are you upset about the writer chick? Are you into her? I'm still confused with that whole situation."

"Her name is Tannon, and I was into her—I thought. I'm not now."

"Why? What happened?"

"She called me a cheater."

Jane laughs loudly. "Jude Martinez, a cheater? God, she doesn't know you at all. You're only the most loyal man I've ever met."

"Thank you."

I take the compliment though it doesn't mean the same coming from Jane. She hasn't had the best examples of what males should be like. Her father, stepfather, and every boyfriend she's ever had have been a complete waste of space. Total dicks.

"She doesn't deserve you then. Don't give her another thought," she says, taking a long drink of the clear liquid in her glass.

Easier said than done.

"We should play a game!" she exclaims.

"I don't know…"

"Please?" She jumps up, running toward the cupboard at the end of the living room and swinging the door open. "We have Uno or Monopoly? Oh, Risk! Or Scrabble?"

She continues to call out games, of which I have a lot. Growing up in a big family, we played lots of games. There was one small TV for the entire house with three local channels, and it was rarely on unless my dad was watching the news or my sisters were watching *Friends*. We didn't have our faces glued to a device like this generation does. Either we were playing outside or, on rainy days, we were playing games.

I love that my sisters are raising their kids the same way. Whenever my nieces or nephews come over to visit, they want to play games. So, I make sure I'm stocked.

Jane returns and plops Clue on the coffee table. "I decided for us. I love this game."

"Okay, set it up."

"I will, but first, I need a refill. Do you want another beer?" She skips off to the kitchen.

"Nah, I'm good. Thanks."

"We should order a pizza!"

I laugh, grabbing my phone, and I look up a local pizza place to input an online order for delivery. Based on the speed at which Jane is drinking, she's going to need some food in her. I'm not sure how much she had to drink at Asher's, but I'm pretty sure this second drink she's making here will do her in. She's a bit of a lightweight, but at a hundred pounds, it kind of goes with the territory.

"I'm on it."

"Get ham and pineapple."

"No way," I call out. "You know that's a hard pass." I'll eat almost anything, but I am not eating pineapple on my pizza.

"Fine," she grumbles. "Just get a supreme then without the olives and a side of ranch. No! Two sides of ranch or three for leftovers, you know?"

"Okay, I'll get four sides just so you won't be without." I grin and type in the order.

"You're so good to me." She comes back to the couch and starts to set up the game. "You're too good for that girl. You know? She probably has issues. Don't most writers have issues? It's like they're all depressed and weird. They're all like suicidal and cut their ears off and stuff."

"Um, you're thinking of Van Gogh, and he was a painter." I chuckle. "And that's quite the blanket stereotype you have going there."

"I'm just saying. You don't pick 'em well, Jude. Remember Stacy? It's like...*why?*"

"Tannon's no Stacy," I protest. "Not even close."

"Well, if she's calling you a cheater, then she sounds crazy to me."

"Let's just play. You go first."

She takes another long gulp of her drink, rolls the dice, and moves her pawn into a room on the board. "I think it's Mrs. Peacock with a candlestick in the library."

"But you're in the kitchen."

"So?"

"So you can only ask about the room you're in."

"But I want to ask about the library."

"Then you need to go to the library."

"I don't want to go to the library."

"Then you can't ask about the library." I let out a laugh.

"Fine," she snaps. "Then everything I said in the conservatory."

"You mean kitchen?"

"Whatever."

I show her the Mrs. Peacock card in my hand and watch as she marks off the candlestick and library on her score sheet, leaving the Mrs. Peacock square blank.

I roll my eyes. "You're in the kitchen, and I could have more than one card in my hand. I only showed you one, and it was Mrs. Peacock."

"Yeah, I know."

I humor her for a few more rounds, as there is no chance in hell of us playing a real game. She's too drunk. Most of my focus is on the movie, which she doesn't seem to notice.

"I think it's Mrs. Peacock with a knife in the library," she says from the lounge on her next turn.

"Go fish," I say.

She nods as if she's just discovered something and makes some more doodles on her score sheet.

The doorbell rings, and I hop up from the sofa to retrieve the pizza. When I come back, Jane is leaning against the arm of the couch asleep.

"Hey." I shake her arm, trying to wake her. "Pizza's here."

"I don't..." she grumbles, half asleep.

I place the pizza in the refrigerator and put away the game. Grabbing an extra pillow and blanket from the closet, I situate Jane so she isn't sitting so awkwardly, and then I cover her up.

I click the remote, turning the TV off, and retrieve a large mixing bowl from the kitchen. I place it on the floor beside her just in case.

As I start to walk away, she reaches her hand out and grabs my leg.

"Thank you," she whispers.

"No problem. There's a bowl on the floor and water on the table here if you need it. Okay?"

"She doesn't deserve you, you know?" she says on a sigh. "No one does but me."

She slips back into a slumber, and I watch her for a moment. Finally, I shake my head and retreat to my bedroom.

Today wasn't the best.

Tomorrow's a new day.

CHAPTER 18

TANNON

At first, the paw to my face is soft, but with each hit, it becomes more forceful. Lucifer's meow is loud and pained—the sound of someone being tortured. Yet I'm the one being assaulted by his deceivingly strong jab to my jaw and shrieks of warning.

"Stop hitting me," I groan and roll over onto my side, burying my face in the pillow. "It's early. Go away."

The light pressure of his paws against my back as he retreats causes me to grin. I won. He's letting me sleep in. Good. It's about time he realizes I'm the one in charge here—not him and his eight pounds of attitude-charged fluff.

"Ouch!" I howl and jolt up, pulling my legs toward me so I can protect my feet. "You bit my fucking toe?" I scream at Lucifer, but he doesn't flinch. He sits, prim and proper, at the foot of my bed and merely warns me with his slanted green eyes. "You are a horrible cat." I throw my blankets off me and stand from my bed.

I check the time on my phone. It's six in the morning. I've been in bed less than three hours, and my head is pounding from the mojitos I consumed after Jude left the party. I wobble before catching my balance as I stand. *Hell, I'm probably still drunk.*

"For the record, I officially hate you," I grumble as I make my way to the kitchen. Lucifer meows softly behind me. He's calling out my lie.

I scrape the canned food out of its container and into a glass dish. Lucifer doesn't like to eat straight from the can. "Here you go, your majesty." I set the dish of food on the ground. My little black devil purrs as he takes his first bite.

I hobble back toward my room as my toe is sore from Lucifer's assault. My nightstand catches my attention as I enter, and I recall what Jude had told me. I hurry toward the small piece of furniture and open the top drawer. BOB lies there in his abandoned glory, but the picture of Jude is gone.

Dropping to my knees, I check behind the nightstand. There's nothing but dusty cords belonging to my phone charger and lamp. I scan the floor to the one side and find nothing, then I move my attention to the small space between the furniture and my bed. Lying on its side, pressed against the wood of the table, is his picture.

I pull it out and turn it over to see the back.

. . .

Tannon,

Sorry to leave so early. I have to work. I had a great time last night. I'd love to see you again. Call me when you can.

Jude

Below his name is his number. Well, damn. Jude's not an asshole, but I kind of feel like one.

I climb back into bed and wrap myself in the blankets. The pieces of information gathered since yesterday change everything. Jude is single. He didn't blow me off. My body still craves him, and his lips are just as amazing as I remembered.

I'll fix everything, or at least I'll try. But first, I need sleep.

"What are you doing still in bed?" My mother's voice is out of place in my sleepy haze. "Tannon."

I open my eyes, blinking to clear my vision. Sure enough, my mother stands over my bed. "Why are you here?"

She shakes her head, disappointed. "We made plans to go apple picking. Remember?"

"Oh, that's right. I forgot." I sit up and lean against the headboard. "Is Branson here?"

"Yes, your brother is in the living room talking to

Cassie. Did you have a late night writing? I don't understand why you're still in bed at noon."

"Yeah."

Something like that.

"Well, get up and get ready. Should I go over and invite Everett and Asher to come along?" she asks hopefully.

"No, Mom." I step out of bed. "Listen, you have to let the Everett thing go. He's just my friend. Neither of us wants it to be more than that. Stop making it weird."

"I'm not trying to. I just figured they might want to come along," she answers, her voice coy.

"I know you, Mother, and I know how your mind works. So stop. Nothing is going to happen with me and either of those boys. Let's just have a family day with you, me, and Branson."

"Well, I already invited Cassie, and she said she wanted to come."

I stop in front of my bathroom. "Cassie's fine. But no boys. I'm going to take a quick shower. I'll be ready in five minutes."

Twenty minutes later, my brother Branson, Cassie, and I are in my mom's car on the way to the orchard. I'm looking forward to getting a large bag of apples. Living in Michigan, I've grown accustomed to the crisp deliciousness of a freshly picked apple. Because of that, I really only eat apples in the fall. The ones in the store never taste as good.

"We're going to an orchard with donuts, right?" Branson asks from the back seat.

"Yes. This place has the best donuts," I answer. There's also nothing like freshly made apple and pumpkin donuts.

"I love the glazed pumpkin ones." Cassie sighs.

"Me too," I agree. "They are probably my favorite. Though the cinnamon and sugar-coated apple ones are a close second."

"Agreed," Cassie says.

"I'll eat them all," Branson offers.

"Well, you need to." Cassie chuckles. "You've grown like a foot since the last time I saw you. You're a senior this year?"

"Yep," Branson answers.

"What colleges are you applying to?" she asks.

"Western, State, Central, Eastern, and Michigan."

"What's your number one?"

"Obviously, the University of Michigan," he says.

"So you want to come here even though I live here?" I ask with a grin.

Branson scoffs. "Just because you refuse to move off-campus at age twenty-six doesn't mean it's not still the best college there is. Your inability to move on is a personal problem, one that I won't let affect me."

"Hey. Rude much? I still live here because it's convenient, and I like the city. I've moved on from college."

"Whatever you say," Branson teases.

"The only person who she speaks to from college is me, so I'd say she's moved on. Lots of people live in Ann Arbor who aren't college students." Cassie sticks up for me.

"That is true," Mom chimes in, "and she's already on her second career. Your sister is doing well for herself."

"Yeah, Bran. You better watch it, or I won't come pick you up when you text me wasted your freshman year." I shoot a wink at my brother.

My mother tsks. "Oh, stop teasing, Tan. He won't be twenty-one, so he definitely won't be drinking."

"You're right, Mom. My bad." I press my lips in a line, trying not to giggle.

Mom pulls into the orchard, where rows upon rows of beautiful trees wear apples like ornaments.

"Ask them which rows are the pink lady apples?" I instruct my mom when she leaves the car to go purchase the bags for our apple collection.

"You know I've drunk before," Branson says when just Cassie and I are left in the car.

"Yeah, we know," I answer. "And I know you'll drink in college...I would keep that fact from Mom, though. Sometimes ignorance is bliss when it comes to her. She prefers to see life through rose-colored glasses."

"And you puking your guts out at your first college party definitely won't be rosy." Cassie scrunches her nose up in a grimace.

Branson frowns toward Cassie. "I won't be puking. I can hold my liquor."

"That's what they all say." Cassie chuckles.

"Well, I'm not like the other freshman newbs," Branson defends himself. He always tries to act older than he is around Cassie. He'd never admit it, but I'm pretty sure he's had a crush on her since he first met her at age ten.

"You're right. You are wise beyond your years, little grasshopper," I say seriously.

"Bite me, Tannon."

"So mature, Bran." I laugh.

The driver's side door opens, and my mom drops into her seat and hands me four white apple bags. "He said that many of the apples have had hail damage this year. They are still edible and taste delicious, but some have divots in the peel. So we'll just need to cut that part out."

"Are there pink ladies left?" I ask.

"Sure are. There are three whole rows of them."

Mom puts the car into gear and starts to drive back into the orchard.

"What is your deal with pink ladies? You're a little obsessed," Branson says.

"Well, they are the best apple in the world. They are sweet and crisp but sour, too. Their skins aren't too tough, and the apple part doesn't get mushy once they're picked. That's the thing about red delicious. They taste incredible straight from the tree, but two days at home in the fridge, and they get mushy and grainy. I like apples that stay crisp," I explain.

"It's just an apple, Tan." Branson sighs.

"No. Not all apples are the same, little brother."

"Whatever. Let's go." Branson opens his door once Mom has parked.

"Look at that perfect group of apples up there." Cassie points toward the top of one of the apple trees.

"I can lift you up there," Branson offers, and I roll my eyes.

"Stop leading him on. He's a child," I whisper into Cassie's ear.

"I'm not, and I know. Ew." Cassie shakes her head and narrows her eyes at me.

Branson bends down, and she steps onto his thigh and then swings one of her legs over his head to sit on his shoulders. He holds on to her shins and stands.

Cassie giggles. "I'm so high up."

"What a cute picture!" my mom exclaims. "Tannon, go stand next to them by the tree. I'll get a picture." I do as she says. "Smile, kids!" Mom snaps some photos from her phone. "Now reach out and pick the apples, Cass, and look back at me and smile."

Cassie plays the part perfectly and lets my mother snap a dozen pictures of her. "These are going to look so cute on Facebook," my mom says. "Tannon, pick an apple and smile back toward me."

"You should get a picture of me taking my first bite of apple, Mom," I say as a joke.

"Oh, great idea. Take a bite!" She holds up her phone toward my face and takes a picture.

"Mom," Branson says with Cassie still on his shoulders. "I'm going to spin in the middle of the rows of trees here while Cassie holds her arms out. Get ready."

Branson starts spinning, and Cassie extends her arms out to her sides in dramatic fashion, giggling toward the sky as my mother continues to take pictures. I can't help but laugh.

"Mom, get me looking through these leaves." I stand behind a branch, and I peer through the opening between the bunches of leaves.

And just like that, our day has turned into the weirdest photo shoot ever. Branson, Cassie, and I do strange pose after pose, laughing so hard. My mother eats it up. She's a sucker for a good photo op and too innocent to realize we're kind of making fun of her. Though it starts as an inside joke between the three of us about my mother, it morphs into an afternoon of fun and laughter.

Apple picking is one of my favorite activities of the year, but this year tops all of the rest. When we leave the orchard, my sides ache from laughing so hard, and I have a full bag of pink ladies. This day really couldn't get any better.

CHAPTER 19

TANNON

"This is so good, Mrs. Lee," Everett says to my mother, who has been in the kitchen cooking since we got back from the orchard. She's made a huge pot of chili with cornbread, and two pans of apple cobbler are currently baking in the oven.

"This is like the most fall meal ever." Cassie takes a big bite of chili. "It's so good."

"I feel bad that Dad isn't here to enjoy it," I say to my mother.

"Oh, he's fine. I made him a chicken potpie this morning before we left, so he has plenty to eat. He's not much for apple picking. Plus, you know how he loves to relax every Sunday and watch the Lions lose."

Asher almost chokes on his mouthful of chili. "Ain't that the truth? I don't think they've had a winning season since I was born."

I don't know much about football, except that our state football team, the Detroit Lions, doesn't win too often—or at least often enough to make the fans happy.

Mom pulls the pans of apple cobbler out of the oven. "I made a pan for the boys and a pan for the girls," she says with a smile. You'll all have plenty. Branson and I should get going, though, since he has school tomorrow."

"What about a pan for me?" he grumbles.

"I'll make you and Dad some at home. We still have plenty of apples." She directs her attention toward me. "Tan, honey, I forgot to grab vanilla ice cream for the cobbler. Is there somewhere close by that you can grab some?"

"Sure, Mom. I can walk down to Fedé's store and get some real quick. It's only two blocks away."

"Okay, great. These are still bubbling hot now. They'll be cooled enough to eat in about twenty minutes, and you're going to want ice cream with them." She raises her eyebrows and grins.

I carry my empty chili bowl into the kitchen and set it in the sink. "Thanks, Mom, for a perfect day." I wrap my arms around her and pull her into a hug.

"You're welcome, love." She pats my back. "Okay, we should be going, Bran. Give your sister a hug."

Branson stands and wraps his arms around me. "Gotta go. Can't wait a couple of minutes to eat dessert. Must go now," he groans, and I chuckle.

"Bye. Love you," I tell him.

Asher stands from the table. "I think I'm going to get seconds of this amazing chili."

"You mean thirds," Cassie corrects him.

"Whatever. I work out a lot. I need calories."

Everett holds his hand to his chest and mocks his friend. "I'm Asher. I'm so hot. I need extra food to feed all of my muscles. I have an eight-pack."

"Whatever, chubs. I've offered to help you out, so don't be jealous. The invitation is always open," Asher says before going over to thank my mother again.

Everett is far from chubby, but it's the running joke between the two. Where Asher's muscles are large and defined from his work at the gym, Everett's muscles are lean. Everett has more of a swimmer's body, and Asher's is more like a boxer's. They're different but both gorgeous.

My mom and brother say the rest of their goodbyes and head out. Once they're gone, I grab my purse. "I'm going to run and get ice cream. Does anyone need anything else?"

"Tissues, maybe? E will need them if we watch another episode of *Survivor* tonight." Asher lets out a laugh.

"Whatever. He had been bullied his whole life," he says in defense, referring to one of our favorite contestants from *Survivor*. "The show was the first time he felt whole and important, then they blindsided him, and it brought back all of his insecurities. It wasn't fair."

I nod. "Tissues...check." I squeeze Everett's shoulder. "I cried too. I totally get it." I give him a wink and head out.

"Mi niña!" Fedé claps his hands together as I enter his store. "You've been a stranger," he tells me.

"I'm sorry, Fedé. I've been busy."

He nods in understanding. "Working hard for your money. Strong, independent woman." He raises a fist in the air.

I chuckle. "I try, at least."

"What can I help you with today, mi amor? I don't have any tamales."

"It's okay. My mom visited today and made dinner. I'm actually here to get ice cream for the dessert."

"Oh, wonderful. Well, you know where that is. Straight back." He points toward the freezer section of the store.

"Thank you," I tell him before heading back.

I cut through the canned food aisle and stop in my tracks when I see Jude. He's wearing an apron and lifting cans out of boxes to stock the shelves.

"Hi," I blurt out.

His back stiffens, and he turns to face me. He's as hot in his street clothes and gray apron as he is in his cop uniform. "Hey," he says with a small smile.

"Do you work here?"

"Not really. I'm not on the payroll or anything, but I

come in when I can to help my grandpa stock the shelves. He's too stubborn to hire help and thinks he can do it all himself, but he's getting old. These boxes are heavy. He shouldn't be doing it on his own."

"Well, that's nice of you."

Jude narrows his stare. "That sounded like a compliment. Weird coming from you. I'm used to random insults."

I sigh. "I'm sorry I called you a cheater, but you can see why I assumed?"

He shakes his head. "Not really, no."

"I found your note, the one you left on the back of your picture. It had fallen between my bed and nightstand."

Jude just nods and goes back to stacking cans of tomato sauce on the shelf.

"I'm sorry." My voice quivers. Jude turns his attention back toward me. "I'm not good with people."

"You're not good with people?" he repeats my words back slowly, quirking up an eyebrow.

"No." I chuckle. "Not really. I'm kind of an introvert. I spend my days wearing jammies in front of a computer screen writing about people who do not exist. I don't get out much, and when I do, it's with the same three people. I haven't slept with anyone in a long time. I haven't dated anyone in a longer time, and the last blind date Cassie set me up on was with a married dude. I don't have a great track record with guys. I thought I felt something special with you, and when I woke up and you were gone—I let my mind think the worst of you. Sometimes, it's easier to be mad than be hurt. I didn't have a right to be hurt because you didn't promise me anything. So then I was mad that I let myself hope for more when I shouldn't have."

I stop talking when Jude begins to laugh.

"What?" I say.

"Do you always ramble this much when you're nervous? It's kind of cute."

"I'm not rambling. I'm explaining."

Jude bites the corner of his lip and grins. "You're rambling."

I let out a long exhale. "Do you accept my apology for calling you a cheating whore?"

He quirks an eyebrow. "You called me a cheater, not a whore."

I shrug. "Well, in my mind, I called you both. Anyway…I'm sorry. Are we good?"

"Sure, Tannon." Jude grins and drops his gaze to my lips.

The familiar pressure in my chest starts to build, but I swallow down the lump in my throat. "I need ice cream," I croak. "Do you want to come over for some apple cobbler and ice cream? We picked the apples today."

"I have a problem," Jude groans. He reaches out and takes my hand in his, rubbing his thumb over my skin.

"What?" The question is barely audible. My throat is so dry.

He licks his lips and looks around us. We're the only two in the aisle, but he leans in closer to me. "When I'm near you, I just want to touch you and kiss you. It's irrational, this need that I have for you, but it's there, and it's strong."

"Yeah?" My voice is breathless.

"I don't think it's healthy, though. I'm not sure we're compatible."

I have no idea what he's talking about. Maybe he's still pissy about the way I acted. Perhaps we'd be a disaster if we dated. At this point, I'd let him fuck me right here in the middle of the canned vegetables just to feel him again. When I'm around him, I lose my mind with lust. It's unlike anything I've ever felt.

"Okay." I step forward until my chest is against his. His rises and falls in time with mine. I close my eyes and take in his smell. It's not cologne, but maybe a body wash that's clean and spicy. His breaths are loud as they leave his mouth. I wet my lips and inhale him—his sounds, smells, and the heat between us. Fully clothed, it's there —an intense warmth that leaves me desperate.

"What do you want, Tannon?" His words are needy.

"You," I breathe out.

He moves in even closer and presses his forehead against mine. His pelvis pushes into my hip, and I can feel how much he wants me too. "Do you know what you do to me?" he whispers against my temple.

"Let's go to your place," I plead and push my hips into his leg. I'm so desperate for release that it aches. If we weren't standing in his grandfather's store, I'd beg him to take me against the wall in the storage room.

Jude's hands grasp my arms and push me back a step, breaking our contact. I open my lust-filled eyes and stare into his.

"Tannon." His voice is deep. "Your body was made for mine."

"I know." God, do I know.

"But I'm not the type of guy who just wants the physical part. If we do this, I want it all. We know we make magic together in bed, but there has to be more than that."

"Okay," I say on a sigh. "We'll cuddle, play board games, talk about our hopes and fears. We'll do it all. Just do me first," I beg without shame. Jude is my drug, and I'm so eager for him it's dangerous.

"Let's do all of those things you mentioned first," he says, and it's like he dropped a bucket of cold water over my libido.

"What?"

"Let's date and see if we even like each other with our clothes on."

"I like you with your clothes on," I quip, "and off." I shrug. "Let's like each other both ways."

"Listen." His greens capture my blues. "I think I really like you, but I want to do this right. I've been in a toxic relationship before, and I don't want to go down that road again. So let's get to know each other, go on some dates, and see if there's more than just the physical there."

"There is," I reassure him. "Trust me." *And fuck me.*

"We'll see." He grins. "So does your invitation still stand?"

"Invitation?"

"You invited me over for some apple thing?"

"Oh, yeah," I say, pulling in a cleansing breath and taking another step back from Jude. I can't think straight when I'm so close to him. "Asher, Everett, Cassie, and I are going to watch *Survivor* and eat some apple cobbler that my mom made from the apples we picked this afternoon. I don't know if it will be weird for you with everyone there, but you're welcome to join us."

"I'm assuming you all watch *Survivor* with your clothes on?" He shoots me a smirk.

"Most days." I grin and roll my eyes.

"Then I think I'm safe," he says.

"You act like sleeping with me will hurt you," I kid.

The smile drops from Jude's face. "You, Tannon, absolutely have the power to hurt me."

"I'm not going to hurt you," I tell him.

He shakes his head. "You don't know that, so you can't promise that you won't."

"Well, you could hurt me."

He nods. "I could. That's why we need to decide if we like each other enough with our clothes on to take that risk."

"I already know my answer."

He presses his lips into a line. The corner tilts up into a grin. "I'm pretty sure I do, too."

"How much more stocking until you're done?" I ask.

"This is my last box."

"Okay. I'll help you, and then we'll grab the ice cream and head back to my place for some dessert and reality TV."

"Sounds like a plan." He looks at me warmly. His face is so beautiful.

For the first time in a long time, I feel good—beyond good. Sometimes, things have a way of working out the way they're supposed to. I hope whatever is starting here with Jude is one of those things.

CHAPTER 20

TANNON

As we walk back to the apartment, the air surrounding us is heavy—with nerves or lust or perhaps both. I find it amusing that telling Jude that I want to have sex with him slides off my tongue as effortlessly as breathing but having a normal conversation is a challenge.

I suppose it makes sense. Sex is all about chemistry. When two bodies fit together effortlessly, it's easy. The need takes over. Chasing one's orgasm is instinct. Yet talking to someone and getting to know him for who he truly is carries stress. More so, it brings out all of my insecurities because what if he decides he doesn't like me.

We close in on the alleyway that leads to my apartment's entry door, the metal tables and chairs outside of the Starbucks now in view.

"So remind me again what I'm walking into." Jude's

voice is light and husky all at once, and despite the innocence in his comment, pebbles form across my skin.

"Well, as I mentioned. It's me, Cassie, and the guys, and we have a date with reality TV from over a decade ago. We're bingeing *Survivor*. I think we're on season seven. The contestants are in the Pearl Islands. This is going to be weird, isn't it?" My words come out in rapid succession.

I need to chill.

Jude chuckles beside me and opens the door to the stairwell, holding it for me to pass. "It will be fine, Tannon."

"Yeah, of course," I say quickly under my breath. *Just fine.*

Asher cheers on a football player on the television as we enter. The room buzzes with classic sounds of the game—the voices of the crowd yelling for their team and the deep timbre of the announcer's calls. The combination of sounds usually lulls me to sleep. Growing up, I could always count on getting a good nap in on the weekend during football season. Watching football was a family event, but no matter how much I wanted to be interested in the sport, I simply wasn't.

I'm not sleepy tonight, though. I'm full of excitement and nerves, and every emotion between rushes through me as Jude Martinez stands at my side. It doesn't take long for my friends to realize that I'm not alone. Cassie jumps up from the couch, and Everett mutes the TV. Four sets of eyes stare toward us. Our friend Quinn sits on the sofa. I had forgotten that Cassie invited her over for *Survivor* night.

"Hey, um...Jude's going to hang out with us tonight." I work to keep my demeanor cool, and I think I succeed. Sort of.

"Sweet. How's it going, man?" Asher addresses Jude.

"Real good," he answers.

Cassie eyes me, attempting to conceal her grin.

"So, I have ice cream." I hold up the bag in my hand.

"Yes," Everett says with a moan and grabs the bag from my grasp before rushing into the kitchen.

"Hey, I know you," Quinn says to Jude. "Alma's my best friend. I've taken several of your self-defense courses."

"Yeah." Jude nods. "I remember. It's been a while since you've been to one. Quinn, right?"

"That's me." Quinn grins. "Well, you and the other officer were such great instructors that I have it all down. All the techniques."

"Well, you should come back for a refresher soon. It's good to practice the moves once in a while so they're fresh in your mind."

"Maybe I will." She stands from the sofa and looks at me. "The guys tell us that your mom makes the best cobbler. My mom does, too. It's one of my favorites."

We all dish up a big bowl of apple cobbler and ice cream and take a seat on the sofa sectional. Jude sits next to me on the end, nudging his knee against mine. Asher finds *Survivor* on the TV's playlist and starts the episode. It's a typical Sunday night for us—food, friends, and TV, yet I'm sitting next to Jude, which, for me, means nothing's typical about it.

"I miss Rupert," Quinn says on a sigh as she stares toward the show.

"Don't even get started, or Everett's gonna start bawling again," Asher teases.

"Hey! It's okay to have feelings, dude. Like...come on." Everett shoots Asher a mock glare.

"We all miss Rupert. He's one of the best people to ever be on this show," Cassie says. "You know he's the only contestant to ever win the million who didn't win the game. It was like a fan-favorite vote that CBS did only once. He spent most of the money to start a teen shelter and help struggling kids. He's like a saint."

"Spoilers, Cass. Not everyone here has seen this season," Everett grumbles.

She raises her spoon and waves it like a flag of surrender. "Sorry," she says before taking another bite of cobbler.

I would normally be all in this conversation, but I can't think straight. I've eaten half a bowl of my mother's dessert before realizing that I haven't tasted any of it. I've been too focused on the man next to me. I'm aware of everything—his breaths, the scrape of his spoon against the bowl, his knee lightly brushing my own as he readjusts on the sofa. Every flipping thing.

God, I have issues.

If I'm going to consume all of these calories, I'm at

least going to enjoy it. There's no point in finishing. Standing, I carry my half-eaten bowl of cobbler into the kitchen and set it beside the sink. Jude walks up behind me and places his empty dish beside mine.

"You okay?" he asks.

I swallow with a nod of my head and turn to face him. "Yeah. No. I don't know," I mutter.

I'm not sure why I'm finding this so difficult, but to be honest, I'm on a path that I've never been on before. I feel like a thirteen-year-old with my first crush when hormones are raging, and my lack of experience creates an almost debilitating doubt as it fights against the intense need to be with the object of my affection every second of every day.

I remember those crushes, and it was rough. Though back in my preteen days, I was an awkward bookworm who fell for my best friend, who just saw me as his nerdy sidekick. I spent hours on the phone with him, internally begging him to see me when all he could talk about was Katie McMillian and her hot body. It didn't matter to him that she was as shallow as they come and could barely string a sentence together. It only mattered that, at thirteen, her breasts had completely developed, whereas mine hadn't even started. Now, I realize that my childhood best friend and I were completely incompatible in the romance department. Yet it was soul-crushing back then.

All of those insecurities circle me now. It's ridiculous. I'm not thirteen, and clearly, neither is Jude. He's here because he wanted to be, and still, I can't chill the hell out.

"Talk to me," Jude encourages as he takes one of my hands in his, swiping his thumb across my skin.

The music from the show can be heard in the living room, indicating that the players are making their way to the tribal council. "We should go back. They're going to vote someone off."

Did those words seriously just come from my mouth? Jude Martinez has my hand in his, and I want to go and watch the fate of a stranger that I actually already watched happen like a decade ago.

The side of Jude's lip raises in a smile, and he lets out a small chuckle. "I couldn't care less who gets voted off, Tannon."

Me either.

"Right." I shake my head, painfully aware that Jude's thumb is still caressing my skin. "It's stupid, really." I finally force words out. "I feel awkward, and I don't know why. It's like I've never done this before or something. For some reason, it's different with you. You make me nervous and doubt myself. I can't think straight around you. I want to touch you all of the time, yet I get that we know next to nothing about each other. You're right. We need to be more than just sex, but..."

I let out a soft groan and chew on my bottom lip in frustration. I would literally kick my own ass if I could. I'm acting like an idiot, and I can't make the insanity stop. Word vomit rich in pathetic unattractiveness has fallen from my lips, and I know that at any second, Jude's going to run. He should run.

If the roles were reversed, I'd run.

He doesn't, though. Instead, he inches closer. Leaning in, he finds my neck with his mouth, and he kisses me there softly. Just once, a small peck before he whispers into my ear. "Let's go back to my place."

Goose bumps erupt all over my body. "But I thought you said...?" I question on a weak exhale.

"Fuck what I said."

I feel his words throughout my entire body, and it's everything I can do not to moan out cries of lust right here in my kitchen.

Instead, I simply nod.

"That's a yes?" asks Jude.

"Yes," I say firmly. "Let's go."

Our exit was awkward as Jude and I mumbled incoherencies intended to be reasons for our departure as we stumbled out of my apartment, drunk on lust and anticipation. It doesn't take a genius to figure out where we're going and why, but it doesn't matter. Asher and Everett can say what they will tomorrow when I'm back and fully sated from my evening with Jude.

We Uber to Jude's house, which is only a five-minute ride from my apartment. He still lives within city limits but not near campus. Ann Arbor is a fairly big city compared to most. It's not Chicago or Atlanta, but it's a good size. The University of Michigan's campus and the surrounding area where the college students live is actually just a portion of the city. Beyond where I live is a normal town with neighborhoods, strip malls, and a Costco.

Jude lives in this part, the non-college part. I suppose most people who aren't current students do except for me, Cassie, and my friends. Though we graduated from the university four years ago, we rarely venture out of our little area of the city.

Maybe that's odd? I don't know, and as Jude unlocks his front door, I don't care to think any more on the subject. We step inside, and the second his entry door closes, he shoves me up against it, his lips finding mine as his hands run under my shirt and across my skin.

I groan into his mouth as I thread my fingers through the short hair at the nape of his neck and pull his face closer to mine. My tongue eagerly explores his mouth, wrapping around his. The kiss is everything. It's deep and needy, and warm and passionate. It's a dance perfectly choreographed for the two of us. The kiss leaves me wet and desperate for so much more.

He pulls his lips from mine. "I want to know you, Tannon, and I want you to know me." Jude's words are husky and drenched in lust. My bra now hangs loosely from my shoulders. I didn't notice him unsnap it during the kiss. Each of his hands cups one of my breasts, his fingers tugging on my nipples, and I moan.

I nod in response to his statement. Words fail me as my legs shake with desire. I want to know Jude, too, and not just what he feels like inside me. I want to know everything about him. Yet, right now, I'm so hyped up with need that everything hurts. Everything feels amazing. Everything needs Jude.

Releasing a hand from my breast, he brands my skin with his touch as he drags his hand down my abdomen until he's unbuckling my jeans. He leans in farther as he slides two fingers inside me. I cry out as his slick fingers alternate between entering me and rubbing the bundle of nerves that need his touch the most.

Bending down, he kisses up my neck and nibbles on the lobe of my ear. "Does that feel good?" he whispers against my skin.

"Yes," I pant. "So good."

"I'm going to make you come, Tannon, and each time I do, I need you to give me something—a piece of you. Can you do that?" He licks the skin of my neck while his fingers move faster against me.

He stops moving his fingers, and I protest.

"I'm going to need an answer," says Jude.

"Yes," I cry. I'm not sure exactly what I'm agreeing to, but Jude can have it. He just can't stop.

His fingers start moving against me again, and they don't stop until I'm screaming my release. I cling to Jude's arms as my body shakes. The pressure of Jude against me keeps me standing, though my legs are weak.

My face falls against his chest with a sigh.

CHAPTER 21

TANNON

Jude traces light kisses up my neck as I come down from my orgasm. I can honestly say that no one has ever made me come with their fingers alone. I've always needed a guy to go down on me and actually know what he's doing with his tongue, or to use BOB while having sex to find my release. Either Jude is a god in the bedroom or I've only slept with imbeciles. I'm probably biased, my brain still cloudy with the hormone-induced haze, but I think it's the former.

The praised one.
That he is.

My back presses against the wall of the hallway, and Jude's lips have worked their way up to my ear. He nibbles lightly on my earlobe before whispering, "I need a piece of you, now."

Pebbles erupt on my skin. The sound of his voice

and his warm breath caressing my skin cause a rush of need to resurface. My body still hums from my release, yet I already need him to touch me again.

This can't be real. This feeling. This desire. This pleasure that Jude brings me. This can't be a casual fling. This can't end because I know I'll never find it again, and I need it. God, how I need it.

I pull in a breath, burying my desperation because it was an orgasm, not a marriage proposal. I have to get myself together. These aren't magical words typed on a page. This is real life. Insta-love doesn't exist outside of romance novels.

Though, clearly, insta-orgasms do, and I'm hungry for another.

"Tannon," Jude whispers again, his soft lips nibbling up my ear. "What do you want?"

"You. Touching me." My declaration is broken and breathy.

"I want that, too, but I need something from you first. Tell me anything. Who is Tannon Lee?"

I expel a sigh. "I'm a daughter, a friend, a teacher, and a writer. I love pumpkin spiced lattes, the colors of fall but the warmth of summer. I love animals, and I'm twenty-six. Is that good?" I plead.

"For now." Jude chuckles dryly. Wrapping his arms around my waist, he lifts me from the ground and carries me into his living room.

Setting me down before his couch, I watch as he pulls off my shoes and slides off my jeans. His stare burns my skin as he removes every piece of fabric that covers me. My chest rises and falls with breaths that never provide enough air. My head spins in a drunken state, needing to feel Jude's hands on me once more.

"Sit," he commands, and I comply. My heated skin presses against the cool leather of the sofa.

Jude's deep green eyes pull me in as he stares at me with a forceful emotion that I can't name. His gaze speaks to lust, need, and desperation, but there's a calmness, too. Acceptance, joy, and something that resembles love. I know it's not, but it feels like it is. My hormones are seeing what they want to see, but I don't care because Jude's stare is everything right now.

His gaze lowers from mine, and I want to cry out, the void of his stare on me almost painful until each of his palms firmly grasp each of my knees and push me open wide. I gasp, my body already trembling as his mouth descends until he's tasting me. My head falls back onto the sofa, my eyes squeeze closed as my brain fills with colors and satisfaction. I scream out into the lust-filled air as Jude's tongue worships me. It's almost too much. The urge to shove his head away from me is overpowered by the knowledge that falling over the cliff that Jude's pushing me toward is going to be indescribable.

And then I fall. My scream cuts through the space as my body vibrates with a forceful release. The warmth radiates from the tips of my toes to my scalp. Jude's tongue doesn't halt until I'm a sated pile of whimpers, my skin slick with sweat.

"I've dreamed about that," Jude declares. "It's so much better in real life." He peppers kisses up my body until his muscled arms hold him over me.

"I need you inside me," I pant out, still coming down from the euphoria of moments ago.

"I need more information." His lip tilts up into a small grin, and it's sexy as hell.

It takes me a few seconds to figure out what he's talking about.

"What do you want to know?" I ask, my brain needing direction as it feels like mush.

"Everything."

"I love the smell of cinnamon. One of my biggest turn-ons is a man who can cook even though I suck at cooking myself. My favorite food is Mexican, and I could eat it every day for the rest of my life. I do want to move off-campus eventually, but I don't see the point right now since I think I'd be lonely without my friends. Everyone thinks opossums are gross, but I love them and feel they are greatly misunderstood. They eat their weight in ticks and are a really cool animal. Is that good enough?" The last sentence comes out as a plea.

"Yeah, that's good." Jude picks me up and carries me into his bedroom.

We make love three times in Jude's bed. Each time is the best I've ever experienced until the next time. Perhaps it's not making love and it's just sex, but to me, it feels different. It feels like more. Every time with Jude is an awakening. I can't believe a connection such as this exists, and I'm terrified to lose it.

Between lovemaking, I tell him about my life, my childhood, and my family, and he does the same. We reveal ourselves to one another between kisses and intense orgasms. I feel more like myself than I've ever felt before with Jude's skin pressed against mine.

I'm utterly exhausted as we have sex again. There's an orgasm waiting eagerly beneath my skin, but I don't know if I have the strength to allow it to crescendo. Jude's tan muscles glisten with sweat as he pounds into me.

"I need you to come with me, babe," he grunts out, his voice low.

"I can't," I pant. "I can't do it again."

"Yes, you can," Jude says firmly.

His hips pick up speed, and he pushes so deeply inside me that I think I'll break. The rhythm is punishing. Reaching up, he grabs my nipples between his fingers and starts twisting and pulling as he pounds in and out of me.

"Oh my God," I cry out.

I can't.

I can't.

I can't.

"Fall with me, Tannon," Jude pleads, his voice a needy growl, and I know he's close.

My body has been wrecked in so many delicious ways tonight. I don't have the energy to come again, but I greedily want to. I need the high that only Jude can give me.

"Tannon," Jude begs. I can feel his body trembling.

"I..." I whimper.

"Let go," he urges.

"I'm..." Words escape me as the heat within me builds.

"Fuck, Tannon." Jude's lust-filled words echo as he pumps harder. "Fuck..." he draws out before removing a hand from my breast and dropping it between my legs. He pinches my clit, and as he comes hard, I fall.

Jude lies beside me as we both breathe heavy, coming down from our orgasms. The air is pregnant with the smells of sex and the sounds of two completely sated people. My limbs are heavy, and my entire body resembles mush. I can't move.

I'm overcome with emotion, whether it be from orgasms or exhaustion. I'm grateful for tonight and terrified for tomorrow. I want nights like this forever, and I know that only Jude can provide them. How far would I go to keep this? To keep Jude? The thought makes me feel ill.

Jude kisses the top of my head and lazily whispers. "You know the drill. Tell me something. I want to know everything."

Words exit my lips on their own accord, and I'm too tired to stop them. "I've never felt this in my life. I don't know if other people experience this with multiple people, but I never have. It's scary because it's so amazing. It's scary because I want it so badly. It's scary because I've been hurt before by a man, in the worst possible way, and I haven't been capable of intimacy since. I'm terrified of what this strong of a connection will do to me if I lose it. I'm terrified of losing you, and I'm not entirely sure I even have you to begin with. I write about soul mates and everlasting love because I don't think any of it's real, and if it is, I'll never have it. I've had the worst happen to me, but I think losing you would be more painful. I've never told anyone about what happened. Not a soul. Yet I'm telling you. Now you have everything."

My words cease as sleep pulls me under. The weight of Jude's arms around me lulls me further toward slumber, and I go toward the darkness willingly.

Somewhere in the dark recess of my mind, I hear, "You have me," and it's a beautiful dream.

CHAPTER 22

TANNON

I STRETCH my arms out above my head. My muscles pull, and my joints crack. I feel like I ran a marathon yesterday. Turning to my side, I find the other side of the bed empty, and a warning starts to go off until I realize I'm in Jude's bed. He can't run out on me when I'm in his house.

I sit up, and the aroma of something delicious piques my interest, causing my stomach to growl on instinct. Scanning the room, I find no sign of my clothes, and an incredible memory of Jude removing them out by the couch last night surfaces. I hop off the bed and open the drawers of Jude's dresser until I find a T-shirt and shorts. I pull the string of the shorts tight so they'll stay on. I dip my chin and pull the plain white T-shirt to my nose. I know it's laundered, but it still smells like Jude. I need to ask him what laundry soap he uses because I never want to use anything else again.

I use the bathroom connected to his bedroom and wipe some toothpaste over my teeth before rinsing with mouthwash. I wash my face before grabbing the hair tie that is always on my wrist and pull my hair up into a messy bun. The reflection that stares back at me seems happy and content, and—besides the small bags under my eyes—fresh-faced. Sex doesn't look too bad on me. I approve.

Fear tries to creep in right before I open the bedroom door, but I push it down. The sole fact that Jude's not going to leave me alone in his house is my saving grace for the confidence I cling to. Bright light shines in my eyes as I step out of the bedroom.

"Hey there, beautiful," Jude says from the kitchen. "Did you sleep well?"

"Better than well, I think," I say as I make my way toward the kitchen. "What time is it?"

"One in the afternoon."

"No way." I giggle. "Man, I look like quite the lazy bum."

"Your body needed the sleep," Jude responds, and though the sentiment is innocent enough, my breath hitches thinking of last night.

He stands in the kitchen in just a pair of sports shorts, similar to what I'm wearing. Yet they are mouth-watering on him and nothing like the baggy, unflattering things on me. His defined arm and back muscles look incredible in the afternoon light.

I shake my head. "What smells so good?"

"I'm making you an authentic Mexican breakfast like my abuelita would make." He grins.

Bringing my hands to my mouth, I gasp. "Seriously? You can cook Mexican food?"

Jude chuckles. "Of course I can. Take a seat. It's ready." He nods toward the dining room table.

He sets a plate in front of me.

"Huevos rancheros for you," he says. "I made the tortillas, salsa, and frijoles from scratch."

My eyes go wide as I look at the beautiful dish before me. Atop the corn tortilla is refried beans, then an over-easy egg topped with salsa and slices of avocado.

"Will you marry me?" I kid before regretting the words that just came out of my mouth. *Why am I so awkward?* "I mean, you seriously made the tortillas? How is that even possible?"

"It's really not that hard." He grins.

"Speak for yourself. I couldn't do this in a million years."

"Well, you've tasted my grandma's cooking. She taught my mother and my sisters how to prepare authentic Mexican food. Then she made sure that I knew how as well. She always joked that if I fell hard for a gringa like my father did, I had to make sure my family was fed properly. The story goes that when my dad and mom got together, my mom couldn't make toast without burning it."

"Sounds like me," I add.

"To be honest, my mom still isn't the best cook, but my father and sisters can make almost anything as well as my grandmother can, save for her tamales."

I chuckle. "Well, yeah...because her tamales are straight-up magical."

"Exactly," Jude agrees. "So, I have some fresh-squeezed orange juice or aqua de Jamaica."

He holds up a pitcher of a purple liquid.

"What's that?"

"In Spanish, it's translated to Jamaica water. We drink it all the time. My grandparents swear it has amazing health benefits and aids in digestion. I guess you could call it a cold tea. It's made by steeping hibiscus flowers until a concentrate is made. Then cold water and sugar are added. Never tell my abuela but I use stevia instead of sugar. That little tidbit would send her to an early grave."

"All right. Well, I trust you. I'll do the purple stuff."

Jude fills my cup with the purple beverage before sitting across from me with his own plate of huevos rancheros, which translated, he says means rancher's eggs. I take a big bite of my breakfast and groan.

"Good?" Jude chuckles.

"So good."

I consume my breakfast—or technically lunch since it's past noon—at record speed with zero shame. I have little willpower when it comes to good food. The Jamaica juice is heavenly, and I'm going to have to figure out how to make it because I'll definitely need more of it in the future.

"You want some coffee?" Jude asks as he clears our plates.

"Yes, please."

He pours us each a mug of coffee and sets milk and sugar out for me before taking a sip of his.

"So you drink your coffee black?" I inquire with a grin.

"Yeah..." He chuckles. "Is that okay?"

"Definitely."

Coffee scale restored.

I make a mental note to tell Cassie. We've been questioning the scale since Malcolm.

We take our mugs of coffee and go out to sit in Jude's three-season room off the kitchen. It faces a peaceful and secluded backyard. Though I know houses are all around, the trees of various heights that border his backyard make it seem so private.

"If I didn't see your neighborhood last night, I would think you lived out in the country. It's so peaceful back here," I tell him.

"Yeah, that was the biggest draw of this house when I bought it. Someday, I hope to live outside of town in the country. I like the privacy, but it's definitely more convenient to live in town with my job. At least here, I can feel like I'm secluded from the world a little."

"I think this is my favorite part of the house," I say. "I would be out here writing all the time if I lived here." Once again, the words coming from my mouth seem so forward, and I internally cringe.

"You're welcome to write here anytime you want. I'm gone a lot with work, so you'd have the run of the house." Jude takes a sip of his coffee.

He must see something in my expression because he places his coffee mug down on the small table before us and takes a seat on the outdoor sofa beside me. He wraps an arm around my shoulders and kisses the side of my head.

"Tannon, don't do that."

I turn on the sofa to face him. "What do you mean?"

"Don't do that thing that you do when you overanalyze everything and start second-guessing things. I meant what I said last night. I'm in. I'm yours. You're welcome here anytime." He places his large hand against my knee, and it causes a shiver.

"When did you say...?"

My question gets lost, but Jude answers anyway. "Right before you fell asleep. I told you that I'm yours."

"But we hardly know each other."

"I know you. The parts that matter, I know, and the rest I'll learn. Sometimes, things just make sense even when they don't." His hand rubs against the skin of my knee.

"What does that even mean?" I shake my head in amusement.

"It means that I want to be with you. I don't know you well, and I haven't known you long, but I can't ignore the chemistry between us. I know you feel it, too."

"Yeah, but..." I start to protest. Why, I'm not sure.

"But nothing. Let's do this. Let's date or whatever title you want to put on it. All I know is that I want to be with you and only you. I want to get to know you. I'm twenty-eight years old. I don't want to play games anymore. I'm not waiting three days to call you back or anything else. I want you now. Can you handle that?" He holds my gaze in his, and it leaves me speechless. "Tannon?"

I swallow. "Yeah, okay. I want that, too."

"Good." He leans in and places his lips on mine. The chaste kiss is over before I registered that it was happening, yet I loved it so much. It was different than our other kisses. It wasn't fueled by insane desire and lust, and it wasn't frantic or desperate. It was the kind of kiss that a man gives to his wife after fifty years of marriage. It was an everyday, real-life, forever love kind of kiss.

CHAPTER 23

TANNON

I let go. With a half sob, I scream into the air that's charged with the scent and flavor of sex, like an electrical storm of raw pleasure. I feel the warmth flush through my body, and I lose my mind to the pleasure it brings.

My fingers move across the keyboard at a record pace. The words are just flowing from me, and it feels great. Yesterday, after Jude dropped me off, he went in to work, and I had a ten-thousand-word day. I can't remember the last time that happened. I suppose it helps that my female lead is at the point in the book where she is starting to fall for the male lead. After the two nights I had with Jude, I can write about intense feelings and good sex.

It's hard to believe it's only Wednesday. Three days ago, my mom made apple cobbler, which led to the ice cream run and Jude. I've been on cloud nine since Jude's little talk with me on his back porch area on Monday when he declared he doesn't want to play games. We spent Monday talking, laughing, and eating. Jude is an amazing cook, and I'd date him for that reason alone. We showered together and worked in a handful of orgasms throughout the day, which was, of course, amazing, but the other stuff was even better. If not better, then of equal importance.

He dropped me off early yesterday, and I haven't been able to wipe the smile off my face since. He's texted me several times over the past two days. After work last night, he had to go home and sleep. He said he had to fight nodding off during his shift. I suppose two days of sex, little sleep, and intense orgasms can do that to a person.

We haven't even been together for a week. I should be cautious and not get my hopes up. Yet I've lived that way my whole life, and it has lent itself to nothing but heartache. I'm going to be different this time for Jude—but most importantly for me. If it crashes and burns, then fine, I'll find a way to get through the wreckage, but until then, I'm going to really try, and maybe, just maybe, I'll get lucky this time.

"Knock, knock," Cassie says sheepish at my door. "Can I come in?"

"Of course," I answer.

"How's it going? Are you still on a roll?" she asks.

"Yes, it feels so good, too. Finally, the words are flowing."

Cassie lets out a loud sigh. "Well, I know I'm selfish and a horrible friend and an even worse publicist for even asking, but would you be willing to take a break and come shopping with me?"

I let out a laugh. "Go shopping with you?"

"Yeah." She shrugs. "Henry wants me to meet his parents. I'm having dinner with them tomorrow after my shift. I've tried on everything in my closet, and nothing is working. I'm really nervous. I need a kick-ass outfit, and I need my bestie's opinions when I try things on."

"You're meeting Henry's parents?" I ask.

Cassie nods.

"Why? I mean, no offense, but I didn't think it was that serious. Is it more serious now?"

She walks over to my bed and falls back against it with a sigh. Lucifer, who was happily napping on my pillow, scowls in Cassie's direction.

"I don't know," she says.

"Well, I think he wants it to be more. The whole, 'let's have dinner with my parents' is a good indication of that. But the question is...do you? Want more?" I close my laptop and walk over to my bed, taking a seat next to Cassie.

"I'm confused. I mean, we've been hooking up for a year now. Neither one of us has been sleeping with other people during that time, but we've never put a label on our relationship. We work together and sleep together. That's about it. But maybe this is what a real relationship is like?" Her voice raises an octave. "Have I been in a real relationship with Henry without even realizing it?"

I shake my head. "I don't think so. Do you talk about stuff? Like your desires? Hopes for the future? Families? Your pasts?"

"No, every time we're together, we're at work or in bed. I thought we were just co-workers with benefits. Then he asked me to meet his parents, and now I'm confused. Do I want a relationship with him? I don't know, but I feel like if I tell him that I'm not ready to meet his parents, then he'll get all butt hurt, and it will end any chance of a relationship between us in the future if, in fact, I decide I want one." She sighs.

"Man, that's heavy." I giggle.

"I know!" She groans and places her forearm over her eyes. "I guess I should've known better. I mean, who has a sexual partner for a year and doesn't want more?"

"You know what I think?"

"What?" she grumbles.

"I think you've been using Henry as an excuse not to move on with your life. You're not using your degree. You're not publishing your book. You're not seeking out a person who could be a life partner. You're serving coffee and sleeping with your boss so you can stall and look productive while not actually doing anything productive at all." I bite my lip, preparing for an argument. I love Cassie more than most people in this world. I want her to be happy, and for some reason, like me, she's scared to take the leap.

She sits up and faces me. "Like you're one to talk," she scoffs.

I shrug in agreement. "I know. I'll admit that I have issues. I'm working on it, though, and I recognize it. Do you? I mean, the only thing you're passionate about is my career, but what about yours?"

"That's not fair," she says quietly.

"Agreed, but it's the truth."

"What should I do, Tan?" Cassie pleads.

"Do what makes you happy."

Her eyes go wide. "I don't know what makes me happy."

"Well, let's start with Henry. Do you see him in your future? Do you want to be in his?"

Lucifer struts between the two of us and rubs his rear end along Cassie's leg, indicating he wants her to scratch his butt. She complies, and he purrs. Though the move seems selfish on his part, I think it's his way of showing affection.

"I'm honestly not sure." She drops her hand from Lucifer's velvety black fur, and he meows accusingly. "Fine, you annoying beast," she responds to Lucifer and proceeds to scratch his butt once more.

"Well, you don't have to decide today. Let's go shopping and get you an outfit just in case. Even if you end up meeting Henry's parents, it doesn't mean you're bound to him for life. If you're not sure, just go. Play nice with the parents and try to figure your feelings out. Okay?"

Cassie nods. "Yeah, that sounds good. Plus, we need a girls' day anyway. You've barely spoken to me since you got back from Jude's. I get that inspiration struck, and you had to write, but it's been very hard for me to wait for all the details," she quips.

"I bet." I chuckle. "I do have some juicy details."

She nods, her eyes wide and accusatory "Yeah, I figured."

I jump up from my bed. "All right, I'm going to shower. Then we'll shop."

"Sounds good!" Cassie says with a clap of her hands.

"So, what are we thinking here?" I ask as I finger through the garments hanging on the rack. "A dress? Pants and a sweater?"

"I'm thinking a cute new pair of jeans that make my butt look awesome and a form-fitting sweater so I will look hot but classy at the same time. I don't want to look like I'm trying too hard. Natural beauty is what we're going for," Cassie answers from the other side of the rack.

"Gotcha. Hot ass. Tight sweater. Cleavage or no cleavage?"

Cassie stops her perusal of the clothes and looks over at me. "What do you think?"

"If your ass is smokin', I'm thinking no cleavage. You have to even things out a little bit." I grin.

"You're right. No cleavage. Plus, with the right bra, I think boobs look amazing in a sweater even without the girls making an appearance," Cassie offers.

"Agreed." She moves on to another rack. "So...best sex of your life?"

"Definitely. Better than the best. Better than I knew existed." I hold up a plum sweater. "What about this one?"

Cassie shakes her head. "Too happy. Okay, so amazing sex. Amazing food. Great conversation. And more amazing sex? Anything I'm missing?"

"Nope. That pretty much sums it up." I grab a cream sweater. "What about cream with your cute brown leather boots?"

Cassie bites her lip. Her head bobs back and forth as she takes in the sweater in my grasp. "Yeah." She nods. "I think that's the one. Let's find the right jeans, and I'll go try it on."

We walk over to the missus section where the brand-name jeans reside.

"And you're like dating? Boyfriend and girlfriend dating?" she ponders.

I shrug. "Yeah, I know. It's crazy. Right?"

Her face lights up. "I think it's awesome. You deserve to be happy, Tan. When are you going to see him again?"

"Thanks. Um, tonight for a late dinner. He's going to the gym after work, and then he's going to swing by and pick me up."

"I'm so jealous." Cassie sighs. "I want better than amazing sex."

"Well, you've been with Henry a year. I'm sure it will taper off for Jude and me over time. It's still new. You know?"

She laughs. "No, I don't know. You remember me telling you about my first time with Henry? In the stock room after close with all of our clothes on and our pants pulled to our knees. It lasted less than a minute. I didn't come with him for two months until I started using my fingers during sex. It's hardly magical."

I think of the times I've been intimate with Jude and how truly incredible they were. Our connection is so good it's almost fictional. I write about great sex, but I didn't think it truly existed. My heart breaks for Cassie. What if that's what it's like for most women? What if that will be what it's like for me if Jude and I break up?

"You deserve more than Henry," I blurt out suddenly. "Don't settle for him, Cass. That's not love."

She smiles in my direction, though the joy doesn't reach her eyes. "I know. Let's go try these on."

One very sexy but classy outfit later, we walk out of the store and into the center of the mall.

"Let's get a pretzel," Cassie suggests.

"Sure," I agree.

We each get a soft pretzel with extra salt and a lemonade.

"What do you think about Asher?" Cassie says out of the blue.

I halt my steps and turn to look at her. "What do you mean?"

She bites her lip with a shrug. "What do you think about him?"

I chuckle. "Um. He's nice. Hot. Funny. Our neighbor. Our best friend. What are you getting at, Cass?"

"I kissed him," she blurts out before covering her mouth with her free hand.

"What?" I shriek.

"It was nothing." She shakes her head.

"Tell me."

"Well, it was at their last party when you left because of your exchange with Jude. We were playing euchre. It was me and Everett against Asher and Elizabeth."

"Who's Elizabeth?" I interrupt.

"Some skank from the gym." Cassie rolls her eyes. "Anyway, we were on the porch drinking...a lot. Elizabeth jumped up after a hand and ran out. I think she was going to get sick. Everett left to go get drinks, so I followed. I was feeling really tipsy, and most people had gone. There were only a few stragglers left. So, I said goodbye to Everett and then went out to the porch to tell Asher that I was leaving. He was looking down toward the alley, so I wrapped my arms around his back and gave him a hug and told him I was going home. He turned to face me, and before I knew what was happening, his lips were on mine, and his tongue was in my mouth."

I bring my hand to my open mouth and pull in air.

Cassie and Asher.

Cassie and Asher!

Cassie continues. "I started to pull away, I did. But it felt so good, Tan. Like butterflies in my stomach good. I haven't been turned on by a simple kiss in forever. So I kissed him back. We made out for a while and then he pulled away, and placed his forehead against mine, and said, 'don't go, ELIZABETH.'"

This time my gasp is loud. "No!"

"Yes!" Cassie drops her head back and groans toward the fluorescent lighting.

"What did you do?"

"I backed away from him and darted out of his apartment and into ours. The next day when I saw him, he was completely normal and didn't act weird or mention it. I don't think he remembers. He must've been too drunk or something."

"But you liked it?" I ask.

"Yeah," Cassie answers. "A lot, but that's weird, right? Asher has been one of our best friends for eight years. It would be stupid to mention it. I don't want to risk making him uncomfortable or changing our friendship."

"I'm not sure." I shake my head, confused. I don't know what to tell her.

"See, it's stupid. That's why I didn't tell you or him. It didn't mean anything. He was drunk, and so was I. It was a kiss. That's all."

"Maybe you should mention it in case he's been thinking about it too. If not, it can just be a funny thing that happened between the two of you. You know? Make a joke out of it," I suggest.

"Ugh. Why is my life so messed up? I don't know what to do with my life. I'm meeting the parents of a guy who I'm completely indifferent about. I'm lusting over one of my best friends, and you—who I can always count on to need me—seem to be living the best life ever, at the moment."

"Seriously. Did we suddenly switch places? I mean, who am I? And who are you?" I laugh.

My forced laughter is cut short when I see two uniformed police officers standing several yards away outside Victoria's Secret. I grab Cassie's arm.

"Look," I urge.

She squints. "Is that...?"

"Yeah, it's Jude and *Jane*." Her name tastes sour coming from my mouth.

"His partner?"

I only nod as I watch the pair interact. Jude's thumbs are settled in his belt. His muscular arms bent to the sides. He's peering down at Jane with a sweet smile. He says something, and she laughs. As she does, she reaches out and splays her hand on his uniformed abdomen.

Cassie and I jerk our heads toward each other at the same time, letting me know I'm not the only one who finds that gesture weird. I look back toward Jude. A tall brunette woman in a black pencil skirt and low-cut blouse has joined them outside the store now. Both Jude and Jane turn their attention toward the woman.

"Let's get out of here," I say, all too aware that my current position of having my life more figured out than Cassie is going to be very short-lived.

Cassie nods, and we head out.

CHAPTER 24

TANNON

He's worthy of the white picket fence and two-point-five kids, and he should have it. I know I need to let him go, but right now, I feel safe in his arms. I listen to his heartbeat below his firm muscles, and it soothes my soul, a cathartic rhythm keeping me centered.

The female lead in my book is starting to pull away, her insecurities becoming too loud to ignore. It's a good read, though, angsty and emotional. My readers will approve, I hope.

My bottom lip bulges out, and I blow up at my forehead. The loose baby hairs above my forehead extend up with my breath. "Time to be an adult, Tannon. Address your problems," I say to myself in the mirror.

I walk out of the bathroom and double-check that I've saved my work before I close my laptop. I ended up canceling with Jude last night after the mall. It's immature, I know, but I simply needed to get my head right. I didn't want to go into the date accusing him of anything. He's a mature grown-up, unlike me. I've accused him of being a cheater before, and it didn't go well for me. I know that he and Jane are close. He's told me as much. She touched him in public. It's not like there was anything sneaky about it. I'm allowing my self-doubts to get the better of me.

I had a night to think about it and lots of typing therapy. My character is currently being immature and annoying to her love interest, who is as dreamy as they come. I may have channeled some of my own immaturity into the scenes I've recently written, but it's better to get them out on paper than to take them out on Jude. I'm a work in progress. I've never claimed to be perfect. I'm handling my doubts as productively as I can.

I still can't shake that something very familiar about the way Jane touched Jude's waist. I don't like it one bit, but I also don't think I should say anything about it. Not yet anyway.

Exiting my room, I meet Cassie in the hall. "Gorgeous," I tell her. She sports the outfit she bought yesterday. "Excited to meet the parents?" I raise an eyebrow.

"Don't start," she warns. "I just need to get through tonight, and then I'll figure out what I want with Henry."

I raise my hands in surrender. "I'm not judging. I mean, my guy is probably screwing his partner, so I don't have room to talk."

"Stop it." She hits my arm. "We've been through this already. It was nothing."

"I know." I sigh.

There's a knock on the door. I look at Cassie. "That'll be Jude. Henry just texted. He's a half hour out."

"Okay." I grab my purse off the counter and step over Lucifer, who is greedily eating the wet food I just put down for him.

It's an extra can than normal, but it's a bribe. Sometimes, he gets pissed when I leave him alone for too long or make him wait for his wet food in the morning, and he retaliates. The last time I stayed over at Jude's, Lucifer peed in my dirty clothes hamper.

I reach down to pet Lucifer. "Tomorrow morning when you don't get a can bright and early at six in the morning, you remember this extra can you're eating now. You have a whole bowl of dry food you can eat if you get hungry. Okay?"

The furry heathen doesn't even acknowledge me, so I know I'm going to come home to some evil surprise tomorrow.

"Have fun," I call out to Cassie.

"You too," she answers.

I open the door to find Jude leaning against the doorframe with one arm, and I have to stop myself from sighing.

"Hey." He smirks.

"Hey," I answer.

He bends down and gives me a short, sweet, forever love kind of kiss, and I melt. Then he threads his fingers through mine, and we exit the building.

"Did you get some epic writing in?" he asks when we step out into the cool night air.

"Huh?" I question.

"Last night. You texted and said you were on a roll with your writing and needed to cancel. So it was good stuff?"

"Oh, yeah. I made a lot of progress. I'm sorry about canceling. It's just when I'm in the mood to write, I need to write."

"No need to apologize. I'm proud of you. I think it's amazing that you can write entire novels. I'm not a fan of writing. I can barely type up my notes at the end of my shift," he kids.

"Like you hate typing them up, or you can't string a sentence together?" I smirk. "What am I dealing with here?"

Jude laughs. "I can write. I'm smart. I finished college, Tannon." He grins. "I just don't like to write."

I nod. "Okay, I can live with that."

Jude leads us down the sidewalk on Main Street. The leaves on the trees that line the road have all changed color. The setting sun highlights the rich gold, burnt orange, and deep red hues.

"How was work yesterday?" I ask him. "I saw a police car at the mall. Were you there?"

"Yeah, I was actually. We responded to a shoplifting call at that bra and panty store."

"Victoria's Secret?"

"That's the one. The shoplifter had already run out of the store and the mall before we got there. So besides taking the report, there wasn't much we could do. Other than that, there were some traffic violations and a noise complaint. It was kind of a boring day, to be honest."

"Have you and Jane ever dated or hooked up?" I blurt out.

Jude turns to face me with a weird smile on his face. "No, we haven't. Why, Tannon?"

I shrug. "No reason. I was just curious. So you've never slept with her? It wouldn't matter to me if you had. I mean, it's in the past."

He reaches up and tucks my hair behind my ear. "I've never hooked up with Jane in any way. She and I are strictly friends. You have nothing to worry about, Tannon."

"Oh, I'm not worried. Merely curious."

"You're kind of cute when you're jealous." He chuckles.

"I'm not jealous," I retort.

Jude places his hands on either side of my neck and moves them up until he's cupping my face. Then he pulls my face toward his and captures my mouth. This time, the kiss isn't chaste. His tongue claims my mouth, and I groan in acceptance. Our lips move together, and our tongues dance. It's needy and delicious and makes my knees weak. I wrap my arms around his neck and pull my body against his. I feel his desire against my waist, and I whimper with need. Jude bites my bottom lip between his teeth and pulls gently as he pulls away.

Still holding my face, he peppers kisses all over my mouth before he places a firm one against my forehead. He clears his throat. "Later." He gets out, and I know he's as affected as I am. "We have something else to do first."

"What are we doing?" I ask, equally annoyed and interested. I just want to go back to Jude's and make love to him until I can't walk, but I'm also curious as to what he has planned.

"My nephew's birthday party," Jude answers, taking my hand in his.

"What?" I hold in a squeal. "Is your family going to be there?"

He chuckles. "Yeah, that's usually how birthday parties work."

"We just started dating. Don't you think it's too early for me to meet your family?" My voice comes out shriekier than I would prefer.

"No, I think it's a perfect time to meet them. Plus, Abuelo insisted I bring his niña to the party. Don't worry, it's just a small family celebration. My nephew Aidan will have his big party with all of his friends this weekend. It's just a dinner, Tannon."

We start walking once more. "Who's going to be there? Let me know what I'm walking into."

"Abuela is cooking the dinner in their apartment above the store. Three of my sisters and their husbands will be there. Plus, my nieces and nephews. There are eight and one on the way. Of course my parents and grandparents will be there. See, a small family gathering." He squeezes my hand.

"Yeah, twenty people, including us. Just a tiny little gathering," I deadpan.

"You'll do fine."

Jude starts to tell me about his sisters. Apparently, his two single sisters, Luciana and Amelia, live out of state pursuing their careers. His three married sisters all live nearby with their families. I hold on to the information that I can, though admittedly, it's not much because his grandfather's store isn't too far from my house.

There's a sign on the front door of the store that reads, *Sorry Friends. Closed early for a family celebration. See you tomorrow.* It's in Jude's grandfather's handwriting, and I find it so adorable. It's just like Fedé to close up shop instead of hiring someone to cover for him for a couple of hours. He's such a hard worker and lives at his store, and I suppose that's literally the case as well. At least, he lives above it.

Jude leads me to the alleyway on the side of the building. Past the dumpsters are two doors. One presumably leads to the back of the store. This is probably where Fedé accepts the deliveries for the store. The other, the one that Jude opens, must lead to the residence.

As we ascend the stairs, I pull my hand from Jude's and wipe my palms against my jeans. Laughter and voices can be heard on the other side of the door.

"You ready?" Jude asks.

I can only nod.

"Have I told you that you look beautiful today?" he says before placing his lips against mine. Pulling away, he says, "They're going to love you."

CHAPTER 25

TANNON

"Jude's here!"

"Tio!"

"Hermano!"

Voices ring out in welcome when Jude opens the door. "Uncle Jude!" A little boy plows into Jude, wrapping his arms around Jude's waist.

"Aidan? I hardly recognize you. Goodness, you look old!" Jude exclaims.

"That's because I'm six now," Aidan says proudly.

"Dude. I can tell. You're huge. Happy Birthday, buddy." Jude runs his hand across Aidan's head. "Hey bud, I brought a friend to your dinner. This is Tannon."

"Hi, Tannon." Aidan exclaims.

"Hi." I smile down at him.

Before anything else is said, a big orange Nerf bullet

hits him in the back, and he turns and runs after the culprit.

"Mi niña. Come in," Fedé greets me with a warm embrace. "You've met the love of my life, Lupita? Si?" He introduces his wife.

Jude's grandma is short and cute. Her long gray hair is up in a bun.

"Yes, we've met a few times. I'm addicted to your tamales. You're the best cook I know," I tell her.

"Well, Jude can cook very well. Don't let him fool you. I've taught him everything I know," she says.

"I cook for her, Abuelita," Jude answers. "But I could never be as good as you." He bends down and gives his grandma a kiss on each of her cheeks.

The apartment is not what I envisioned at all. I guess I'm not sure what I expected an apartment over a convenience store to look like but not like this. It's huge. Besides the doors at the far end of the space, which I can assume are the bed and bathrooms, the entire floor plan is open. It's as big as the store. There are a couple of sitting areas with sofas throughout. The kitchen area is massive, extending most of the length of the sidewall. The sink and countertops face out over the city streets. Everything is colorful and happy. The décor reminds me a bit of some Mexican restaurants I've been to but more sophisticated. The massive wooden table runs parallel with the kitchen counter, and I'm sure it can easily seat thirty people.

"Tannon, this is my dad, Javier, and my mother, Debbie." Jude begins the introductions to his family who are lined up to meet me. "My eldest sister, Maria, and her husband, Juan Carlos, my other sister Marcela and her husband, Ben, and my sister Amara, and her husband, Victor." Each person greets me with kisses on each cheek.

"Hi." I wave sheepishly to the group. "I guess I should be taking notes. Please forgive me if I need to be reminded of names."

Jude's pregnant sister, Amara, waves her hand through the air. "Don't worry, babe. We'll remind you if you forget. There are a lot of us to remember." She chuckles. "Plus, our baby brother has never brought home a girl, so we're all just excited to meet you."

I turn to Jude, an eyebrow raised. "He's never brought a girl home before?"

"Never," his sister—*Maria?*—answers.

Marcela grabs my hand. "Come sit with us. We have so many questions. Jude, grab us some drinks." She calls over her shoulder to her brother as she leads me to one of the large leather couches.

Amara sits across from me. Her hand absentmindedly rubs her round belly.

"When are you due?" I ask her.

"December twenty-fourth," she says with a sigh. "It's going to be a Christmas baby, which sucks for the baby, but I'm just so ready to have him or her out of me."

"You didn't find out what you were having?" I ask.

"No, we wanted it to be a surprise. It's our third, so Victor kind of wanted to find out this time, but I really like the surprise. There are so few true surprises anymore. You know?"

"A Christmas baby will be wonderful," Maria says to her sister. "We promised you that there would be no Merry Christmas/Happy Birthday presents."

Debbie, Jude's mom, speaks from behind me. "Are we ever going to live that down? That was a rough year for us." Debbie's voice is teasing. She walks around the sofa and sits in a chair adjacent. She looks toward me. "You see, Tannon, our youngest daughters Luciana and Amelia were both born in December, almost exactly a year apart. They were our Irish twins. One year when finances were particularly tight, the girls got a combined Christmas and birthday gift, and none of my children will let their father or me forget it."

"Yeah, because it's horrible, Mom." Marcela laughs.

"It can't be that horrible. I think you all turned out just fine, regardless of the horrors and combined presents you lived through," Debbie defends herself with an eye roll.

"Well, if you noticed, your two absent kids are the Christmas twins. I don't think they're over it, Mom," Amara says with a serious face.

Debbie's mouth falls open.

"I'm kidding, Mamacita." Amara grins and leans forward to rub her mom's arm.

A foam bullet flies by my face.

"Gianna!" Maria yells. "Nerf war over there. If you hit an adult, you lose the guns. You know the rules."

"Sorry, Mom." A little girl with long auburn braids yells out an apology as she runs past us, a group of giggling kids on her tail.

Debbie turns to me, returning to our conversation. "The girls are out west pursuing their dreams. They'll be back when they find love and settle down," she says to me by way of explanation. "God knows I can't shake these three."

"Touché, Mother." Maria laughs.

Jude enters the area, both of his hands full with beer bottles. He hands one to each of us and a sparkling water to Amara. I thank him and hold the bottle of beer in my grasp.

I hate beer, like I can't even get one down. I'd gag. Anyone who knows me knows that I hate beer. Here I am, meeting Jude's family simply because we've had a handful of sexual encounters. We barely know each other. It's been less than a week. He's never brought a woman home to his family, yet he's brought me, and he doesn't even know that I hate beer.

Panic begins to rise from my gut. I swallow to keep it at bay. This is all moving way too fast. Chill, Tannon. Nothing you can do about it now.

Jude takes a seat beside me.

"So how long have you two been together?" Debbie asks.

"We just started dating recently, but we've known

each other for a couple of months. Tannon actually hired me for a job," Jude says.

"Well, I didn't actually hire him. My roommate did." I smile at the memory. Though I was mortified to run into Jude in just my skimpy sleepwear at the time, I have to admit it makes a good story now.

"Oh, this sounds juicy. Tell us everything," Marcela says, leaning in toward Jude and me.

Everyone has joined us in the seating area now, besides the children and Javier and Abuela, who work in the kitchen area. Jude and I take turns narrating the story of how we met right down to me running into a boxer brief–clad Jude while in my pajamas. The women think it's incredible that I write romance novels and pull up Amazon on their phones to one-click my books.

Fedé says. "I told you mi niña was very talented. She's a catch, this one."

I smile warmly at Fedé before addressing the women. "They're spicy, my books, and fiction," I warn them, putting an emphasis on the last word. In my first book, my main character has sex outside a nightclub against a brick wall, and I once had a girl from high school ask me if I had based that scene on my life. *That's a negative, Jenny.*

"Oh honey, I can't wait. The more spice, the better," Debbie says while tapping on her phone. "Right, honey?" she yells over her shoulder to Jude's dad in the kitchen.

The sisters let out a collective groan.

"Stop, Mom. You're going to scare her away," Amara says.

"Obviously, she knows we do it, Amara. I have six children, and you didn't all get here by means of immaculate conception."

"Mom! Ew. No. None of us wants this conversation to go any further," Maria chastises her mother.

Debbie turns her attention back to me. "All I'm saying is that I can't wait to read your words, love. I'm really looking forward to it."

"Thank you. That's really sweet."

The conversation moves from me and my books to Marcela's husband, Ben. The group is teasing him about some mistake he made at work. Apparently, he thought he was messaging a co-worker to complain about his boss, but he accidentally sent his boss the message. Everyone is laughing, and it's contagious. My cheeks are starting to ache from smiling so much. I can see why Jude is such a great person. He was raised by really cool humans.

Javier calls over, telling us it's time to eat.

We make our way into the kitchen. I place my full bottle of beer on the counter next to the sink, grab a plate, and line up behind the rest of the family. There's a long line of food in ceramic bowls on the counter. I fill my plate with salad, Mexican rice, beans, tortillas, guacamole, and salsa. There are various meats as well. Everything looks and smells incredible, and I can't wait to eat. Jude brings me over a tall glass of Jamaica juice, and I give my thanks. It's quickly becoming my new favorite drink.

Piling a corn tortilla with all the fixings, I take a big bite and have to stop myself from groaning. Ben sits across from me with a knowing look.

"It's good, right?" He nods toward the tortilla in my hand. "If you like Mexican food, you've hit the jackpot. Abuela's food is better than any restaurant you'll find."

I grin. My mouth stuffed full.

"I told you," Jude says beside me, in agreement with Ben.

"So good," I manage to say when I've swallowed.

I eat until I can't eat anymore and then sit back and watch the birthday festivities. Marcela brings over the cake for little Aidan. It's a baby Yoda *Star Wars* cake.

The family starts to sing to Aidan in Spanish, of what I can only assume is some sort of Mexican birthday song.

"Estas son las mañanitas, que cantaba el rey..."

When the Spanish song is finished, they immediately go into, "Happy Birthday to you! Happy Birthday to you! Happy Birthday, dear Aidan..."

I sing along during the latter of the two.

Aidan blows out his candles and opens presents. Jude dropped off a sweet Lego set for Aidan earlier from both of us, which he absolutely loved.

We eat cake and laugh some more, and when Jude

and I leave, everyone hugs me and kisses my cheeks as if I'm already part of the family. I've spent one afternoon with these people, and I already love them.

As we descend the steps out to the alley, I really hope I get to see them all again.

CHAPTER 26

TANNON

I'M quiet on our drive back to Jude's house. There's so much about the evening that I want to take in—

the personalities of Jude's family, the stories, the overall feeling of happiness. I had so much fun, and that's why I hate this nagging feeling inside my gut. It's a warning of trouble to come.

"You're awfully quiet," Jude says to me as he unlocks his front door.

I walk in.

"Just thinking about the night," I respond with the truth.

"Did you have fun? Did my sisters give you a hard time? I didn't mean to throw you to the wolves. They mean well. They just love to pry," he offers by way of explanation.

"No, it was great. Everything was. Your family was

the coolest, and I mean that, Jude. They are some of the most awesome people I've ever met." I take a seat on the couch, and Jude sits beside me and looks me in the eye. "I'm not surprised, given how awesome you and your grandpa are, but I was still so impressed. I love your sisters and your mom. They didn't make me feel uncomfortable at all. You're so lucky to be a part of that big, supportive, fun family. The food was great. Seeing a birthday celebrated in two languages was awesome. Everything was just perfect."

"I sense a but," he says cautiously.

"There's no but," I lie.

"Just tell me, Tannon," he coaxes.

"Did I meet your family too soon? I mean, we're newly dating, and tonight was special. I loved every minute of it. What if I don't get to see them again? Maybe we should've waited for this step."

"Is this because of the beer?" Jude's eyes squint down at me.

"What do you mean?" My voice raises an octave.

Jude laughs. "It totally was, wasn't it? So, you hate beer, don't you? Maybe I didn't know that fact about you yet, Tannon, but who cares? It doesn't mean anything bad. Plus, I know it now."

"I know. It just showed me how much we still have to learn about each other," I offer.

"Exactly." He grins. "We have tons more to learn about each other, which we should. We just started dating, as you keep pointing out." He shoots me a wink.

"I took you to meet my family tonight because for the first time in my adult dating life, it felt right. I can't explain it. I simply wanted my family to meet you and you to meet them. I don't need to know what your favorite alcoholic beverage, favorite color, or favorite animal is for you to meet my family, Tannon. There's no quiz involved. Just my favorite people in the world meeting my favorite girl."

"That's a pretty bold statement," I tell him. "You could decide that I suck and hate me by next week." I chew on the corner of my lip.

"Then I'll hate you next week, but right now, I think you're pretty fucking awesome, Tannon Lee." He takes my hands in his.

"I think you're pretty cool, too."

"Good, and that whole thing you did with your beer was adorable by the way."

"What do you mean?"

"You know, the way you held it during the whole conversation with my family and then how you quietly snuck it onto the counter when you thought no one was watching. Next time, just say, 'Yo, dude! I hate beer.'"

"Yo, dude! I hate beer? Who talks like that?" I giggle.

"You get the point. Be who you are, Tannon. I promise you, that's all I want."

"I just didn't want your family to realize that we don't know each other well," I admit.

"They all started somewhere in their relationships,

too. It would've been fine. So, do you hate all beer or just certain brands?"

"All beer. It's disgusting."

"Noted." He grins. Leaning in, he presses his lips against mine.

I sigh at his touch, and all is well with the world.

I pull away. "It's mojito, pink, and pig."

"What?" he questions.

"You mentioned that you didn't know my favorite drink, color, or animal. It's mojito, pink, and pigs."

"Pigs?" He smirks.

"Yes, they are adorable with cute little flat noses. I've always loved them."

"What color pink? Like hot pink? Baby girl pink?"

"Any pink. I love all the shades."

"Good to know." He stands from the sofa. Extending his arm toward me, I take his hand, and he pulls me up.

"I feel like a hot shower," he states as we walk hand in hand toward his bedroom.

"I could definitely go for a hot shower."

"Good."

The sun filters in through the closed blinds, creating thin tiger stripes across Jude's arm that lies across my bare waist. My body still hums with pleasure from our festivities last night. I've come to realize that the physical portion of our relationship will never be an issue. I don't know if two people are more compatible in this area than us. We just need to figure out the rest.

"Hey." I run my palm across Jude's five o'clock shadow. I admire how beautiful he looks. I love the little bit of rough hair on his face. He's always so clean-shaven for work.

"Hey." He opens his eyes with a squint and instantly pulls me toward him, his bare skin against mine.

"Don't you have to work this morning?" I ask, afraid that he forgot to set an alarm.

"No, I'm on second shift today. I don't go in until two," he says lazily.

"Oh, good. So I have you all morning?"

"You do. I normally go to the gym, but I don't feel like it. I want to stay here with you instead."

I smile against his chest and run the tip of my finger across his pec. "I approve of that plan."

"I'm glad."

"I could make you breakfast," I offer.

"Oh, yeah?" Amusement lines Jude's voice. "I thought you didn't cook? What are you going to make?"

"Well, I'm pretty good at toast if you have a toaster, and I'm a pro at cereal," I say, causing Jude to let out a chuckle.

"Okay, how about egg and avocado on toast?" he suggests.

Sitting up, I pull the sheet around me and stare down at Jude. He's like a Grecian god, his tanned muscles spread across the white sheet. I'm kind of obsessed with him. It's true.

"Hey, I said toast. Plain toast with butter. Whatever you just mentioned isn't toast. It's some sort of meal."

He reaches an arm forward and slips his hand under the sheet to caress my knee. The physical contact causes goose bumps to erupt down my arms.

"How about we cook together, and I'll show you how to make egg and avocado toast? It's incredibly easy," Jude suggests, his thumb tracing circles against my skin.

I rub my palms against the skin of my arms, warming away the shivers. "Okay, sounds like a plan."

Opening the door of Jude's dresser, I pull out a clean white T-shirt. "You don't mind that I go into your drawers to find clothes, do you? You can tell me if some places are off-limits. I don't mean to snoop through your stuff. I get that you may want to keep some things private."

Jude finishes pulling on a pair of boxer briefs and eyes me curiously. "Of course I don't mind. It's just a dresser drawer full of T-shirts. What do you think I'm hiding in there?" He grins.

"I don't know." I shrug, pulling the shirt over my head. "You're a guy. You might have stuff."

"Like porn?" He raises an eyebrow, and his lip tilts up in a smirk.

"Maybe?" I grab my panties off the floor and pull them on. "Guys have that stuff sometimes—like magazines or naked pictures of old girlfriends, or whatever—

and if you did, you might not want me going through it. I'm just trying to be respectful of your space."

"You're so cute." Jude walks over to me and holds my hips in his grasp. Bending down, he gives me a soft kiss. "I'm not really into porn, and there's nothing I have that I'd mind you seeing. You can rummage for clothes in any drawer that you see fit."

"You don't watch porn?" I tilt my head back and squint up at him.

He smiles. "I mean, I have, of course. I don't watch it often, though, especially when I'm with someone. I much prefer the real thing." He drops his hands to my ass and squeezes each of my butt cheeks, pulling me against him.

A yelp escapes, and I press my hands against his chest to catch my balance. "Well, that's good." I lean in and kiss the space between his pecs. "I think we have better than porn sex anyway."

"Hell yeah, we do."

I wrap my arms around his neck. He bends and kisses me. Short little kisses. Again and again. I sigh and sink further against him.

"We could delay breakfast a little bit," I say against his mouth, nodding toward the bed we just vacated.

I feel Jude's grin against my lips. He pulls away a fraction and smacks my butt lightly. "No, we need to eat, and I promised you a cooking lesson."

"All right, fine. I take a step back and scan his chest.

"I'd like my cooking instructor to remain shirtless throughout the lesson."

"I can do that as long as you remain in just this." He squeezes my ass cheeks once more.

"Deal."

I follow Jude into the kitchen, and he gets out the bread, eggs, avocado, salt, pepper, and turmeric.

"What's turmeric?" I read the label of the glass spice container.

"It's a really mild spice. I like it on my eggs, and it's supposed to be good for you." He shrugs.

"Hmm, I've never heard of it." I place my hands on the counter and pull myself up to sit on it.

"You'll like it," he reassures me. "So what do you typically have for breakfast at your place?"

I bite my lip. "Besides coffee? Because I have to admit, that is often my breakfast. Sometimes, I'll have cereal. Fruity Pebbles is my favorite."

"Fruity Pebbles?" He chuckles.

"Yeah." I cross my arms against my chest. "Do you have a problem with Fruity Pebbles?"

"No, no problem." He laughs. "I just think it's funny is all."

"Are you telling me that you don't buy Fruity Pebbles?"

"Never," he says, putting the slices of bread in the toaster.

"Well, that's just sad," I tease. "Because it's the best." I kick my legs out in front of me as Jude hits the knife into the avocado peel. I know I should be helping, but he looks so damn sexy in his briefs slicing an avocado, and I just want to watch him. I could definitely get used to breakfasts with Jude. "Do you want me to help you do something? I'm going to be honest, I really like watching you. It's such a turn-on, but I can help if you need it."

He stops slicing and puts the knife down. His green eyes capture mine, and my heart starts to race. He renders me needy with a single glance. My chest rises as I breathe deeply.

"You turned on, Tannon?" Jude's voice is gravelly, his need mirroring my own.

I chew on the inside of my cheek and nod.

He steps over to me and positions his body between my legs. His hands clasp my thighs. I lean forward and put my lips against his. He fists my thighs and kisses me hard. Wrapping my hands around his back, I splay them across his shoulders and pull him closer, circling my legs around his middle.

His mouth leaves mine, and he kisses down my neck. I drop my head back against the cabinets behind me with a groan. He rotates between kisses, sucks, and licks as he gives the sensitive skin of my neck his attention.

"What do you want, baby?" he asks, his teeth nibbling against my shoulder.

"You," I moan, my core now throbbing with need.

One of his hands slides up my thigh. "Let's see how bad you want me." He pulls my panties to the side and slips two fingers in. I release a cry and push onto his hand.

"Oh fuck, Tannon. You're so ready." Jude's mouth captures mine, and his tongue mimics his fingers' movements below. His free hand slips under the T-shirt and cups my breast.

I grab at his back and shoulders, desperately trying to pull him in closer, and my hips thrust toward his hand. I cry out each time his fingers rub inside me. I'm crazed where Jude is concerned, and I'm not self-conscious in the slightest. It feels too good to care.

Jude pulls my bottom lip between his teeth. "I want to come together," he says against my lips. "I want you right here. Just like this." He pulls his fingers out and runs them up until he's rubbing them against my bundle of nerves. I throw my forehead against his shoulder and whimper. The sensations coursing through me are starting to build, and I'm racing toward a delicious release.

He rubs his fingers in circles, and the warmth that I've come to crave with such an intensity starts to fill me up.

And then he stops.

I groan in protest.

Jude pulls his hand out of my panties and provides a quick kiss on my lips. "Give me five seconds. I'm going to go grab a condom."

I open my lust-filled eyes to find Jude retreating toward his bedroom. "Don't move," he warns playfully.

Not a chance.

I close my eyes and rest my head back against the cabinet. Waiting.

What is it with Jude and kitchens? I've never found the room particularly arousing, but two of my greatest memories now take place in one with him.

"Thanks for standing me up, asshole." A perky voice throws metaphorical ice water on my libido because it's so out of place here in my utopia of sex and Jude.

It belongs to a woman.

CHAPTER 27

TANNON

It takes my brain, saturated with lust and longing, a second to register the fact a woman is walking into the kitchen. As she rounds the corner, I close my legs and sit up, attempting to appear as natural as a woman in a T-shirt and panties sitting on a counter can look. I'm certain my flushed skin gives everything away.

"Oh, hey. Who are you?" asks the high-pitched voice belonging to Jane, a tiny woman with short blond hair.

I've seen her a few times now, but it's always been from a distance, and I guess I never realized how fairy-like she appears. She can't weigh more than a hundred pounds, and her haircut is oddly reminiscent of Tinker Bell. If I didn't already know she was a police officer, I would've never guessed that she had it in her to be one. A preschool teacher, yes. A cop, not so much.

Then I register her words. Who am I? *Who are you*

barging in here like you own the place right when I was about to make sweet breakfast love to my boyfriend on his kitchen counter? I press my knees together to clue my body in that it's not happening now, thanks to Tinker over here.

I attempt to swallow, but my mouth has gone dry. "Tannon," I answer.

"Uh, Jane. What are you doing here?" Jude emerges from the bedroom in shorts and a T-shirt, obviously having thrown some clothes on when he heard Jane's voice.

"What are you doing here?" she responds with a tsk of her finger. "I was at the gym waiting for you."

Jude lifts an arm and runs his hand along the back of his neck. "I texted you last night letting you know that I wasn't going today."

"You did? I guess I didn't get it." Jane shrugs.

I stare from Jude to Jane, and I'm frozen, a statue of confusion. Should I hop off the counter and go get some pants? Should I stay put and act normal? Should I hit this girl over her head with a pan for intruding on my Jude time?

Probably not the latter, but man, it's tempting. Who just walks into someone's home unannounced?

Jude reads my mind. "Jane, you should've called. You just can't walk in here."

"Oh, sorry. It's just never been an issue before. You gave me a key."

Is this woman actually that dense?

Jude sighs, and I can tell he's pissed. Which makes me feel better. If he was cool with this twit barging in whenever she felt the need, that would be a problem.

"Are you making breakfast? I'm starving. Unlike you." She makes a show of pinching some nonexistent fat on Jude's abdomen. "I got in a good workout this morning."

And I hate her.

This could be a problem.

Jude looks at me in question. I give him a shrug and a small smile. What else can I do? Throw the pixie out of the house?

"Yeah, we're making eggs," Jude answers flatly.

Jane doesn't seem to notice his tone. "Oh, good! I love your eggs." She looks toward me. "Aren't his eggs the best?"

I supply a smile before hopping down from the counter. Jude's shirt covers my ass, but I still feel very exposed.

"Oh, I'm Jane, by the way," she says to me.

"Yeah, I saw you at a self-defense class before." The idiotic reply leaves my mouth, and I excuse myself and walk briskly toward Jude's bedroom.

Once inside his room, I opt to take a shower and get my own clothes on. I know I have every right to traipse out there in Jude's baggy, *Yeah, we had sex all night* clothes, but I feel weird. Jane's presence here is really annoying me, if I'm being honest.

I ignore the laughter coming from the living room

and close the bathroom door. After dropping Jude's T-shirt in the hamper, I shimmy out of my panties and step into the hot spray of the shower. I let the scalding water carry my annoyance and any shred of desire I still had crawling on my skin down the drain. I guess I won't be having mad orgasms with Jude this morning, and I just have to get over it.

The door of the bathroom opens, and seconds later, Jude opens the shower door a crack.

"Hey, I'm sorry. I texted her last night. I don't know why she came over." His words are heavy with an emotion somewhere between annoyance and regret.

"It's okay," I lie and provide a smile. "Not a biggie." I'm not a pro with relationships, but I recognize that it's too soon to play the angry girlfriend card.

"It is big, though, and rude. It doesn't make sense because I told her that I would be spending the morning with you in the text. She says she didn't get it, but that's strange," he explains as I run my soapy fingers through my hair.

"It is what it is. I'm fine."

"It was bad timing." His gaze roams my wet skin.

I laugh. "It could have been worse if she'd come a minute or two later."

"True," Jude agrees. "Or a minute earlier." He wraps his palm around my neck and pulls me in for a kiss. "I'll make it up to you."

"Damn straight, you will." I kiss Jude again before he leaves.

After I've showered, I put on my outfit from last night and run a comb from Jude's bathroom through my hair. I feel better equipped to handle Jane when I'm in actual clothes. I step out of Jude's bedroom to find the two of them sitting at his table with empty plates in front of them.

Jude stands up when he sees me and gives me a kiss before offering me his seat. He removes his plate and brings me back a fresh cup of coffee.

"Thank you," I tell him.

"Your breakfast will be ready in a minute," he says.

"So, do you live nearby, Tannon?" Jane asks.

"Yeah, in town. Above the Starbucks, actually."

She takes her fork and moves around some crumbs on her plate. "That's convenient."

"Yeah, it is."

"So what do you do for a living?" Her brown-eyed gaze seems uninterested.

I take a sip of coffee. "I'm a romance author."

"I told you that already, Jane," Jude says from the stove.

Jane presses her lips in a tight smile before responding to Jude. "Oh, that's right. You did. I forgot," she says to Jude before addressing me. "That must be an interesting job."

I can't tell if she's being genuine or not, but I give her the benefit of the doubt since she's Jude's best friend. "Yeah, it is," I say again.

Jude places a plate with avocado egg toast in front of me.

"This looks delicious. Thank you," I say.

He kisses the top of my head and then sits down beside me.

Jane asks me question after question. She now knows about my parents, brother, roommate, friends, college education, pet cat, exercise routine (or lack thereof), coffee habit, writing process, and future ambitions.

"Jane, enough with the interrogation." Jude chuckles.

"I'm not trying to interrogate. Sorry. I just want to get to know you." Her sugar-sweet response is directed toward me.

"No worries," I say to the both of them.

"You can always ask me anything, too," Jane offers.

"Great, thanks." Truth be told, maybe I'm a bitch, but I have no desire to ask her questions right now. I know I shouldn't let her rub me the wrong way, but she is. I'm sure she's a great person. Jude wouldn't be friends with an evil witch. Hopefully, the next time I see her, it starts off under different circumstances. Maybe I'll feel like getting to know her then.

We've chatted the morning away, or at least Jane has. "I better get going. Have to get home and shower before work. I'll see you soon, Jude," she tells him. "It was great meeting you, Tannon."

"You too," I lie.

After the front door has closed behind Jane, I turn toward Jude, and he laughs.

"Come here," he extends his arms, and I gladly step into them.

He wraps me in a tight hug and kisses my forehead.

"I'm sorry our morning sucked," he says.

"It didn't suck," I grumble.

"It did, but as I said, I'll make it up to you."

I perk up. "Now?"

Jude's deep chuckle vibrates against my body. "No, not now. I have to shower and get dressed for work before I drop you off at home."

"Ugh, fine."

"Believe me, it wasn't how I wanted to spend our morning either, but we'll have many more mornings together." He talks about our future so nonchalantly like it's a sure thing. It equally freaks me out and makes me so happy.

None of my past relationships have been very serious. Regardless, none of those guys spoke to our future. Maybe that should've been a sign that those relationships were doomed from the start. I could've saved myself a lot of time.

As the words leave his lips, I can only hope that our relationship is, in fact, a sure thing and that I'll always feel the way I do now about this man before me.

"It's fine, really. I'm glad I got to spend some time with her." I make my words as convincing as possible.

"She's important to you, and therefore, she's important to me."

"Is that why you wanted to learn so much about her?" He smirks.

"Hey." I playfully smack his chest.

"I'm kidding. You'll have time to ask her all sorts of questions later. She was a little off today anyway."

"How so?"

"I don't know. She was just rubbing me the wrong way, so I know she was probably annoying you a little. I promise she's normally super easy to get along with."

"You should probably take her key," I warn. "I definitely won't like her if she interrupts counter sex again."

"Noted." He chuckles before kissing me again. "Me either."

CHAPTER 28

JUDE

I break down the last of the boxes and toss them into the recycling dumpster behind the store. Today was mainly re-stocking ramen noodles and boxes of mac and cheese, which my abuelo argued that he could do by himself. While it's true that he could easily handle a box of noodles, I'd rather do it.

One of my abuelo's strongest attributes is his work ethic, but it's also a bit of a downfall. He should be retired and enjoying a quiet life with his family, not working from open to close. He says he loves it, and he also swears that a man should work or he'll die. He's told us all the story of his father, my great-grandfather who retired at the age of ninety-two, and died a month later. One could argue that he passed because he was ninety-two, but Abuelo said it's because he stopped working.

We've all tried to reason with him but always end up just letting it go. Abuelo is one stubborn man.

"Well, the college kids noodle supply is restocked," I say.

"Oh, good."

"Is there anything else I can do to help?"

He shakes his head. "No, Jude. I'm good down here. Your momma and sisters are upstairs visiting. You should go say hello."

"Well, you call me if you need anything. Okay? I don't want to come in here again and see you holding a carton of juice on top of a ladder."

"I'm not in the grave yet, boy. I'm fully capable."

"I know you are, but it makes me feel good to help. Please just call me."

He nods, but whether he'll actually reach out is yet to be seen. It hasn't happened yet, which is why I try to stop in whenever I can and stock the shelves before he has a chance to.

"Te amo, Abuelito," I tell him I love him before I leave.

"Te amo, Jude," he says before I step outside.

Opening the next door over, I take the stairs two at a time up to my grandparents' home.

The women in my life all call out my name in greeting as I enter. "I heard you were up here," I say.

"Were you down helping your abuelo?" my abuelita asks.

"I was. I've shelved all that there's to shelf until he gets another shipment."

"Thank you, mi amor."

"Anytime." I give her a kiss on each cheek in greeting.

"We just finished eating. There's spaghetti on the table. It's still warm," my mom says.

I dish up a plate of spaghetti and grab a few corn tortillas. With my fork, I scoop a pile of spaghetti onto my tortilla and wrap it up before taking a bite. I learned young that everything tastes better in a tortilla. My grandma serves all meals with tortillas as her mother in Mexico did before her. It's normal to me, but my mother told us how strange it was to her when she first started dating my father.

With my plate in hand, I take a seat across from my sisters on the sofa. "So, what are you ladies all talking about up here?"

My grandmother hands me a glass of agua de melon—melon water made with cantaloupe.

"You." My sister Marcela grins. "Well, you and Tannon to be precise."

I take another bite of the spaghetti taco. "Okay, let's hear it."

"We love her." Amara grins, rubbing her belly.

"We do," my mom says. "She has this awesome vibe to her. She just seems like a good person. Plus, she makes you happy. She must since you finally brought a girl home."

"Good." I chuckle. "I'm glad you're not feeling the opposite because I really like her, too."

"You have a good sense about people. If you like her, that means she's good," Maria adds.

The nightmares of my past come to mind, and I scoff. "Well, you all haven't seen some of the women I've dated."

"Exactly," my mom says. "Because you haven't introduced us to those women. The fact that you wanted us to meet Tannon means she's a keeper."

I look around the space, suddenly aware that there's no screaming. "Where are all the kids?" I ask.

"The older ones are in school, but I had Victor take the little ones to the park after we ate. It was too much noise." Amara makes a face.

"You know it's about to get noisier." I laugh, nodding toward her large belly.

She shakes her head. "I know. Please don't remind me."

"So what did Tannon think about all of us?" Maria asks.

"She loved you all. She thinks we have the coolest family."

"Well, obviously." Maria nods.

"She's loved Abuelo for years, you know? And Abuelita by extension. So I think she was happy to meet the rest of you. She had nothing but great things to say about everyone."

"Do you see her a lot?" Maria inquires.

"Whenever our schedules allow it. She's busy writing a book right now, and you all know my work schedule. But, all in all, yeah—I'd say we see each other a lot."

"So things between you are serious? They're going good?" Marcella asks.

I nod. "Really good."

"So do you think she's *the one*?" my mom asks, her eyes wide.

"It's a little too soon to know that, I think." I take a sip of my melon water and place it on the side table. "We haven't been dating that long."

"No." My abuelita takes a seat beside me. "You know already if she is."

I've grown up hearing stories of love at first sight and soul mates. Both my grandparents and my parents claim it was love at first sight for them. Both couples were married very soon after meeting and are still happily married.

My three eldest sisters have since claimed the same.

So who am I to question it?

The truth is, I want to believe in it, but I think it's more complicated than they pretend it is. Or maybe because it's a different time, the whole *the one* philosophy doesn't come into play until later. I think life is more complicated than it used to be. Do I have a deeper connection with Tannon than I've ever had with anyone else? Yeah, I do. But sometimes I worry that we're so physically compatible that I'm not seeing the parts where we're not.

There are pieces of Tannon that she hasn't completely shared with me, a trauma in her past that I think she's still dealing with today. I saw it in her the first time I laid eyes on her at one of my classes. She's been hurt, and she's put up walls. I feel them coming down a little more every day, but I also see her insecurity around our relationship, which I think stems from her past.

"I don't know," I say. "It's complicated."

"Do you love her?" Amara asks.

"Yeah," I answer almost immediately because I do. Logic tells me it's too soon, but I do. I love her.

"Have you told her?" Marcela leans forward, resting her elbows on her knees.

"No."

"That's a problem." My abuelita tsks.

"It's not always black and white," I say. "I think she has a history, and I'm just trying to be respectful of that and give her time."

"That's true. Everyone has a history," my mom adds. "There may be things you need to work through, but it's either wrong or right. If it's *right*, if she's the one for you, you already know it, and all the other stuff won't matter in the end because she's the one."

"But it matters in the fact that we may not be in a place where we can be as happy as we can possibly be because all that other stuff"—I circle my hand through the air—"is placing a cloud over our relationship. I'm not saying it is right now, but I'm afraid it will. I'm worried about it."

"Because you don't want to lose her?" Amara's smile is warm.

"Right." I nod. "Everything's great right now, but I'm afraid of what unresolved issues from our pasts could do to our future."

"Then resolve them," my abuelita says, her tone matter of fact.

"It's not always that easy," I say.

My grandmother shakes her head. "Of course it isn't easy. Love isn't easy. It's hard work. Your grandfather is the love of my life, yes, but it doesn't mean we haven't worked for everything we have and everything we are. Anything worth having in this life will come with challenges. Love is the greatest challenge of them all and also the most rewarding. Fight for it and for her. If she's your one...you get ready for battle and don't let her go."

CHAPTER 29

TANNON

"I can't believe you two aren't coming," Everett grumbles. He's sitting at our kitchen table flipping through our local hardware store's weekly ad that he grabbed from a pile of junk mail. "Our party won't be the same without you," he says to Cassie and me.

"Why, because then you won't know anyone in your apartment?" Cassie jokes from the couch. She and Asher are watching an old version of *Family Feud* on the Game Show Channel.

"That's a low blow," Asher argues weakly beside her. He's sprawled back on the couch, resting his head against his outstretched arm. "True. But low."

"Why keep having parties? We're not in college anymore. I don't get the draw of wanting to fill your apartment with drunk strangers, especially when you have to clean up after them the next day. How about you just hang out with people you actually know and like?" I suggest while scraping a can of gourmet cat food into Lucifer's dish.

Lucifer paces at my feet, meowing like a cat in heat.

"Here you go, crazy cat." I place the bowl down on the floor.

"Not on the lips!" Cassie yells at the TV.

Asher laughs. "Richard Dawson was a player, man. I wonder how many contestants he slept with?"

"He kissed everyone. It had nothing to do with wanting to sleep with them. That was just how he greeted people," Cassie defends the game show host.

"Nah, he was hooking up. I'm sure of it. Don't you think, Ev?" Asher says.

"Oh, absolutely," Everett agrees. "Player status, for sure."

The sight of Everett staring intently at the ad insert causes me to laugh. "Are you looking to do some landscaping or home projects anytime soon?" I ask him.

Everett flips through the rest of the pages and tosses the ad back on the pile of junk mail. "No, just bored and mad that you're standing us up."

"Just admit it," I tease. "You're pissed because we're the only ones you ever talk to at your parties, and now you're going to be forced to mingle with all the weirdos you invited."

"Whatever," Everett mumbles and stands up from the table.

He plops down on the couch next to Cassie.

Cassie and I are going on a double date tonight with Jude and one of his work buddies, Bennett. She broke it off with Henry the day after meeting his parents a little over a month ago. She decided not to settle, which I knew she never would have, anyway. Cassie isn't the settling type. She's chosen to drop the subject of the drunken kiss between Asher and her, as well. She states that his friendship is way more important than exploring a kiss that didn't mean anything.

The past month has been amazing for me. When Jude's at work, I'm writing. When he's off, we're together. I get to know him a little better every day, and each day, I fall deeper. My newfound relationship with my hot cover model has come with an incredible writing streak. Words are flowing, and they're good. At least, I think they are. An author never knows until the book is published if the words are, in fact, good.

I've felt bad that I've been gone so much over the past month. I still make time for my friends but not as much as before, and though I know it's only natural to spend more time with my significant other as I get older and the relationship becomes more serious, I still carry some guilt. Especially now that Cassie is single. I want her to be as happy as I am—hence the double date, which also happens to be a blind date.

"I'm starting to get nervous," Cassie says. "What if he's a total tool? I can't believe I let you talk me into this."

"Jude promises that he's cool and reassures me that

all the girls think he's cute," I tell her.

"Blind dates are stupid. Who goes on them anymore?" Cassie protests.

"Anyone who swipes right on Tinder." Asher chuckles.

"Yeah, but at least you have a picture and a conversation beforehand. You don't go in completely blind," Cassie says with a pout.

"Sometimes you do," Everett adds with a chuckle. "There isn't always time for conversation, and sometimes pictures are not what they seem."

"Ew," I add.

"Yeah, tell us about it," Asher says.

There's a knock on the door. Cassie's eyes dart toward mine, and I shoot her a smile.

"Can't back out now," I tell her.

I open the door to find Jude and his friend Bennett.

"Hey, beautiful." Jude greets me with a kiss.

I shake Bennett's hand, and then we introduce him to Cassie. She's pulling out her classic flirtatious smile and tucking her long dark hair behind her ear. At least I know she thinks he's cute, and I agree he is. He's not as broad-chested as Jude, but you can tell he works out. Dark blond hair, chiseled jaw, blue eyes, megawatt smile —yeah, he's your hot-ass boy next door. If his personality is halfway decent, Cassie will be in heaven.

"All right, boys," I say to our friends on the couch.

"But it's almost the fast money round," Asher argues.

"Fine, but lock up and make sure Lucifer doesn't get

out." My fat cat has never even attempted to exit the apartment. I think he knows life outside of these walls will not provide him three cans of wet food a day. Still, it makes me feel better to remind the guys to be cognizant of my fur baby.

"And enjoy your party," Cassie teases, her voice jovial as she grabs her coat and purse and follows Bennett out the door.

"Stop by after your date," Everett calls out to the group of us.

"Oh, we'll sure try." Cassie's voice is laced with sarcasm as the door closes behind us.

"So what's the plan?" I ask when we exit the door to our stairwell and are greeted by the freezing December wind. I pull my coat tighter around my middle.

"We are going to have dinner at the Real Seafood Company and then go out to see a Christmas light display," Jude tells us.

"Oh, that sounds great. I love that restaurant," Cassie says, and I have to agree. It sounds like an incredible date.

I hope Bennett and Cassie work out because, truthfully, I'm a little annoyed that I'm sharing my first Christmas light experience with Jude with a basic stranger. I wish tonight was only Jude and me. See, this is why this double date is important. I'm becoming obsessed. There's a fraction of remorse in my gut for wishing I was just with Jude. Not a ton, but some...if one were to really look.

The restaurant is fun, and the food is delicious. Cassie is her normal talkative self, and the conversation between her and Bennett seems to be going well. He's outgoing like her, so they're hitting it off.

"How's Amara?" I ask Jude as Bennett and Cassie start a pretty detailed debate on the best way to crack crab legs.

"Still pregnant and miserable. Doctor doesn't think she's going to go early."

"Oh, that sucks. She might get that Christmas baby after all, then." I think back to Jude's pregnant sister and the conversation about her not wanting to have the baby on Christmas.

"Well, her first two were late, so there's a chance."

The remainder of dinner is smooth. Cassie and I excuse ourselves to go to the restroom while the boys pay the tab.

"What do you think of Bennett?" Leaning over the sink in the restroom, I reapply my lip gloss in front of the mirror.

Cassie teases her fingers through her long hair, breaking up some of the curls. "He's cool."

"Cool?" I furrow my brows.

"He's hot, obviously, and nice and stuff."

"What a glowing review." I chuckle, tossing my lip gloss back in my purse.

"I don't know. It's weird. I'm not a fan of blind dates. It feels forced, like we have to get along because we're stuck in this situation together for the next several hours. You know?"

I turn toward her. "So are you missing Henry or Asher?"

Her eyes widen. "Neither."

"Cassie..."

"I'm not missing Henry. Yeah, I was comfortable with him, and it was easy, but I don't miss him. And there's no reason to *miss* Asher. There's no me and Asher. You know that."

"Look me in the eye and tell me that you haven't compared Bennett to Asher tonight, not even once."

"You're ridiculous." She tosses her hair behind her shoulder. "We need to go. They're waiting for us." She walks past me and out the bathroom door.

"You didn't answer the question," I sing-song, following her out.

Jude heads into a local coffee shop and gets us all a hot cocoa.

"This is a nice touch." I hold up my to-go cup of hot chocolate. My other gloved hand rests in Jude's grasp as we continue down the sidewalk.

Christmas light displays, ice sculptures lit up with an array of colors, and trees that have lost all their leaves are strung in lights on both sides of the street. It's beautiful and romantic.

Cassie and Bennett walk in front of us. They stand a few feet apart from each other. Bennett is laughing about something Cassie's said.

"Laughter's good, right?" I ask Jude.

"Yeah. I think so. Not everyone's first date is as intense as ours." He shakes his head, a wicked grin on his face.

"What first date?" I purse my lips.

"Your kitchen." His voice lowers.

I nod slowly, releasing a sigh. "Ah, yes. That was a heck of a first date. Kind of impromptu, wouldn't you say?"

"Definitely not planned."

"But memorable."

"Hard to beat."

I lean into Jude's arm, wearing a smile on my face.

Cassie turns around to face us. "We're going to make an appearance at E and Ash's party after this. You two in?"

Jude looks at me to respond.

I shake my head. "No, we'll probably just call it a night and head to Jude's."

"All right, suit yourselves." Cassie shrugs and faces forward.

"That's not a good sign," I whisper to Jude. Knowing Cassie, if she were really into Bennett, she'd want to spend time alone with him. I feel like the party is a buffer for her with lots of people to interact with so she won't be forced to spend all her time with Bennett.

"Well, not everyone's compatible," Jude answers.

"Yeah, I guess not."

CHAPTER 30

JUDE

Tannon's arms cage my face in as she clings to the back of the couch. Straddling me, she moves up and down, sliding onto me—fierce and intense—in a perfect rhythm. Her delectable taut nipple hangs in my mouth. I suck it in greedily, tasting the salt on her skin. She drops her head back, and a jet of pleasure escapes her lungs as she moans. The fueled air around us is saturated with lust, need, want, and the desperate desire to fall hard into the oblivion that hurts so good. The high that our bodies were made to bring each other.

I brush my thumbs across the top of her thighs, burning her skin with my touch until I reach the bundle of nerves begging to be stroked. Everything about Tannon Lee feeds this heated frenzy burning within me. She's straight from a dream that was made for me. A fucking goddess. Her curves, the silkiness of her skin, and the unrestrained sounds falling from her lips as she picks up her pace fuel a crazed need, desperate for release.

Rubbing her clit, I thrust my hips as she falls against me. The cadence of our skin slapping with each thrust increases in tempo. Her pants become louder, and I know she's close.

"Jude." My name escapes her lips in a reverent plea.

"You feel so good, Tannon. So fucking good."

I need this woman more than anyone in my life. I'm addicted to her, to her smells, her sounds, her touch. I ache for her, constantly.

My free hand digs into the soft flesh of her hips and ass. I guide her over me, urging her down—faster, harder, deeper. The force of her movements builds, and she whimpers as she takes me in, every inch in long forceful thrusts.

She starts gasping for air, releasing the pained cry that lets me know she's about to fall over into ecstasy, and I'm ready to fall with her. Tannon coming is the sexiest fucking thing I've ever seen in my entire life. It pushes me over the edge every time.

"I'm com..." She cries out, her body trembling above mine.

"Fuck..." I groan as my release hits hard, and blinding light flashes behind my eyelids.

I circle my arms around her back, slick from sweat, and hold her to me. My face rests between her breasts as we both breathe deeply, allowing the tremors of pleasure to work through our muscles, across our skin, and to every nerve.

She falls against me, boneless, and cradles my face, her mouth finding mine. Our tongues dance in a seductive rhythm as we kiss until our lips ache. God, she's everything. She's the whole package, and I'm hers. Mind, body, and soul...she can take it all.

I pull away from the kiss and tuck a strand of her long blond hair behind her ear. She leans into my hand as I run the back of it softly over her cheek. She's so beautiful it makes my chest hurt. I want her always.

"I love you, Tannon," I finally say what I've been feeling from the start. "I love you."

She presses her lips together. "I love you, too." Her voice is quiet as her words come out on a shaky inhalation. She leans in to kiss me again, and I can't remember a moment in my life when I've felt this happy.

Tannon's it for me. She's *the one*, my *happily ever after*, my *love at first sight*. Whatever my family wants to call it—she's it. The truth is, I've known it from the start. I knew it before I'd uttered a word to her at that initial self-defense class. An insane pull in my chest has led me to Tannon from the beginning.

This pull was new and foreign. I hadn't experienced it before, so I didn't know how to process it. I know now that it's love. The connection that's existed between us from the start was fate pulling us together.

She's mine.

And I'm hers.

I finally understand my horrible history with women. Every woman before Tannon was a wreck because I couldn't settle until the universe brought us together, until it brought me her. I'm just grateful it finally did.

She leans back, removing her lips from mine. "You should probably take that off." She looks down at where we're still connected, wearing an adorable grin.

I give her a chaste kiss. "You're probably right." I lift her off me and make my way to the kitchen as I remove the condom and toss it in the trash.

My phone buzzes repeatedly from where I left it on the coffee table.

I return to the living room and pick it up to find text messages from Jane.

Hey! Let's get together tonight.
I miss you.
We never hang anymore.
Can I come over?

I shoot her a quick text, telling her that I'm busy tonight and I'll talk to her tomorrow. I would've preferred to leave her messages unanswered as all I care about is getting Tannon to my bed. But, knowing Jane, had I ignored her, she would've shown up at my door in a matter of minutes.

I finish typing out the text and extend my hand to Tannon. "Ready for bed?"

She smiles. "Yeah."

Tannon's soft body molds into mine. Her bare ass presses into my dick, and it takes everything in me to let her sleep. It's early. The sun's hesitant rays peek through the blinds, casting a glow against Tannon's pale skin. I feather my lips against her shoulder, needing to feel her but wanting to let her sleep.

We passed out in this position after fucking ourselves into exhaustion last night. Her ass against me with my arms wrapped around her middle. The delicate crook of her neck against my lips. An effortless fit.

I've been slacking on gym time these past few months, but I can't feel guilty because I've definitely been getting my workouts in. Making love to Tannon is the best cardio there is.

She twitches beneath my embrace and starts to mumble in her sleep.

A smile finds my face, wondering what she's dreaming about. I'm in deep with this one, and there's nowhere I'd rather be. Everything about her turns me on, even her dreams.

Her vocalizations become louder, and she thrashes her arm out. I scoot back, startled, and give her space. She screams, a full-blown, panicked scream. Fear slices through my heart. I grab her arms and shake her awake.

"Tannon," I say gently, trying to suppress the dread I feel for her. She breathes heavily, releasing a cry of terror, her body now covered in sweat. Heavy concern bubbles in the pit of my stomach. I shake her more forcibly. "Tannon. Wake up."

Her eyes spring open, and she gasps, sitting up in bed. Her terrified eyes dart around the room until they fall on me. The horror in her expression fades away as realization dawns. She pulls in a shaky breath.

"Hey, are you okay?" I ask.

"Yeah." She moves her head to the side, pulling the blanket up over her naked body. "Just a bad dream. Sorry."

"You don't have to apologize."

My chest hurts seeing her like this. Visibly shaken and afraid.

"You can talk to me." My words are gentle.

She bites her lip. "It's nothing. Really." She sighs. "You know. I think I'm going to take a shower. Alone, if you don't mind."

She hurries from the bed, shutting and locking the bathroom door behind her. The click of the lock, a foreign sound between us, causes the hairs on my arms to rise. I let out a breath. Something's not right. I feel it.

Sitting on the side of the bed, I rest my head in my hands. This is the first nightmare Tannon's had while I've been with her. It was new and unsettling, but it wasn't foreign to her. This isn't new territory for her. I could see it in her expression when she finally woke. She'd been there before, and if I had to bet—I'd say a lot.

I pull on a pair of shorts and make my way to the kitchen to start the coffee pot.

Opening the cupboard, I remember that I bought a box of Fruity Pebbles for Tannon, more so as a joke than anything. When we first got together, she told me it was her favorite breakfast.

I'm thinking she may appreciate a bowl full of sugar this morning after the night terror she had. Sugar is one of her favorite food groups, second to caffeine, which I'll also have ready for her.

My jaw clenches as I watch the coffee drip into the pot at an irritatingly slow pace. Unease ripples across my skin as I push down the unsettling feeling that rests in the pit of my stomach like a pile of cement.

It's fine, I tell myself. Or it will be. It was just a dream.

Tannon emerges from the bedroom, her wet hair drips against her shoulders, soaking the shirt she wore over here last night. The hollowed expression stealing her beautiful features causes bile to rise up in my throat.

It's not fine.

CHAPTER 31

TANNON

Jude's face falls when he sees me, and it breaks my heart. The last thing I want to do is hurt him. I wasn't lying when I said I loved him last night. I do. God, I do. I love him so much it hurts. But, because I love him, I need to let him go.

I thought I was ready. I hoped I was. After last night, or I suppose this morning, it's clear I'm not.

I'm not sure what it was. Maybe our spoken words of adoration took our relationship to a new level, making the stakes that much higher. Perhaps it was Jane and her needy texts bringing out all my insecurities. Or a combination of everything.

Jude loves me. He doesn't want Jane. I know this. Yet she's constantly pushing herself between us, inserting her perky little pixie self where it's not wanted. I don't think Jude would ever cheat on me, but that doesn't mean Jane won't mess things up. She's been creating tension between us from the start. Maybe I'm weak, but I can't handle the stress and uncertainty that Jane brings.

Especially now.

Now, words of love are being thrown around, making everything so much more serious. This is no longer mind-blowing sex with a hot man. This is my life. My heart. Everything I am is invested in Jude and our relationship. If we crumble, if we break—I'll break, too.

The terrors of my past cling to me, pulling me under so I can't breathe. I can never be the woman Jude deserves until I emerge from the depths of darkness, until I'm free.

Jude closes the distance between us. He doesn't say a word as his arms circle me pulling me into a hug. I lean into his firm chest, smelling his skin and embracing his warmth. *I love him.* Tears fall as he rubs my back.

"It will be okay." He kisses my head. "Whatever it is, we can work through it. I'm here for you. I love you."

Jude is an amazing man, the best, and he deserves to be happy. I can't make him happy when I'm so broken. Holding on to him is selfish.

He leads us over to the sofa, and I turn to face him. He holds my hands within his strong grasp.

"I was raped in high school—"

He inhales a sharp breath. "Tannon, I—"

I shake my head. "No. Please let me finish."

He nods, and I pull air into my lungs, fortifying my resolve. I can do this. *He deserves to know.*

"I was on spring break, dancing with a cute guy. I drank a little too much, and it happened. I couldn't stop it. I tried. I really, really tried... but I couldn't." Tears filled with the memory of that night roll down my cheeks. "It messed me up, Jude. It's not even the event that has me so broken as much as the way it made me feel. Helpless. Alone. Weak. Unlovable. Tainted. Ugly."

Dipping my head, I close my eyes. My back quakes with sobs. Hearing the truth of my reality spoken out loud for the first time is intense and just...sad.

I lift my head, my solemn gaze holding his pained one. "I've never told anyone." I shake my head. "Not a soul. Not my mom. Not Cassie. Not a therapist. No one. Well, besides Lucifer." A dry chuckle escapes my lips. "I used to have really bad night terrors. You know, reliving that night as if it were happening again. They're so real... so completely terrifying. They've decreased over the years, less and less, as time goes by. I think writing helps, too. I don't know why the vivid and horrifying nightmare came back today. Something changed, and my insecurities festered. I don't think it was one thing, but maybe a combination of many. It reminded me why I've never been in a serious relationship. Why I can't."

Jude can no longer stay quiet. "Tannon. No."

"I'm sorry." My voice breaks as more tears fall. "I'll never be able to be the woman you need—the partner you deserve. He ruined me," I cry. The pain in my chest is so raw that it's suffocating. "I've tried so hard to heal into a woman worth having, but I can't get back the piece of my soul that was stolen. I hate being jealous and insecure. I hate that I can't love freely without this weight of doubt pushing me down, reminding me at every turn that I'm not good enough. Not for you. You, Jude"—I hold my hand to his face, and a light stubble tickles my palm—"are so good. You're strong, and kind, and beautiful inside and out. You deserve to find your equal. I owe that to you."

Tears soak my skin, falling fast now. I blink hard to bring Jude into focus. He's so perfect, and it kills me that he can't be mine. I'll love him forever and miss him always. The pain in his eyes tells me that maybe a part of him will miss me, too. I don't think anyone will ever fill my heart and nurture my soul the way Jude does. It's devastating, but I can't change the hand I've been dealt.

"I wish it could be different, I do. Believe me when I say I've tried to change who I am. For years, I've struggled to get myself back. But she's gone." The last words break as I swallow a sob. Jude opens his arms for me, and I fall into them. His strong embrace pulls me close, and my body shakes as the pain escapes in a torrent of tears.

Jude strokes my back in long, slow motions. He kisses the top of my head as I keep it buried against his chest.

"When I was a little girl, I dreamed of you. I knew I'd find you someday, and I'd know, not by the way you looked but the way you made me feel. My dream, so long ago, was fleeting, but the utter wholeness I felt when I met you there stayed with me, and I've been searching for it ever since. I've craved it so badly that I've written entire novels in an attempt to replicate that feeling. With you, I almost feel whole. With you, I could almost pretend that the darkness isn't there, but I love you too much to do that to you."

I can't believe I'm saying goodbye to Jude. Every ounce of my being wants him, yet I have to let him go. I know I do.

Jude pulls back and tucks a piece of my hair behind my ear. "Look at me, Tannon."

Releasing a sigh, I sit up to look at him. He swipes the pad of this thumb under my eye, wiping the wetness away. "I don't want her." His finger repeats the motion under my other eye, erasing my tears. "I don't want the version of yourself that you lost. I only want you, the person you are here and now, darkness and all. Horrible things happened to you, and I'm so sorry. I wish they didn't. No woman deserves that. Yet you're wrong...you see, your soul can't be stolen. It's only yours to give."

He touches my temple. "Your mind." He lowers his hand, splaying it across my chest. "Your heart and soul. The essence of who you are as a person. They are yours to give. No one has the power to steal them. No one." He shakes his head. "You are the greatest thing to ever happen to me, and I want you like you are. I'm here for you. I'll help you. I'll stand by you as you work through this, no matter how long it takes. I'll stand by you forever."

"That's what I'm afraid of," I whisper, my words full of sorrow. "I won't ruin you, Jude. You deserve the world, and I can't give it to you. I wanted to. I had almost convinced myself I could, but the nightmare this morning brought it all back, reminding me that I'll only bring you down. I have to fix myself first...and I don't know if that's possible."

"Please. Please don't do this, Tan. You don't have to be alone in this. I want to be here for you. You could never ruin me. Love doesn't work like that. As long as we love each other, we can get through anything. Loving you—all of you—will always be a privilege."

I stand from the sofa with a shake of my head. "I'm sorry."

"Tannon, wait." Jude follows me to the door. "Please. Stop. Let's just take a second to regroup. We can figure this out. Okay? Come on." He reaches for my hand, but I pull it away.

I touch my fingers to my lips and then press them against his.

There are so many things I want to say, so many things I want him to know, but it all hurts too much. So, instead, I simply say goodbye.

CHAPTER 32

TANNON

Maybe I shouldn't be here? The closer I get to her hospital room, the more nervous I become. I can't tell if my presence here is wildly inappropriate or acceptable. But I felt like I had to come. I wanted to come.

I hold the planter of beautiful pink poinsettias in my grasp. It's a little cheeky but cute.

I rap my knuckles lightly outside Amara's hospital room.

"Come in." Her voice, though tired, is filled with joy.

"Hi," I say, entering.

She wears a genuine smile, and it makes me feel better about my decision to come. "I wanted to stop by. I'm on my way to my parents' but couldn't leave town without wishing your new little one a Merry Christmas and Happy Birthday." I hold out the pot of pink Christmas flowers.

Amara chuckles and then shakes her head. "And so it starts."

I place the planter on the window's ledge and then peek in at the new baby girl in her arms. "She's beautiful."

"She's perfect. Isn't she?" Amara asks with that astounding joy that new mothers always have after bringing a miracle into the world. "I just love her." She kisses the baby's head.

"What's her name?"

"Emerson Grace." She grins.

"I love it."

She nods toward the door. "You just missed everyone. Victor took the kids to the cafeteria for some food, and the whole family followed. You know eating is a group activity in our family." She chuckles. "It's not a usual Christmas brunch, but it will do, huh?"

"It's one they'll always remember."

"That is true." She nods. "Do you want to hold her?"

"Sure."

Amara hands me baby Emerson. She's beautiful—olive skin, chubby cheeks, and lots of dark hair.

"I didn't have this much hair until I was three." I chuckle. "She's a lucky girl."

"Yeah, all the babies in our family are born with lots of hair. It's adorable, but the old wives' tale about horrible heartburn during pregnancy with babies with lots of hair is true, or at least in my case it was. That part's not so adorable."

We sit in silence for a moment, and I take in the baby.

"You know, Jude's downstairs with the family." Her voice is hesitant.

I press my lips together and nod.

I figured he'd be here. I prayed I wouldn't run into him. Not because I don't want to see him. I do. I miss him like crazy. But because I'm not sure what to say to him yet. I haven't figured out how to get to where I need to be.

"He said you guys are taking some time?" Her voice is hesitant.

I nod again, keeping my eyes on the baby.

Leave it to Jude to make our breakup, and my part in it, sound less horrible than it really is.

Amara continues. "I think I may know a little bit about what you're going through."

I raise my head and lock eyes with Amara.

"Jude didn't say anything. But when I inquired deeper, as a nosy big sister I tend to do quite often, he simply said that you were working some things out from your past."

"Yeah," I answer.

"Did someone hurt you?" she asks gently.

My eyes widen at her question, and panic starts to rise from my gut.

"Because someone hurt me." She gives me a knowing look.

I hold the baby against my chest, hating that I have

this tiny living and breathing reason I can't just run out of here.

"I was sixteen. It was a college guy who worked at the store for my abuelo. His name was Kyle. Such a douche name, right? Should've been my first warning sign." She chuckles dryly, but there's no humor in it, only pain. "Anyway, I was infatuated with Kyle. He was older and handsome...my first crush. I would sneak by the store whenever I knew my abuelo wasn't working because that meant Kyle was. Even then, Abuelo hardly took any days off from work, but he trusted Kyle. Everyone did. He was a part of the family, almost, you know? You've met us. When we like someone, we pull them in."

Amara looks down at the blanket covering her body. I want to tell her that she doesn't have to go on, but I'm frozen to the spot where I sit with Emerson. I can't make the words come.

"Kyle and I were friends, and I thought my crush on him was a secret. I was young, and there was no way I should've been crushing on a college guy and definitely not acting on it. It would've been wrong. But Kyle knew, and he used it to become closer to me. He made me feel special and beautiful. Then one day, when I was helping him in the store when my abuelo was out, it happened in the storage room. I cried and begged and tried to fight... you know, all the things one does, but he was too strong. He said I'd asked for it, no—begged for it. He called me a tease and every other name he could think of. He threatened to tell everyone that I was a whore if I said anything. I was so ashamed. I had planned to keep quiet and not tell a soul, but Jude found me shortly after in the storage room. He was only twelve, but he knew what had happened."

"Amara..." My voice breaks.

She continues. "I was in a rough spot for a long time. My family tried to help, but I was set on destroying myself. I couldn't live with the shame. I started skipping classes, hanging out with the wrong people, doing drugs. Horrible things. You know what saved me?"

She looks at me, a tear falls down her cheek, and she shrugs. "Love."

"Victor?" I ask, and she nods.

"Through his love, I was finally able to start loving myself again. I get it, Tannon. I get the shame and fear and all of it, but as someone who's been there and has come out on the other side, I'm telling you it's so much better on this side. I was not to blame. You are not to blame. That sin is on them, those who hurt us. We simply have to let love in because love drives out the hate in our hearts...it's the only thing that can."

"Thank you for telling me that, Amara." I swallow. Standing, I hand the baby back to her.

"Jude's a good one." She shakes her head, a proud smile on her face. "You know all those classes he does?"

I nod.

"He does those so other women won't have to go through what we have. He became a police officer to help people. If there was ever a man who could love you through your worst demons, it's him...and trust me, he loves you."

"I know he does." I wipe an errant tear. "I love him, too. I just need to work through some stuff on my own first. I think love will help me, but I want it to come from me first."

"I understand that," she says. "Just know that we're here for you. You can talk to me anytime."

"Thank you. I appreciate that so much," My gaze darts toward the door. "I really do need to get going. My brother's out in the car waiting for me to drive us back to my parents' for the holiday."

"Well, thank you for coming to visit."

"Yeah. She's perfect." I motion toward baby Emerson. "Merry Christmas, Amara."

"Merry Christmas, Tannon. I hope to see you soon."

"Me too." I wave before exiting the room.

I rush down the hallway. My mind is on overdrive with everything that Amara just told me. I'm so confused. I want to run to Jude and throw my arms around him. Knowing that he's here in this hospital, and I'm so close is almost more than I can bear. I miss him like crazy.

I hit the down button on the elevator. Within a few seconds, the elevator dings, and the doors slide open.

Jude stands before me, a coffee from the café downstairs in his grasp.

He's wearing a pair of worn jeans that hang off his

hips just right. The gray long-sleeved thermal clings to the muscles across his chest and arms. When he looks into my eyes, my soul burns. He's so incredibly handsome. Every piece of me ignites with electricity, wanting every piece of him.

"Tannon." My name comes out on a gasp.

"Hey. I wanted to visit the baby before heading home. My brother's waiting in the car." The words fall from my lips at a rapid pace, and I bite the inside of my cheek.

The doors of the elevator start to close, and Jude extends his arm to stop them. He takes a step forward so he's in the threshold. "I miss you." His emerald greens pull me into his orbit, where it's hard to think about anything but how much I love him.

"I miss you, too."

Without thought, I step toward him and sink into his warm embrace. He holds me against his chest and presses his lips to the top of my head.

The elevator starts to buzz, and he leads us inside before the doors close. He extends an arm and presses the button for the lobby.

"Are you doing okay?" he asks on an exhale.

"I'm getting there."

"Please come back to me as soon as you can."

I wrap my arms around him and relish the calm his touch brings. The elevator chimes again, and the doors open.

"Here, it's just like you like it." He hands me the coffee, following me out of the elevator.

"How'd you know I was here?"

"I didn't. I was bringing it up to Amara, but it's what you always order. You two are a lot alike. I can go get her another one."

"Okay, thanks." The corners of my mouth tilt up into a smile.

Jude kisses the top of my head again before stepping away. "I love you, Tannon Lee." He smiles.

My grin grows wide, and I lower my chin. "I'll see you soon."

"I'm counting on it." He turns away.

I hug my coffee to my chest and walk out of the hospital feeling a whole lot lighter than I did when I walked in.

CHAPTER 33

TANNON

THE FINAL COVER of my new book, the one I've yet to finish, taunts me from my computer screen. It's not my normal artistic type of cover, but it's still stunning. It's eye-catching and sexy, and I love it. Cassie won in the end.

I caved and put his gloriously defined abs on the cover of my book, breaking my heart in the process. He's so much more than a six-pack, yet it doesn't matter because he's no longer mine.

Or at least not at this moment.

It's been a month.

A long, torturous, horrible month.

I keep telling myself that tomorrow will be easier.

After I saw him on Christmas, two weeks ago, I felt like my breakthrough was coming, but it's yet to arrive. I'm not sure what I'm waiting for, but I'll know it when I feel it. I refuse to go back to Jude as the same broken girl who walked out on him. Something has to give.

I'm so deep in my confusion that I'm not even sure why I ended our relationship in the first place. I'm second-guessing everything. Nothing makes sense anymore. I'm lost, and that fact alone is the only thing I'm certain of. The rest is just noise.

I'm broken, and I don't know how to fix myself.

The mind is one of our greatest assets, but it's also my greatest enemy. It tricks and confuses, belittles and shames. It makes me feel I'm not good enough when my heart knows I am.

I replay the words that Jude spoke in my head. The bits and pieces I remember make sense, and I start to question what I'm even doing. *I'm here for you. I'll help you. I'll stand by you as you work through this, no matter how long it takes. I'll stand by you forever.*

I can't escape this darkness around my heart, this voice in my head that tells me I'm not enough.

The thing is, I know it's a lie and a result of my experience. It's not real. It's not who I am. The pieces that Jude loves are the real me. I feel almost crazy because I can't let it go. The guy who took it all probably doesn't even remember my name, and here I am, remembering every line of his face as he still tortures me all these years later.

Why do I allow it? I'm not that girl anymore. I'm not weak.

The darkness screams so much louder than the light. It always has.

I touch the computer screen where Jude's body is on display on my new cover. It's not even his inverted v or defined abs I crave. It's his heart. No one has loved me the way Jude Martinez loves me.

The past few weeks have been rough, but Jude continues to let me know I'm not alone. He's texted words of adoration. Sent notes filled with love. Flowers. Candy. Hell, he's even sent Lucifer's favorite wet food and Lupita's fresh tamales. He's covered his bases, making sure I know he's not going anywhere.

He's waiting for me, and I'm trying so hard to get back to him.

Cassie plows into my room with a bag in her hand. "Uber eats just dropped off your favorite burrito from your favorite Mexican restaurant. I'm guessing you didn't order this?"

I shake my head.

She lets out a frustrated sigh, putting the bag of food down on my desk. "Why won't you call him? You're clearly miserable. He obviously loves you. You still haven't told me why you broke up. I'm missing something here. What's going on?"

"It's complicated."

Her eyes dart to Jude's cover on my screen. "Right. I see that." She places her hands on her hips. "Well, I really wish you'd talk to me. This isn't like you. You're kind of worrying me, to be honest."

"I need to figure some stuff out, Cass. It's personal. Okay?" Raw emotion lines my face, causing Cassie to frown.

"Okay." She sighs. "Well, remember I'm going up north this weekend with Bennett to go skiing. Are you going to be okay? I can cancel. You know what...? I'm going to cancel."

"No," I protest. "I'm fine. Actually, I could use a couple of days alone to pound out the rest of these words and finish this book."

She nods. "Yeah. It's been a long time since your last release. It'd be good for you to get that book out."

"See? I have work to do. So, go. Have fun."

"You'll call me if you need anything or need me to come back early? You promise you're okay?"

"I promise."

She studies my face, squinting her eyes. "Okay, but I demand proof of life photos every couple of hours. If I text, you better answer, or I'm calling 911."

"I'm not suicidal, Cassie." I chuckle dryly.

"Well, I don't know what is going on. And I would never forgive myself if anything happened

to you." Her eyes fill with unshed tears.

Guilt threatens to consume me. Ashamed, I stand from my desk and throw my arms around Cassie in a hug. "I'm sorry. I've been a horrible friend this past month. I'm not trying to worry you. I'm just working through some stuff. Okay? I really am happy to have the apartment to myself to write. Let me finish this book, and we'll talk. I promise. Go, and have a fun weekend."

"Okay." She pulls back, a small smile on her face.

Some words are a struggle. I've had whole chapters or even entire books where I've had to fight for every single word to materialize. The inspiration didn't come naturally. Those are the worst kinds of books to write. They come slowly, and each sentence is a battle.

That's not this book.

The minute Cassie left for the weekend, I started to type, and I've barely stopped.

I write until my fingers cramp, and then I stretch them out and write more. I move from my bed to the sofa and to my desk, and then I repeat the rotation. Tears fall as the words materialize effortlessly across the screen, and I let them. I pour every emotion into this story...and it's freeing.

My words.

My feelings.

My heartache in these pages.

My truth.

Mine.

It's setting me free.

Each paragraph brings my shattered heart another piece of hope and healing. The end of the book flows from my fingers. My female lead has found acceptance and love. She's no longer allowing the demons of her past to steal her joy.

My journey has been full of pain and regret, and it's been anything but easy, but no one ever promised life would be easy. Life is not easy, but it's good, so good. Wishes are a reality because mine came true, even the ones I didn't know to ask for. I'm able to let go and forgive myself for all the wrong decisions I made. Although my life didn't go the way I had dreamed it would when I was young, it turned out better than I could have imagined in the end.

Forgiveness, acceptance, and love are a reality. And as I look into Deacon's eyes filled with infinite love as he waits for me at the end of the aisle, I am so blessed to say that I know that reality all too well.

Words have always been my escape. I've written versions of my happily ever after out for the world to read. I've created swoon-worthy men who would do anything for the woman they love. I write about soul-crushing love. My novels are often heart-wrenching and messy because that's real life.

Nothing in life comes wrapped in a neat little bow, especially love. Love is hard, and the journey is often riddled with obstacles that break our hearts or try to steal our souls. Mine did. Yet true love is always worth the fight.

I see Jude in every male hero I've written. It's as if I was manifesting him into my life all along. He's kind, sexy, smart, and beautiful...and I deserve to be loved by him.

I'll say it again. *I deserve to be loved by him.*

I'm in no way *healed* by any means, but I'm different than I was a month ago or even two days ago. It's crazy how much fighting for a fictional character allowed me to find my own strength. Waging war on her demons gave me the fortitude to stand against mine.

She was this broken character that I was determined to fix, and in doing so, I can finally let it all go, and move on. Words are magical that way. They have the power to heal.

This is why I write.

As I type, *The End*, I smile as my chest heaves with sobs.

It's not the end but merely the beginning.

My fingers tremble as I save the document, my finished story. *It's done.*

I email it to Cassie. The subject line reads: I finished!

I close my laptop and turn off the lights before crawling into bed. Relief-filled tears slide against my skin and pillow. Lucifer crawls into bed with me and snuggles against my chest. I hold him to me.

"We're okay," I say, kissing his head.

I've lived off caffeine and emotion for the past few

days with very little sleep. I'm exhausted, but my heart's happy. Tomorrow, I'm going to start fighting for myself.

Sleep starts to pull me under almost immediately. I'm content in that knowledge that the terrors won't come tonight because for the first time in a long time, I'm no longer afraid.

CHAPTER 34

TANNON

THE WEIGHT I've been carrying around since I was eighteen years old has been lifted from my heart. Everyone heals differently, in their own time and their own way. No definitive rule book exists for trauma and mental health, at least not one that consistently works, because we each internalize our struggles differently.

We experience trauma in our own way, so it only makes sense that we will heal on our own terms.

It hasn't been easy, but I've put in the work. I've attended self-defense seminars to make myself feel safe. I've read books on the subject. I've snuggled my cat, and no one is ever going to convince me that the healing attributes of pets, and their unconditional love, aren't one of the best forms of therapy there is.

Ultimately, I wrote it all down...and finally, let it go.

An alternative pop rock station plays through my

Bluetooth speakers, and I sing along to Green Day. Lucifer glares at me as I do a little spin on the kitchen floor before I scoop the canned food into his dish.

"You're an asshole, and I'm happy. All is finally right in the world again." I rub his head, and he growls at the intrusion.

Today is the day I get Jude back.

I've showered for the first time in five days. Honestly, that had less to do with the funk I was in and more to do with the fact I was in complete writing mode. Toward the end of a book, it's just me, my yoga pants, stained T-shirt, messy bun, laptop, and caffeine. There's a method to the madness.

My hair is dried and straightened. I applied mascara and brushed my teeth. Like, I'm seriously winning at life right now. *Kudos, Tannon. Kudos.*

"Tan!" Cassie steps through the door and drops her luggage at her feet.

"Hey! Did you have fun?" I tap my phone to mute the music.

She closes the distance between us, wearing a serious look on her face. "I finished it. I read it while Bennett was skiing yesterday. I made him ski by himself because I couldn't put it down. I love it!"

"Yeah?" A huge smile finds my face. Cassie always loves my books, but if she didn't, she'd tell me. She's always the first person who reads it when I'm finished. She's a good luck charm in that way.

"Yeah." She presses her lips together. "It's one of

your best. Your readers are going to love it so much, but..." Her voice falters, cracking on the last word. She drops her gaze to her feet, and when she looks back up, there are tears in her eyes. "That's your story, isn't it?"

My lips tremble, and my eyes water. I release a breath and nod.

"Tannon," Cassie cries and wraps her arms around me. "I'm so sorry. I'm so, so sorry."

"It's okay," I whisper, hugging her back.

She takes a step back. "I knew it was. It was too raw to be fiction. I cried through most of the book. You were on every page. It was heartbreaking but beautiful, too."

"Yeah, I mean...I just felt like I had to write it. I'd written my story before, years ago, and erased it all. But I couldn't move on. So, I wrote it again. It helped."

I follow her to the living room, and we sit cross-legged on the sofa, facing one another. For the first time, I tell my best friend everything. Because for the first time, I can.

Facing the mirror, I rub the freshly applied lip gloss in. "This outfit's good, right?" I'm wearing a pair of skinny jeans and a thin, v-cut navy blue sweater.

"You could wear a garbage bag, and Jude would welcome you back with open arms. You know that, right?"

I run my fingers under my eye, making sure I catch

any rogue mascara flakes. "I know, but I still want to look good."

"You always look good. I do love that sweater, though. It brings out the blue in your eyes." She pulls the straightener through the back of my hair, catching a few pieces I'd missed earlier.

"Perfect. I need to hear about your weekend before I go."

Cassie looks at my face in the mirror. "Seriously, no. You have more important things to do right now than hear about my weekend."

"But I want to hear about your weekend. Jude has waited four weeks for me, so he can wait a couple more minutes. Plus, I don't even know if he's home."

"Why don't you text him?"

"Because I want to surprise him. Surprises are always nicer, right?"

She blows out a breath, amusement lines her features. "It was fine." She shrugs. "Fun."

"Fine? Fun? Sounds great," I scoff, tossing my hairbrush, lip gloss, and mascara into the makeup bag and zipping it shut.

"It was." Cassie unplugs the straightener and follows me out of the bathroom. "We skied. We ate at the yummy restaurant at the lodge. It was a good time."

"So, you're liking him?" I didn't see an immediate love connection when she and Bennett went out with Jude and me a few weeks ago, but I'm glad she's happy.

"Yeah. He's cool. Cute. Nice....all the things."

"What's one thing you love about him?" I ask.

She plops down on my bed as I look through my closet for my brown boots.

"His smile. He has the most gorgeous smile."

"What's one thing you hate about him?" I call over my shoulder, tossing shoes around. The left boot is in my grasp, but the right one is MIA.

"The way he kisses."

I halt my search and look over at her. "You hate the way he kisses? That's not good."

"No. I mean, he does the other stuff really well, an entire league above Henry. So, there are no complaints there. It's just...when he kisses, he sticks his tongue in my mouth and kind of...leaves it there, just fat and doing nothing. He doesn't move it with mine or push it in and pull it out as our lips kiss. It's just there...plopped in my mouth like a dead fish. He's honestly the worst kisser ever. It's so weird. I can't even adequately explain it."

I tilt my head. "Kissing is kind of a big deal, Cass. It sets up the whole chemistry of a relationship." I continue my search for the missing boot.

"I know, but he does everything else so incredibly well. It's so weird. Like how can he navigate around my body and make me feel so good but can't master a skill I learned when I was thirteen?"

"Maybe you should talk to him? Work on kissing or something?"

"Yeah, I probably will."

"Where in the hell is my other boot?" I groan, tossing my hands up.

"Have you looked under the bed?"

I raise a brow. "Why?"

Cassie kicks her legs over the side of the bed. "I don't know. There's always random stuff under the bed. So, when all else fails, look there."

Crouched on my hands and knees, I peer beneath the bed. "Did you hide it or something?" I ask, pulling the missing boot from beneath the bed.

Cassie laughs. "No, I swear. It's just a good place to look."

I eye her suspiciously.

"Why would I hide a boot?" She giggles.

I pull both boots on.

"Okay, I'm ready."

"You look great. Good luck!"

"Thanks," I say with a wave. Pulling on my winter coat, I quickly request an Uber and walk down the stairs to the street.

Ramone and his red Toyota Camry should be pulling up in a few seconds.

I follow the GPS tracker as it nears my location.

Wet snow falls from the sky, dampening my hair which I now realize was pointless to straighten, but I can't find it in me to care. In a matter of minutes, I'm going to be in Jude's arms, and my world will be right again.

It's time for my happily ever after to begin, and I'm ready.

The little blue car icon flashes across my screen, indicating that my ride has arrived. I raise my gaze and spot Ramone in his Camry across the street. I wave, letting him know I see him, and step into the street to cross.

Tires screech.

Horns blare.

There's a rush of events so intense that my mind can't make sense of the sudden torrent of input. A force knocks into me, and I'm in the air, or I think I am? Everything's in slow motion and confusing all at once. There's no pain but a clear understanding that it's coming. Snowflakes fall from the gray sky, each unique one tumbling toward me. All at once, the snowflakes are gone, and only the slush-coated pavement is in my sights.

All I can think about is protecting my head. I raise my arms to cover my skull, or I think I do. The impact doesn't come, or maybe it does, but all I see is blackness.

CHAPTER 35

JUDE

LEAVING the domestic dispute that took way longer than anticipated, I drive back through town toward the station, ready for this shift to be over.

"We could do Good Luck Charlie's or Connor O'Neill's? What do you think?" Jane lists bar names from beside me.

"I think I'm just going to head home," I tell her.

"Come on," she protests. "You never go out with me anymore."

"It's not as fun as it used to be."

The reality is, I'm over it. Going out to bars and drinking isn't how I want to spend my time. I've seen life through a different lens since Tannon. Now that she and I are *taking some time*—which is what my official stance is whenever anyone asks about her—if I'm not working, at the gym, or with my family, I want to be at home waiting for her. Because she'll come back, I know it. She has stuff to figure out, things that only she can, and when she does—which she will—she'll be back.

I miss the hell out of her, sure. But not like I would if we were to break up. This separation isn't permanent. I'm not sure why I'm so confident in that fact, but I am. I believe with everything in me that I'll be married to Tannon Lee someday. I fell hard for her, and she fell right along with me. She's it for me.

A call comes over the radio, needing traffic redirection around an accident scene involving a vehicle and a pedestrian. An ambulance is en route. These types of calls aren't uncommon in this city, with as many college students as we have crossing the roads on a daily basis.

I reach for the walkie.

"No." Jane halts my hand.

"We're right here," I say to her before responding to dispatch.

"No bar, but let's extend this already horribly long workday with another call," Jane grumbles as I turn on the lights.

"What'd you want me to do?" I let out a laugh. "We're literally a block away. It would've been shitty to ignore it. Don't worry. It won't take that long."

"That's what you always say."

I park the police cruiser across the intersection to stop traffic from blocking the ambulance. Its sirens can be heard in the distance. Jane and I exit the vehicle, and she goes off to direct the vehicles. Years of experience have us falling into our roles without the need to talk it over. I'm the one who moves toward the victim, and she secures the location.

As I jog toward the commotion, I steal a glance toward Tannon's window. The accident is right in front of her building. Shamelessly, I hope to catch a glimpse of her.

"Excuse me." I move through the people looking down toward the pavement.

I step into the clearing and drop my gaze.

My entire world stops.

Adrenaline takes over as I shut my heart off. I can freak out later. Right now, I need to do everything I can to help save her.

I drop to my knees and press my pointer and middle finger to her neck. There's a pulse. Thank God.

She's unconscious. Her long blond hair is dirty from the road and red with blood. Her beautiful features are hidden beneath a veil of crimson. There's so much blood that if I didn't know every curve of her body, I never would've known it was her.

"What happened?" I yell out. A kid, not much older than eighteen, starts talking fast. He says he didn't see her. "Were you preoccupied? On your phone?"

He doesn't answer, which is answer enough.

I'm fuming.

The paramedics arrive, and I move people back as they get her onto the gurney. I can't tell what's injured, and that's what scares me the most. I have no idea how grave this is.

"I'm going with her," I say to the paramedics and follow them into the ambulance. "Give your information and statement to Officer Grenada," I say to the kid and point toward Jane.

Jane's confused stare finds mine before the doors of the ambulance close.

The woman drives the rig as the man sits in the back with Tannon. I stay out of his way as he works on her. He hooks her up to an IV bag before wrapping gauze around her head. "Looks like a head wound. Those bleed like crazy," the guy says. "Her blood pressure's low," he adds.

"Loss of blood?" the woman asks from the driver's seat.

"Probably," he says.

I listen to their exchange but don't say a word. I can't take my eyes off her. I'm frozen in this place that doesn't seem real. This can't be happening. The past month comes back to haunt me. Why did I waste so much time? Why wasn't I with her, fighting harder for her? The prospect of losing her before I've truly had her causes bile to rise up in my throat. I swallow it down. My eyes sting, and I realize I'm crying.

The paramedic shoots me a concerned look but returns his attention to Tannon as we come to a stop in front of the emergency room entrance.

There's a blur of activity, and besides answering the

limited questions I know the answer to, I feel useless as she's wheeled back.

Cassie, Everett, and Asher find me pacing in the waiting room. I texted Cassie the moment Tannon was taken back a few minutes ago.

"What happened?" Cassie shrieks.

I tell her what I know, which isn't much.

"I can't believe this." She shakes her head. Asher pulls her into his chest as she cries. "I called her parents. They're on the way."

"Okay, good. That's good. She's going to be okay," I say to reassure myself more than anyone.

"She was on her way to your house," Cassie chokes back.

"Really?"

"Yeah, she's better. Happy. She wanted to surprise you and win you back."

I press my fist to my lips to stop the hysteria from breaking loose. I take a deep breath. To think we were moments from being back on track. Moments from our happily ever after. Had she stepped off the curb a second later.

One *moment* is all it takes to change everything.

"She never lost me," I tell Cassie, my voice thick with emotion.

"I know." Cassie takes my hand in hers.

"She's going to be okay," Everett says, and I hold on to his words, needing to believe them.

Time clicks on in slow motion. Tannon's parents and

brother arrive, as do most of my family, except for the children who stayed home with my brothers-in-law. I didn't ask my family to be here. In the confusing minutes after first arriving at the hospital, I shot off a text to Cassie and my mother. I don't know why I texted my mother. I guess it's instinct when hurting, even as a grown man, to reach out to one's mother in a time of need.

"You guys didn't have to come," I say to my family. "It could be a while before we know anything."

"Of course we came. We want to be here. We love Tannon," my sister Amara says.

The whole group of us sits in the waiting room. Abuelo has a box of potato chips that he passes out. Food is always the answer to stressful situations in our family. If I wasn't so stressed out, I'd find it cute. Tannon's family really doesn't know what to do with the chips, so they all kind of hug the bags of chips against their chests as they stare at the doors waiting for a doctor to come out.

Finally, a doctor emerges from behind the closed ER door. We all stand with a collective sigh. The doctor looks around at the group of us. "I'm looking for Tannon Lee's family?" she says.

"That's us. I'm her mother, and this is her father." Tannon's mom clings to her husband's arm. "But we're all her family."

"Okay, well...Tannon is going to be just fine."

Screams erupt, and the room fills with cheers and

hoots and hollers as we all hug each other. Cassie sobs into Asher's chest, and Everett hugs them both. My sisters jump up and down and clap their hands while I hug my parents. We're loud and obnoxious, and it's the happiest I've felt in my whole life.

The group of us eventually quiets our celebration, and the doctor continues with a huge smile on her face. "So, she hit her head pretty hard and has a concussion. There was a large gash in her head which was actually a good thing because it helped relieve pressure from the impact. We stitched up the lesion on the side of her head. The scar won't be visible when it heals as it'll be covered by her hair. She fractured her wrist but will be out of that cast in a few weeks. All in all, she's in pretty good shape for what she went through."

"Will there be lasting effects from the concussion?" Tannon's mom asks.

"She might have some dizziness, confusion, and headaches for a couple of weeks at the most, but she should be good as new once she heals."

"Oh, good! Thank you so much." Tannon's mom shakes the doctor's hand. "Can we see her?"

The doctor looks around. "Yes, but just a few at a time. Okay?"

Tannon's parents and brother follow the doctor back, and although I understand it, I hate it. I can't stand that I have no claim to Tannon as her family. I can only see her if her parents allow it, which they will, but the fact that I couldn't get to Tannon if I needed to drives me crazy.

I pace the waiting room.

"La verás pronto, mi amor," *You'll see her soon.* Abuelita says to me.

"I know. I just can't stand waiting."

The minute hand on the analog clock in the waiting room clicks twenty times, and finally, Tannon's family emerges.

"She's asking for you," her mother says to me, all smiles.

I rush back to Tannon's room. She lies in the hospital bed, her hand and wrist are in a cast, and she wears a bandage around her head. But even still, she's the most beautiful woman I've ever seen.

"I'm so glad you're okay." I hurry to her side and pepper soft kisses all over her face. "I love you. I love you. I love you."

"I was making my way to you." Her weak voice is lined with amusement.

"Hell of a detour, babe."

"I'm sorry. This isn't the reunion I'd imagined." She raises her arm and cups my face.

I hold her hand to my face and turn to kiss her palm. "I'm just so glad you're okay."

"I finished my book," she says.

"Yeah?"

"And it helped me. I finally feel good."

I kiss her hand again. "I'm so happy."

"So you'll take me back?" she asks.

I run my thumb gently along her cheek beside a long purple bruise that runs the length of her face. "I never let you go, Tannon."

She smiles, her eyes brimming with tears. "We're going to be so happy."

I lean down and kiss her forehead. I want to lay in bed with her and hold her, but I know she's sore, so I settle with clinging to her hand. "We are."

"I have something else to tell you." Her voice shakes, and my heart picks up a beat.

"Okay," I urge.

"Well, they ran some tests before the X-rays, and it turns out, I'm pregnant." Her eyes dart nervously to mine.

"Are you serious?" I breathe out, shocked.

"Yeah. Is that bad?"

"No." I shake my head. "Of course not. It's a surprise but not a bad one. Oh, my God. Are you serious?" I exclaim, a smile coming to my face.

Tannon grins.

I release her hand and tug my fingers through my hair. "We're going to be parents?"

She nods and lets out a laugh. "Crazy, right?"

"The best kind of crazy."

I feel around my uniform, tapping my pockets, in search of something. I settle on the handcuffs, and dropping to one knee, I hold the circle cuff up toward Tannon.

"Oh my God. What are you doing?" She sits up further in the hospital bed.

"Tannon Lee, I fell in love with you the moment I first saw you. For me, it wasn't even a choice. My soul connected with yours because you are my other half. Our love story is fated, inevitable from the start. Our first kissed sealed the deal, and I knew that you were the one. It doesn't matter what trials life throws our way. I will always be your biggest supporter. I will always protect and love you unconditionally. Yes, this is soon. We haven't been dating long and are kind of coming off a break." I grin, and Tannon chuckles with tears in her eyes. "But I can't care because I know that I'll never love another woman the way in which I love you. This isn't just because of the baby. I've wanted you to be officially mine for a while, but now, there's no reason to wait." I hold my handcuff higher. "Tannon Lee, will you make me the happiest man alive and be my wife?

"Yes!" she squeals.

I stand and kiss her with as much passion as I can without hurting her. Pulling back, I take her hand in mine and lock the handcuff around the cast-free wrist.

"It's how I always dreamed it would be," she teases, her smile beautiful and carefree.

"Do you want to tell people or keep it a secret for a while?" I ask.

"Tell people." She grins.

"Okay, good. Me, too. Wait here."

She shakes her head. "I'm not going anywhere."

Outside of Tannon's room, I get the nurse to agree to five minutes with our whole family in the room with us. I retrieve them from the waiting room.

They file into Tannon's room, giving her hugs and words of love.

Finally, Cassie says. "Why are you wearing a handcuff?"

Tannon lifts her arm and shouts, "We're getting married!"

There are some gasps, cheers, and shocked faces.

Arm still raised, she follows it up with, "And we're having a baby!"

The space erupts with laughter and screams, and questions from Tannon's parents and friends. The nurse rushes in to quiet us down. She ushers the family out of Tannon's room and back toward the waiting room.

Tannon catches my stare from across the room amongst the chaos, and nothing but uninhibited joy resides in her smile. The announcement was wild, unconventional, and absolutely perfect. We're going to have one hell of a life, and I'm going to love every single moment of it.

CHAPTER 36

TANNON

It's been a month since I walked in front of a car like a complete dumbass. I still don't know what happened, but I definitely didn't see that car before I stepped off the curb. Maybe he came out of nowhere. Maybe my mind was so singularly focused on getting to Jude that I had blinders on. I'll never know, and it doesn't matter anymore. I'm completely healed. My headaches are gone, and my cast is off.

The best part of this past month is the beautiful diamond ring on my finger and the baby in my belly.

We were nervous that the trauma of being hit by a car would affect the pregnancy, but thankfully, it didn't. I just had my first ultrasound. The baby is two months along and, according to my app, the size of a raspberry. On the ultrasound, the baby looked like a little bean alien, and he or she was adorable—definitely the cutest bean alien I've seen. Jude and I are going to make cute kids.

It's all happening so fast, but at the same time, it feels so right.

I moved out of my apartment, which has been the only difficult thing. Not because I don't want to live with Jude but because I'm going to miss living with Cassie. At nine years together, we had a good run. I still see her all the time, and I always will. She's the best friend I've ever had, and she's still only a few miles away.

I carry the box my mom sent us to the guest bedroom closest to the master, which will be the nursery. She sent me a pile of my old baby blankets. I'm not sure why she couldn't wait until our weekly visit to give them to me, but my mother has zero chill when it comes to her first grandbaby. She's already planned half the baby's life, and we don't even know the sex of the alien bean yet.

"Tannon," Jude calls from the entryway.

"I'm in the nursery," I say loud enough for him to hear me.

A minute later, he's standing at the threshold, looking delicious in his uniform. I'll never tire of the way he looks in his police gear. Simply gorgeous.

"Welcome home, my love. Mom sent some of my old blankets." I hold up a multicolored crocheted one.

"That's sweet." He closes the distance between us and circles my waist, pulling me in close. "I missed you."

"I missed you, too." I stand on my tiptoes and give

him a kiss. My insides immediately heat like molten lava, and I deepen the kiss.

He sighs into my mouth, threading his fingers through my hair.

Slowly, he slides his hand up my shirt until he's popped my bra up and over my breasts, giving his hand full access to my chest.

Jude was overly careful with me when I first came home from the hospital. I think he was afraid I'd break. It was frustrating because after a month apart, all I wanted was him. Now that my cast is off and my bruises have healed, my timid lover has all but disappeared, leaving the insatiable man I fell in love with to worship my body every night, which he does quite well.

He tugs on my nipple before lowering his hand to the waistband of my sweatpants. I tremble in anticipation of his touch.

All at once, he stops. "He's doing it again." He sighs against my lips.

I look behind me to see Lucifer sitting atop a dresser, glaring at us from eye level.

"Let's go to our room." I grab Jude's hand, and we hurry to our bedroom and close the door behind us before Lucifer can follow.

After making quick work of removing our clothes, Jude is sliding his thick length into me in record time. Tilting my head back, I moan at the feel of him inside me. *I will never tire of this.*

"Fuck, Tannon." He sucks on my neck. "You feel so good."

As if on cue, a loud, obnoxious meow starts from just outside our bedroom as Lucifer scratches the base of the wooden door with his claws.

"Ignore him." I move my hips harder against Jude.

He kisses me hard, mirroring the actions below.

The sounds of sex are all around us. Satisfied moans. Skin slapping as we chase our release. Sighs of pleasure as every hair on my head stands on end with my impending orgasm.

"O-o-W-O-U-H-u-u," Lucifer yowls like a wild cat outside the door. His deep roar is louder than the noises in the bedroom.

"I hate him," Jude growls.

"Ignore him," I urge once more. "Focus on me." I'm desperate to reach the summit where my trembling muscles are leading me. I need the fall. I grasp his face and kiss him hard, pounding my hips against his body.

To a one-cat symphony of snarls and yelps outside our door, we fall into ecstasy.

Jude drops against me, panting. He trails light kisses across my chest. "He's the worst."

"I know."

"He does that on purpose."

"I know." I trace my fingers in light circles along his muscled back. "He's an asshole."

"We need a better system here. He's kind of ruining things." Jude rolls off me, his back falling against the bed.

"He's just letting me know that he's mad. This past month has had a lot of change for him. He'll settle down."

"He has his own fucking room with new cat trees facing the window to the backyard and endless toys and treats. What else does he want?"

"To bother us." I chuckle.

"Well, it's working."

I roll over and prop myself up on my elbow. With my other arm, I run my fingers through the short hair above Jude's ear. "Tell me about your day. Any craziness?"

"Let's see. The little old lady in the apartments on 4th called in a noise complaint again, and once again, it was the TV that she left on in the bedroom making the noise."

"Not again." I laugh. "Aw, bless her heart."

"I know. I can't even be annoyed. She's so sweet."

"What else?"

"Besides the normal drunken fights between college kids and traffic stops, it was a pretty uneventful day."

"No one got hit by a car walking to their Uber?" I tease.

"No, thank God." He pulls me atop him and kisses me.

I lean up on my elbows caging his face in with my arms. "I love you."

"I love you," he says. "Oh, and remember we have Gianna's birthday tomorrow at Abuelo's."

"Got it." With Jude's large family, there's always a celebration going on.

"And Abuelita wants you to sign off on the food for the wedding."

I shake my head. "I don't need to. She's never made anything that I didn't love. I'm sure what she has in mind is perfect."

"That's what I told her, but I'll tell her again."

It turns out I'm the opposite of high maintenance as a bride. All I care about is promising my life to Jude. The rest is just icing on the cake. Jude's sisters and Cassie have taken our wedding planning on as if their lives depend on it.

I'd honestly be completely content going to the courthouse tomorrow and signing our marriage certificate, but I think everyone in our lives would murder us if we did that. Both families are really looking forward to this wedding.

"That reminds me. I'm going dress shopping with Cassie and my mom on Saturday," I tell Jude.

"Sounds good." He kisses the tip of my nose and then rolls us over on the bed so he's on top, causing me to laugh.

I expect to hear Lucifer meow outside our door but not the "Jude!" that sounds instead.

"You've got to be kidding me." Jude rolls off me. "This has to stop."

I throw my sweats and T-shirt on, and Jude grabs

some joggers from the dresser. Lucifer rushes into the bedroom the second that Jude opens the door.

Not wanting to deal with Jane today, I lay on the bed and snuggle with Lucifer. He's much more affectionate now that he has competition, and I have to admit I like this new cuddly version of him.

"You can't just come in to my house whenever you want." I hear Jude say from the living room. "This isn't just my house anymore."

Jane responds, her voice low, and I can't make it out.

"No," Jude says forcefully. "Things are different. I'm sorry that's hard for you, but they are. Tannon is my number one. Don't come between us, Jane. I've told you before, and I'll tell you again. I will always choose her."

After a few more exchanges, the front door slams loudly.

"Awkward," I sing-song to Lucifer.

He purrs and licks his paw as if to say, "Totally."

Jude opens the bedroom door. "It's safe to come out, now." He chuckles dryly.

"Are you sure?" I quirk a brow. "It sounded intense."

"Yeah." He sighs. "But I think it will be better now."

"What'd she want?" I rub behind Lucifer's ears.

"Same stuff. To hang out. I'm not spending enough time with her, yada yada."

"You're with her a minimum of eight hours a day."

Jude lays on the bed, facing me. "I know. I'm starting to think her feelings go beyond friendship."

"You think?" I laugh. "I could've told you that."

"I'm sorry. She'll get on board eventually, or she won't be in my life."

I reach out and cup his jaw. "It's okay. We'll give her time. I kind of feel bad for her. I mean, you're easy to love, Jude."

He kisses my hand and holds it to his lips. "So are you."

CHAPTER 37

JUDE

Before the main meal, the mariachi band serenades the reception as the guests mingle with drinks and appetizers in hand. The melodic songs carry an air of nostalgia for me as I've grown up listening to my abuelos singing the same tunes my entire life.

I've never actually been to Mexico, but its culture is embedded into who I am. My abuelos have surrounded my sisters and me with the food, music, and traditions of their birth country. I've always wanted to visit but growing up, my parents could never afford to fly the eight of us down.

"Thank you," I say to the bartender as he hands me a bottle of beer.

The reception hall is beautiful. The ladies in our lives came together to create a magical ambiance for our wedding celebration. The ceremony held in the local, gorgeous Catholic church, per my abuelos' request was incredible. Though it was a full Mass and over an hour long, it flew by.

Tannon is across the dance floor chatting with my family. All five of my sisters and Cassie wear the same rose-colored flowy bridesmaid dress. The sight of my wife takes my breath away just as it did when she first appeared at the end of the aisle in the church during the ceremony. She's so incredibly beautiful. I'm still in awe that she's really and truly mine.

At almost five months pregnant, she's starting to show. The white satin of her dress lies against her small belly and somehow makes her even more stunning.

It's hard to believe that nine months ago, I walked into her apartment to do a photo shoot as a favor for a friend, and now I have everything I've ever wanted. It's been a whirlwind, but as my abuela has always said, once you know—you know. I don't need more time to know that Tannon is the person I'm fated to be with. I feel it in every fiber of my being. Her presence fills every hole and vacancy within me. She makes me feel truly alive—a true mate to my soul.

I'm so lucky to have her.

"She looks so beautiful." Jane appears at my side.

"Yeah, she does."

"The ceremony was perfect." She looks around the hall. "Everything about today is incredible. You did an amazing job planning it all."

I release a chuckle. "Yeah, we didn't plan much. It was my family and Cassie."

"Well, they did a great job."

"They did." I nod.

"Look, Jude..." Jane's voice trembles with nerves. "I know we had a little awkwardness between us for a bit there a few months back, but I want you to know that all of my feelings are in the past, and I'm a hundred percent thrilled for you and Tannon. You're my best friend, and I love you. I want nothing but the best for you, and it looks like you found it. I'm sorry I ever made it weird. I was in a bad place, and I just had to try. I mean, you're easy to love." She looks down before her gaze holds mine once more. "Looking back, I wish I'd never said anything, but unfortunately, I did. I hope someday you can trust me as your friend again."

I take her hand, squeezing it gently before letting it go. "We've been over this already. It's all good, water under the bridge. We're friends, Jane. We always will be. There's no need for any more apologies. I promise. Go, have fun." I grin.

She smiles back, relieved, and dips her chin before heading back to her table. At her departure, my gaze immediately finds Tannon again.

Tannon's face turns to the side, and a smile finds her lips when she notices my stare. She turns back to my sisters, and her mouth moves in explanation before she returns her blue-eyed gaze to me and begins to head in my direction. She looks like an angel as she closes the distance between us.

My body moves toward her on instinct until we're a breath apart.

"Hey," she says, the sides of her lips tilting up.

"Hey, my beautiful wife. What were you over there talking about with my sisters?"

"You." She grins. "What are you over here thinking about all by your lonesome?"

"You." I take her chin between my thumb and forefinger and tilt her face up, my mouth capturing hers.

She circles her arms around my middle and leans her face against my chest. "The ceremony was incredible. Don't you think?"

"I do." I kiss the top of her head. "It was absolutely perfect."

"I know I said that I didn't care about any of the details of our marriage, but I'm really glad your family and Cassie ignored me and planned something so stunning anyway. This is so much better than a courthouse."

"It is," I agree.

The servers start setting out giant clay bowls of food on the table. Having attended many family celebrations in the past, I know the bowls will be filled with rice, beans, warm tortillas, salsas, and various meats—a taco lover's dream.

Tannon inhales. "Oh my gosh. It already smells so good in here."

. . .

"You know Abuelita will never let you down in the food department." I give her a wink. "Let's eat." I take her hand in mine and lead her toward the long table of food. The wedding party starts to line up behind us.

Once our plates are full, we make our way to the head table that sits slightly elevated atop a platform and overlooks the rest of the tables.

"I've always thought these head tables were so funny," Tannon says after taking a bite of rice. "It's like we're royalty looking down on our peasants in ancient times."

"Well, you are my queen," I say with a smirk.

"Ah, so cheesy, Mr. Martinez. But so cute." She squeezes my hand.

Cassie leans over from the other side of Tannon. "Hey, when you two lovebirds are finished eating, we need to go down and get all of our photo booth pics taken while the common folk below are still eating. I mean, that photo booth was my main contribution to this event, and I don't want to stand in line all night waiting to get all the pics I want. You know?"

I laugh under my breath at Cassie's reference to the guests being common folk. She and Tannon are so close, their friendship and personalities completely in sync, that it's hard to believe that they haven't known one another their entire lives. They're more like sisters than friends, and I love that Tannon has a friend as loyal as Cassie in her life.

"Okay, but I want another taco first," Tannon tells her.

"I'll grab it for you." Cassie stands from the table. "A little bit of everything?"

"You got it." Tannon nods. "Load me up, babe. I'm eating for two."

Cassie scurries off to the food table, cutting to the front of the line. She says something to my cousin Alfred who was at the front of the line, which I'm sure has something to do with her urgent mission to feed my wife.

"You know you can only use that eating for two excuse for another four months," I tease. Tannon knows that her appetite and love of food are one of my favorite things about her. She'll never need an excuse to go up for seconds or thirds if she wants.

"No because then I'll need a second helping because I'll be breastfeeding, and after that, I'll be an exhausted mom needing more energy, and by then, I'll probably be eating for two again. It's a vicious cycle." She scrunches her nose, and I can't help but laugh.

"God, I love you," I say.

"And I love you."

I lean in and whisper into her ear. "You know it's really fucking sexy to hear you talk about carrying our babies, both now and in the future. I love that we created a perfect little human—part me and part you—and he or she is snug and happy inside your belly. You are everything to me, Tannon. Everything. I'll never have enough of you."

I gently kiss the soft skin below her ear, and her skin pebbles as I lean back into my seat.

Her chest rises as she inhales a long breath, her cheeks flush.

"Um, my love...what are you doing to me?" she asks, her voiced heated as she swallows.

I lift my shoulders in a shrug. "I'm just telling you how I feel." I play coy. I *am* telling her how I feel, but at the same time, I know how my words affect her, especially now when her second-trimester hormones are running rampant.

She closes her eyes and pulls in another breath before squeezing my knee. "Meet me in the bridal suite in one minute," she whispers under her breath and stands from the table.

"But your food's going to be here any minute," I say.

"Fuck the taco." And with that final sentiment, she's exiting the ballroom.

I wait a long thirty seconds after she's departed, then hastily sneak out of the room before any of my family can pull me into a conversation.

I slip into the bridal suite and lock the door behind me. Tannon pushes me against the door and pushes up on her tiptoes. Her mouth takes mine in an all-consuming kiss. Her tongue greedily entwines with mine as we let out a collective moan. Fuck, everything about her turns me on.

"I love that you're mine forever. I love that I can have

you whenever I want." She sighs against my lips. "I need you so much, Jude."

"I need you, babe."

Holding her waist, I spin her around so that her back is against the door, and then I drop to my knees and start lifting her dress.

"No." She grabs my shoulders. "As much as I'd love that right now, I just need you inside me. Cassie's going to come looking for me for pictures any minute. We can explore each other's bodies in great detail in Mexico tomorrow, but right now, I just need it fast."

I stand. "Mexico?"

The only part of the wedding that Tannon was adamant about planning was our honeymoon, and she wanted it to be a total surprise.

"Oh, shit. I ruined it," she whines.

"Tan." I run my palm across her cheek. "I can't believe you planned our honeymoon in Mexico. That's so perfect, it's unreal. Thank you."

"Well, I'm not telling you any of the details until tomorrow. Forget I said anything. It was the lust talking. You know I have no control of myself when it comes to you. But I will say, it's going to be amazing." She smiles wide.

"I have no doubt." I lead her toward the sofa. I pull my pants to my ankles as Tannon steps out of her panties. I sit back on the couch and motion for Tannon to join me. She hikes up her dress and straddles my hips before sliding down onto my length.

She squeezes my shoulders and throws her head back in a moan as she takes me in fully. I let her control the movements and cadence as she finds the toe-curling combination. I need her to feel exactly what she wants to feel at this moment because she is and will always be... my queen.

CHAPTER 38

TANNON

I haven't been able to wipe this smile off my face since the night of our wedding. It was so fantastically incredible in every way, I fear that this content grin will become a permanent fixture on my face—which, I suppose, isn't awful. It's a reminder of everything that I have, and I'm so grateful.

The wedding was, by all definitions, perfection. Every aspect, from the ceremony to the ballroom where the reception was held to the food and music, was amazing. It will always be the best day of my life—well, the birth of our baby might top it, but for now, the wedding is still the best day ever.

Jude and I are so fortunate to have so many great humans in our lives, family and friends who love us unconditionally. Every person who attended our wedding made it that more unforgettable. I've always dreamed that the person I ended up with would have an incredible family, and Jude has the best. I would've married Jude regardless of the type of family he came from because he's my person, a hundred percent. But I'd be lying if I didn't say that the fact that his family is so wonderful isn't icing on top of the already delicious cake.

The first several days of our honeymoon were spent at an all-inclusive five-star resort with our own private patio facing the Pacific Ocean in Puerto Vallarta. We spent our days eating the mouthwatering local cuisine, napping, swimming in the ocean, and making love until we passed out from exhaustion. It was everything I dreamed it would be. I couldn't have written a better honeymoon if I had tried.

That's the thing. I've written so many love stories about fated souls that are as beautiful as my imagination could create. Yet my life with Jude tops them all. It goes beyond exquisite words on a page. It's real and unpredictable—raw and right. There's so much love that most of the time my chest aches with it as it bursts from my heart. The combination of words to describe the magnitude of my love for Jude doesn't exist. He will forever be my happily ever after—the hero of my one true love story. The best one in my life.

I've written over a million words, and I'll write millions more in this lifetime, and none of them will be as sweet as my Jude story.

"All set." Jude hands me my boarding pass and takes my free hand as we walk toward security. Most of Jude's family comes from and currently resides in Querétaro, Mexico, which is in the center of the country and our next destination.

I think it's important for people to know where they come from, and when I found out that Jude had never visited his grandparents', Fedé and Lupita's, birthplace—I knew we needed to go. Jude may be an American, but this country lives in his blood, as it will in our child, and I want him to know it.

His family suggested taking a bus from Puerto Vallarta to Querétaro, but we opted for the one-hour plane ride instead of the twelve-and-a-half-hour bus ride. There are limits to what this pregnant woman wants to do on her honeymoon, and sitting on a bus for almost thirteen hours is a hard pass.

Once we're buckled into our seats, Jude takes the book that I bought him on Querétaro out of his backpack.

"Shall we read up?" he asks.

I wrap my hands around his arm and lean into his side. "Absolutely."

He flips to the page where we had left off previously. There's a picture of the eighteenth-century aqueduct that the local people call Los Arcos, *the arches*.

"My great uncle Carlos lives a block from Los Arcos," Jude says. "I'm told they're pretty cool. The seventy-four arches are ninety-four feet tall and four thousand and two hundred feet long or 1.28 kilometers. Abuelita told me that in the early seventeen hundreds, the richest man in Querétaro was in love with a nun and asked her what he could do to win her love. She knew that many people in the dry city didn't have local access to water so she told him that providing water to the people would make her happy. So, he commissioned the construction of the aqueducts, which took twelve years to complete. Abuelita says that for the building technology available in the seventeen hundreds, twelve years was super quick."

"That's quite a gesture. Did they end up together?" I ask.

"Apparently not."

"Aw. Poor rich guy."

Jude turns the page in the book. "I don't know how rich he was after paying for that enormous piece of architecture."

"Are you nervous to meet your family?"

Jude shakes his head. "No, more excited than anything. I've spoken to them all many times before. When I was young, it was over the phone, and now it's via Skype. Technology has a way of making us seem so much closer. I'm just thrilled to be able to hug them. You know?"

"Yeah. It's going to be great."

The plane ride is quick, and moments later, the captain is already announcing our descent. He speaks in Spanish, and I'm jealous that Jude can understand him, but I can't. Learning the language is something I want to do.

We step off the plane and retrieve our luggage while Jude texts his great-uncle Carlos, Fedé's brother.

"Mi sobrino nieto al fin!" *My great-nephew at last.* A loud voice booms from across the baggage claim area.

A strong man with a kind face, and a smile identical to Fedé's, opens his arms and wraps them around Jude before kissing him once on each cheek.

"Y tu hermosa novia!" *And your beautiful bride.* He hugs me and repeats the same greeting, kissing me on each cheek. "Bienvendia!" *Welcome.*

"Hola," I manage with what is probably the worst accent ever.

Carlos smiles wide and releases a chuckle. "Don't be nervous, my lady. We all speak English, the whole family. Not the best, I'm sure but good enough. Yes?"

I nod. "Oh, very good."

"We are so happy to have you both here, and Nieto, a lifetime of watching you grow through letters and pictures...and now, you're finally here. My wife, Esmeralda, is home making the dinner. You like Mexican food? Yes?" he asks us both.

"Yes," Jude says. "Especially her." He hitches his thumb in my direction. "I think she married me for Abuelita's cooking," he kids.

"Lupita has always been a great cook, even when she was just a girl."

"You knew her?" I ask.

"Oh, yes. Our families were very close. Neighbors, you see. Still are. You will meet lots of family from both sides. My brother and Lupita were in love from an early age. We all knew they would wed."

"I can't wait to hear the stories." I grin, following Carlos and Jude outside. "Fedé was my friend before I knew Jude. I've loved his stories."

"And Lupita's tamales?" Carlos says with a chuckle.

"Yeah, those, too," I say.

"Well, you will have many of both while you're here. Esmeralda's tamales are almost as good as Lupita's, but when we're back at the house, the story will go that they're better. Yes?" He raises a brow before shooting me a wink.

"Of course." I smile back.

The breeze from the Gulf soothes my soul like a comforting blanket of salt, warmth, and possibilities. The palm-frond roof of the cabana blocks out the blistering sun, leaving me in a comfortable shade. Who knew it was possible to be this content?

"Here you go, my love." Jude hands me a fancy fruit drink with a piece of sliced pineapple in the shape of a star on the rim.

I take a sip. "So good. Mango and pineapple?"

"Yes, it is." He takes a seat on the lounge chair beside me and sets his bottle of Corona on the small table beside him.

I've become quite accustomed to having a fancy

nonalcoholic drink in my hand over the past two weeks. To be fair, my drinks are nothing more than juice with some frills—cute little umbrellas or shaped fruit pieces as garnishes. But I love them.

I'm high on life, Jude...and juice. This baby is going to have quite the sugar tooth someday, I have no doubt.

"Oh my gosh. Feel." I place my hand on my belly, where the baby Bean is currently putting on an aerobatic performance.

Jude kneels in the sand beside my lounge chair and places his strong hand over my bare belly. I've chosen to be one of those women who wear my normal bikinis and let my baby belly show loud and proud for the world to see. And honestly? I've never felt more beautiful.

"I think Bean likes the pineapple." Jude chuckles. "Baby is literally jumping for joy in there."

"I know, but I'm thinking I should probably drink some plain ole water at some point." I grin.

Jude shrugs, a gorgeous smile crosses his face. "That might be good."

"I don't want to go home tomorrow. I want to live here forever." I stretch my arms out above my head as Jude leans in and kisses my belly.

We spent the incredible five days in Querétaro attending one fiesta after another and meeting so many people—aunts, uncles, cousins, and friends of all ages. Our days were filled with hugs, laughter, stories, and an abundance of adoration from all of Jude's extended family. They're all as equally wonderful as his Michigan family. We promised to get down to Mexico more often and bring the rest of his family with us next time.

It's been a perfect two weeks. The first part was spent lounging beside the Pacific Ocean in Puerto Vallarta, and we're ending it at a private resort in Tampico where we're relaxing beside the Gulf of Mexico. For our first trip to this country, we've seen a good variety of places.

Jude peppers kisses up my belly and across my chest until he's at my lips. "Well, you can write from anywhere, right? Someday, when you make it big, which you will, we'll pack up the kids and buy a beach house. I'll cook and clean our oceanside oasis and take care of the kids while you pound out some words. Then we'll spend all our free time by the water where you can drink juice until your heart's content." He presses his lips to mine.

"I love that dream." I smile against his mouth.

"Then we'll make it happen." He holds my face in his grasp. "I want all your dreams to come true."

I look at his tanned face and big, bright eyes. He's so incredibly handsome and continues to take my breath away.

"You've already made all my dreams come true," I say with truth in every word. "You're the Prince Charming who I thought only existed in fairy tales. You make me so happy, Jude. Everything from here on out is just a bonus to our already amazing life. All I need is you."

"All I need is you," he says.

"Well, and baby Bean."

"And baby Bean," he agrees.

"And Lucifer."

His face scrunches up. "I don't know if I can go that far."

I release a chuckle. "Come on. He's growing on you."

He kisses me softly. "All I need in this life is you and our family—whatever that may end up looking like."

"Six kids and Lucifer?" I raise a brow.

He shakes his head and laughs, all deep and sexy. "I'm all in. Always."

Every beat of trepidation or hesitancy my heart has carried over the past several years is gone. I no longer hold on to any fear. I'm confident that I can face anything this life has to offer as long as Jude is by my side. And he will be. Forever.

I'm the person I've always hoped to be—one who is whole, happy, and free.

That's the greatest dream of them all.

EPILOGUE

JUDE

Tannon awkwardly jogs across the wet sand where the ocean meets the beach. She's fake screaming as Eli hobbles behind her giggling. His pudgy arms extend in front of him, giving him balance as he totters after her.

He started walking just a couple of weeks ago at eight months old. He's strong and has great motor control for his age, and I love it. It's silly that I feel so much pride when I compare my son to other eight-month-old babies who are only crawling.

Tannon loves to remind me that it's not a competition, and Eli and any future children we have will do things on their own time. But, still—my boy is strong, and it's awesome.

"I have the juice!" I hold up the glasses as I call out.

Tannon looks toward me, and a smile spreads across

her face. She scoops Eli into her arms and jogs over to the cabana.

We're celebrating our one-year wedding anniversary at the same resort in Tampico where we ended our honeymoon. The first two days of our anniversary trip were spent with family in Querétaro, but the remainder of the week will be here with sun, sand, and as Eli is now screeching...juice.

"Ju! Ju!" He claps his hands together as Tannon holds him in her arms, laughing at his excitement. Yes, juice, or Eli's version of it, was his third word, only preceded by mama and dada. He just said it for the first time yesterday when he tried fresh-squeezed orange juice for the first time.

"Daddy got us juice, baby boy!" Tannon exclaims.

She sets Eli down on the edge of the double loungers and holds the cup of mango juice to his mouth. He lips the rim of the glass as she tips the cup up. Half of the liquid streams down his chin and neck.

"You know you've created a monster." I chuckle.

"I know. I'm afraid I might have," Tannon agrees with a grin.

Up until this trip, Eli was exclusively breastfed... now that he's been introduced to what's basically sugar water, we're in trouble. But Tannon wanted him to celebrate our anniversary dinner with us, so she ordered us all fancy juice drinks at dinner last night.

"I'm hoping when we're back home, and out of this environment, he'll forget all about it." She leans down toward Eli. "Right, my little love? It's just a little vacation treat."

Life this past year has been nothing short of perfection.

Tannon and I slipped into married and parental life with ease. Everything from the mundane tasks to the big events seem easier when we're together. My soul is lifted now that it's connected to hers, and my world is brighter, better—fucking amazing.

It's all so cliché to say, but I feel my life truly began the moment she came into it. It's as if my soul was waiting for her all this time.

I grab a towel and dip the corner into the melted water of our ice bucket to wipe Eli's face clean of juice residue. "All clean," I tell him before kissing his chubby cheek. Our son is beautiful. He's a perfect combination of the two of us in appearance, and I love getting to know him more and more as he grows into himself every day.

Tannon scoots back against the cushions of the lounger, and I sit beside her, rubbing circles on the soft skin of her thigh with my thumb. We face the water, watching the waves hit the shore as she nurses Eli. It's a different vibe than last year when we were here for our honeymoon, but at the same time, the theme is the same —love. And this time, there's even more of it.

When Eli was born, a whole new part of my heart opened up, and more love than I knew existed exuded from every pore of my body. Its comfort is my constant companion and circles me in protection as I go through each day. Love really does make everything better.

Tannon props a sleeping Eli against her shoulder and pats his back. She leans her head against my shoulder and takes in a deep breath. "I love our life."

I rest my head atop hers. "Me, too."

In all my wife's books, she's written a lot of love stories with beautiful happily ever afters, but ours is my favorite.

Dear Readers,

I hope you loved Tannon and Jude's story! A couple of years ago, I got this idea to write a story about a romance writer since I have some experience in that area. Ha-ha. I wasn't ready to leave the Bared Souls world, so I slowly started introducing these characters in the past two books. I think they are great additions! And it was so fun to write about a romance author—so much of myself can be found in these pages.

In fact, you can find pieces of myself in all my stories. Each one has some snippet of reality woven into the pages. Readers often ask how I get the ideas for my novels, and the truth is that the inspiration for a story usually comes from my life. I'll take a moment, a snapshot of my past, and create an entire novel around it.

If you're one of my diehard readers, you will have noticed that the book that Tannon was writing throughout this novel was *Fragment*, the second book I published. I was going to create a fictional piece for the purpose of this novel, but then thought...why not use one of my real books? When *Fragment* was first released, I had many readers message me to thank me for the content of that novel. If you haven't read it, know there are some hard parts, for sure. But ultimately, I wrote *Fragment* because chapter two (if you know you know) was my story, my history. And just like Tannon, writing it down was therapeutic and allowed me to let it go. That's the beauty of words, isn't it?

I am always truly humbled when I receive messages

thanking me for writing about a certain topic. Yes, I love to write angsty, emotional novels because I, myself, love to feel. Sometimes a good ugly cry is the best therapy. In the end, I write these stories because I want you to know that if you've gone through anything that I've written about, you're not alone. And if you haven't gone through something similar, it allows you to put yourself in someone else's shoes who has, even for a moment.

So, if you're reading this—thank you! I was a special education teacher for fifteen years before becoming a full-time author, and this is the hardest job I've had. Yet I love it so much and pray I can do it forever. Thank you for reading and allowing me to keep doing what I love.

The next book will be Cat's story (Yay!!! And it is a fun one!). Everett, Cassie, and Asher's stories will follow.

Thank you again for all your love and support. It means the world to me.

Thank you so much for reading.

Make your journey a beautiful one.

Love,

Ellie

ACKNOWLEDGMENTS

To my girls—Gala, Suzanne, Christine, Elle, Karrie, Amy C., Kylie, Amy E., and Kim—You all are so awesome. Seriously, each of you is a gift, and you have helped me in invaluable, different ways. I love you all so much. XOXO

To my cover artist, Letitia Hasser from RBA Designs—Thank you! Your work inspires me. You are a true artist, and I am so grateful to work with you. People do judge a book by its cover, so thank you for making mine *gorgeous*! XO

To my editor, Jenny Sims from Editing4Indies—Thank you for always fitting me in! I am so grateful for you and everything you have done to make this book the best it can be.

Lastly, to my loyal readers—I love you! Thank you for reaching out, reviewing, and sharing your book recs with your friends. There are seriously great people in this book community, and I am humbled by your support. Your messages breathe life into my writing and keep me going on this journey. Truly, thank you! Because of you, indie authors get their stories out. Thank you for supporting all authors and the great stories they write.

You can connect with me on several places, and I would love to hear from you.

Join my readers group: www.facebook.com/groups/wadeswarriorsforthehea

Find me on Facebook: www.facebook.com/EllieWadeAuthor

Find me on Instagram: www.instagram.com/authorelliewade

Visit my website: www.elliewade.com

Remember, the greatest gift you can give an author is a review. If you feel so inclined, please leave a review on the various retailer sites. It doesn't have to be fancy. A couple of sentences would be awesome!

I could honestly write a whole book about everyone in this world whom I am thankful for. I am blessed in so many ways, and I am beyond grateful for this beautiful life. XOXO

Forever,

Ellie <3

ABOUT THE AUTHOR

Ellie Wade resides in southeast Michigan with her husband, three children, and three dogs. She has a master's in education from Eastern Michigan University, and she is a huge University of Michigan sports fan. She loves the beauty of her home state, especially the lakes and the gorgeous autumn weather. When she is not writing, she is reading, snuggling up with her kids, or spending time with family and friends. She loves traveling and exploring new places with her family.